GREEK MYTHS AND LEGENDS

GREEK MYTHS AND LEGENDS

TALES OF THE GODS AND HEROES OF ANCIENT GREECE

SIRIUS

SIRIUS

This edition published in 2024 by Sirius Publishing, a division of
Arcturus Publishing Limited,
26/27 Bickels Yard, 151–153 Bermondsey Street,
London SE1 3HA

ISBN: 978-1-3988-4417-9
AD012239UK

Printed in China

CONTENTS

INTRODUCTION

Emilie Kip Baker (1873–1951) was married to Franklin T. Baker, founder of the Department of the Teaching of English at Columbia Teachers' College. She published a number of volumes of re-told myths and legends with the aim of making the stories accessible to the widest audience but had an enjoyable but educational purpose at the heart of her storytelling.

This collection of stories was first published as *Stories from Old Greece & Rome* in 1913. In this edition we have used the Greek names for deities, rather than the mix of Greek and Roman names that Emilie Baker used in her re-tellings. So, for example, the king of the gods is Zeus, rather than Jupiter, his wife is Hera, not Juno and the sea-god is Poseidon, not Neptune. A list of alternate names is given at the end of this introduction.

It is thought that Greek myths began to spread through oral storytelling during the classical period, beginning c.480BCE. The myths subsequently developed into literary figures and archetypes, which were later adopted by the Roman Empire. As the empire grew more powerful and expanded, so did their religious beliefs and cultural figures. Over the following centuries, the practice of worshipping the Greek and Roman deities faded and became dissociated from the literary characters.

It is these figures and their origins and stories that are the focus of the collection of favourite Greek myths collected in this volume. Beginning with their origins, most of the earlier tales are primarily about the gods, although the story of Pandora and her calamitous curiousity is key to many of the following stories. We meet the sun-god, Apollo, in three stories: Apollo and King Admetus; Apollo the Musician and The Love of Apollo. Other gods, including Athena, Artemis, Hermes and Aphrodite are introduced in their own stories in which other famous legends feature, such as that of the brilliant weaver, Arachne and the brutal tale of Niobe, slain by Athena. Hermes features in a story about his theft of Apollo's favourite cattle, while the flighty Aphrodite is found breaking the hearts of both gods and men.

Some of the most famous legends are concerned with the Underworld, including Hades' abduction of Persephone, daughter of the harvest goddess, Demeter as well as Orpheus and Euridice, two lovers kept apart by death.

There are the Greek heroes too: the extraordinary strength and labours of Heracles, son of Zeus and the princess Alcemene. We learn of his slaying of the terrifying Minotaur and the cleansing of a stables left uncleaned for thirty years! The brave Perseus defeats the snake-headed gorgon, Medusa through avoidance of her fatal gaze, while Bellerophon slays the Chimera, a monstrous combination of lion, snake and goat. Jason and his crew of Argonauts travel in search of the Golden Fleece, a symbol of kingship and authority. Finally there is Theseus, legendary founder of the city of Athens and Oedipus, tragic king of Thebes beset by a horrifying prophecy.

Emilie Baker gives a delightful introduction to Greek myths and legends, hopefully encouraging the reader to learn more of these wonderful stories.

The gods and goddesses

Greek	Roman	Role
Zeus	Jupiter	King of the gods
Hera	Juno	Queen of the gods
Poseidon	Neptune	God of the sea
Ares	Mars	God of war
Athena	Minerva	Goddess of wisdom and war
Demeter	Ceres	Goddess of the harvest
Apollo	Apollo	God of the sun, music, archery, prophecy and healing
Artemis	Diana	Goddess of the hunt, wild animals, chastity and childbirth
Aprodite	Venus	Goddess of love, sex and beauty
Hephaestos	Vulcan	God of fire
Hermes	Mercury	Messenger of the gods
Dionysos	Bacchus	God of wine, vines, fertility, and festivity
Hades	Pluto	God of the dead and the underworld
Eros	Cupid	God of desire, erotic love and affection
Hestia	Vesta	Goddess of the hearth
Dionysos	Bacchus	God of wine and festivity
Pan	Pan	God of wild beasts and the forest

I

IN THE BEGINNING

In the days of long, long ago when men built altars, and burned sacrifices, and worshipped their gods in temples of pure white marble, Zeus, the greatest of the gods, sat upon his throne on high Olympus and looked down upon the doings of men. The topmost peak of Mount Olympus was covered with clouds – so high it was above all the hills of Greece – and its slopes were thickly wooded. Just how high the mountain really was could only be guessed, for no man had dared to climb even as high as the first cloud line; though the story goes that once upon a time a wandering shepherd, looking for a strayed lamb, had ventured far up the mountain side and had soon lost his way. He groped about blindly, as the mists began to thicken all around him, and the sound of his own footsteps terrified him in the dreadful silence that seemed to be suddenly creeping over him. Then a mighty tempest broke over his head, and the mountain shook to its very base. From the hand of wrathful Zeus fierce thunderbolts were hurled, while the lightning flashed and gleamed through the darkness of the forest, searching out the guilty mortal who had dared to climb too high.

No human eye had ever seen the glories of Olympus, no human foot had ever stepped within its sacred halls, where the ceiling was of gold and the pavement of pearl and the thrones of the gods shone with a thousand glittering jewels. Here

> "the gods have made, So saith tradition, their eternal seat;
> The tempest shakes it not, nor is it drenched
> By showers, and there the snow does never fall.
> And in the golden light that lies on all
> Day after day the blessed gods rejoice."
>
> *The Odyssey*, Book VI

Of the life that was lived among the dwellers on Olympus, not even the poets could claim to know; but sometimes a tired soldier dozing by his camp fire dreamed dreams of this wonderful country where the immortal gods walked by night and day; and sometimes a lonely fisherman, looking across the blue waters of the Mediterranean to the crimsoning sunset, saw visions of youth and beauty and life that lasted for ever and ever and ever.

It was long before the memory of man that the gods first came to live on Mount Olympus, and it was still longer ago that all the great powers of the universe fought with each other for the right to rule the world. In this mighty war, which rent the very heavens with the crash of battle, Zeus at last conquered all his jealous enemies, and made himself ruler of the gods and of the world. On that day he established his dwelling place on Mount Olympus, and set the earth below him for a footstool. From his throne in the high heavens he looked down upon the kingdoms that he had portioned out to each of his brothers; and he saw Poseidon, the god of the sea, driving through the waves on his chariot drawn by huge, misshapen sea-beasts that beat up the thick white foam until it glistened on the sea-king's beard and on his crown of shells and seaweed. The other kingdom was so far away that even the all-seeing eyes of Zeus were strained to catch any glimpse of the shapes that moved noiselessly there, for this was the realm of Hades, god of the underworld, that dread country of darkness and unending gloom, where no ray of sunlight ever came, and where the sad spirits of the dead wept for the lost world of love and light and laughter.

Sometimes the great billows of clouds that rolled at the foot of the red-gold throne shut out for a moment all sight of the earth at his feet; but however thickly the mists gathered, Zeus could always see old Atlas standing on the shore of Africa with the heavens resting on his bent shoulders. This giant had stood so long that forests of huge trees had sprung up around his feet, and they had grown so tall during the ages and ages that had passed, that their topmost branches reached to the giant's waist and almost hid him from the sight of men. No one offered to relieve him of his burden, not even his two brothers, Prometheus and Epimetheus, to whom had been given the less difficult task of creating man and placing him in the rich gardens of the earth. There was every kind of plant and animal life in the gardens, and all things were very beautiful in this morning of the world – so beautiful that the gods, who must forever dwell in Olympus, felt sad that no eyes like their own could look upon the green meadows and flower-covered hillsides. So they bade Prometheus and Epimetheus fashion a being which should be like and yet unlike themselves. There was nothing but clay out of which to make this new creature called man, but the brothers spent much time over their task, and, when it was finished, Zeus saw that the work was good, for they had given to man all the qualities that the gods themselves possessed – youth, beauty, health, strength – everything but immortality.

Then Prometheus grew ambitious to add even more to the list of man's blessings; and one day, as he sat brooding by the seashore, he remembered that there was as yet no fire on the earth; for the only flame that burned in all the world was glowing in the sacred halls of Zeus. For a long time he sat on the seashore, and before night fell he had formed the daring plan of stealing some of the divine fire that burned for always and always on Mount Olympus, and carrying it to the earth that men might revel in its warmth and light.

It was a bold thing to dream of doing, but Prometheus forgot the fear of Zeus's wrath, so determined was he to carry out his plan; and one night, when the gods were in council, seated around the great red-gold throne, he crept softly into the hall, unseen and unheard. The sacred fire was burning brightly on a hearth of polished silver. Some of it Prometheus secreted in a hollow reed and hurried with it back to the earth. Then he waited, with terror at his heart, for he knew that sooner or later the vengeance of Zeus would search him out, even though he fled to the uttermost parts of the earth.

When the council of the gods was over, Zeus looked down through the clouds and saw a strange light on the earth. For a while he did not realize that it was man, building himself a fire; but when he learned the truth, his wrath became so terrible that even the gods trembled and turned away in fear. In a moment Prometheus was seized and carried off to the Caucasus Mountains, where he was securely chained to a rock, and a hungry vulture was sent to tear out his liver and devour it. At night the vulture, having gorged itself, slept on the rocks above its victim's head; and at night the liver of the wretched Prometheus grew again, only to be torn out and eaten by the vulture as soon as the sun rose. This terrible punishment kept on for years and years; for though Zeus heard the cries of Prometheus, and many tales were told of his sufferings, the ruler of the gods never forgave the theft of the sacred fire, nor would he set Prometheus free. But the story tells us that at last there came an end to this cruel vengeance, for Heracles, son of Zeus, went wandering one day among the mountains, found the tortured Prometheus, and broke his chains, after killing the vulture that had been enjoying this hateful feast.

Though the gods were rejoiced at his freedom, the name of Prometheus was never spoken on Mount Olympus for fear of Zeus's all-hearing ears; but on the earth men uttered his name in their prayers and taught their children to honour the Fire-giver as one of the greatest among heroes.

2

THE STORY OF PANDORA

In the early days of man's life on the earth, when everything was beautiful and new, there was no sickness anywhere, nor any pain, nor sorrow. Men lived to be very old and very wise, and everywhere was happiness such as has never been since in all the world. Now Zeus had not forgotten about the stealing of the sacred fire, and it angered him that man should light his own fires and kindle the cheerful blaze which should by right be glowing only in the halls of Olympus. The suffering of Prometheus had not softened his wrath. He would not be satisfied until punishment was visited upon those who had received the stolen fire. Accordingly he called a council of the gods and spoke to them of his desire. Though none of the deities wished to see misfortune brought upon the race of man, they did not dare to dispute the will of Zeus. So they agreed to carry out the plan that he unfolded, and before many days had passed they had fashioned, out of the same clay from which man was made, a creature that they called woman. To her each of the gods gave a gift such as softness, or grace, or wonderful fairness; but Zeus added one other quality, curiosity, and he gave the woman the name of Pandora, which means "the gift of all the gods". Then he bade Hermes, who is the messenger of the gods, take this new soft thing down to the earth and give her to Epimetheus for his wife. Now Epimetheus had mourned apart from his fellows ever since he learned of his brother's dreadful fate; and he sat day and night in the cool silence of the forest, brooding over his sorrow. But one day he saw some one coming toward him, led by the hand of Hermes, and all at once he forgot to be sad; for the sunlight was shining on the woman's golden hair, and her white arm was stretched out to him in greeting.

For some time Epimetheus and Pandora lived happily in the gardens of the earth, and every day Epimetheus thanked the gods for their last and best gift to man. He never tired of watching Pandora chasing butterflies through the tall meadow grass, or making cups out of broad leaves, that she and Epimetheus might drink from the clear, cool spring. One day as they were resting under the trees and eating their simple meal of dates and wild honey, they saw a traveller coming toward them. He was walking very slowly and seemed heavily burdened with what appeared to be a large box. While he was yet some distance off, Pandora ran to meet him and asked him to come into the shade and rest. The stranger was old, and the chest that he carried bent his shoulders almost to the ground. He looked hungry and thirsty and tired, so Epimetheus urged him to stop and rest, and offered him some freshly gathered dates. But the traveller – who was none other than Hermes in disguise – replied that he could not tarry with them, for he had a long distance yet to go. He asked them, however, to take care of his great oak chest, for with that burden off his shoulders he could hurry on and reach his journey's end before nightfall. He promised to come back for the chest a few days later. Epimetheus and Pandora were delighted to be of service to a stranger, and promised to guard the chest with great care. The traveller thanked them and turned away; but just as they were saying goodbye, he mysteriously disappeared, and whichever way they looked there was no trace of him to be seen.

Epimetheus was not at all eager to know what was in the mysterious chest; but as soon as they sat down again under the trees, Pandora began to ask a thousand questions as to who the traveller might be and what the chest contained. Epimetheus begged her not to think any more about it, as nothing could be learned of the old man or his burden; but Pandora refused to be silent, and talked still more of the probable treasure that they were guarding for the stranger. At last Epimetheus got up angrily and walked away, wearied with her insistence. Pandora then went over to the chest, and kneeling down beside it, she examined the exquisitely carved figures that were on all its four sides. Then she studied the fine golden cord that bound the chest. It looked soft enough, and yet it was very strong; for it was made of strands of twisted gold and was tied at the end with a curious knot. There was no lock to be seen, and apparently nothing hindered eager fingers from opening the lid when once the knot was unfastened and the golden cord unwound. Pandora's fingers itched to try her skill on the knot, and she felt sure that if she worked at it long enough, she could finally loosen it. The figures carved on the lid were groups of dancing children, and in the very centre was one figure whose face was so strange that Pandora sat for a long time staring at it. Now and then she turned away, and when she looked at the face again, it had a different expression from the one she had seen on it before. She knew that this carved thing was not alive, and yet each time she gazed into the strange eyes of the wooden face they were quite unlike the eyes that had smiled or frowned or mocked at her before.

She went to see whether Epimetheus had come back, and finding that he was still away, she returned to the chest again, but would not let herself be tempted into so much as touching the golden cord. As she stood wondering what to do, she thought that she heard some little voices coming from inside the chest, and they seemed to say:

"Open, Pandora, please, please open and let us out."

Pandora looked quickly around to see whether Epimetheus were in sight, then she came a bit nearer to the chest and put one hand on the golden cord. Again she heard the small voices, this time very distinctly, and they said:

"Open, Pandora, please, please open and let us out."

Pandora's heart was now beating fast. What *could* be in the chest? What poor imprisoned creatures were calling to her, begging her to set them free? She put both hands on the golden cord, then she looked guiltily around; but no one was in sight, no one was watching her except some inquisitive squirrels who were peering down at her from the branches just above her head.

Swiftly and deftly she untied the knot, which yielded easily to her eager fingers; but even then she hesitated, fearing the anger of Epimetheus.

The little voices cried again:

"Open, Pandora, please, please open and let us out;" but still she hesitated, not daring to raise the lid. Just then she heard her husband calling to her, and she knew that there would be no chance now to explore the contents of the mysterious chest. She must wait for that pleasure until another time; meanwhile she would take just one peep inside to be sure that the voices were not mocking her. So she raised the lid very gently, but no sooner had she made the smallest opening than out poured a host of tiny creatures like brown-winged moths; and they swarmed all around her, biting and pinching and blistering her soft skin until she cried out in fear and pain.

She tried to fight them off, and rushed away to find Epimetheus; but the tormenting little sprites followed her, buzzing about her ears and stinging her again and again. In vain she strove to brush them away, for they clung to her dress, her hair, and her poor swollen skin. When she reached Epimetheus she was crying bitterly, and it did not need any questioning to find out the trouble, for the malicious little creatures were so numerous that hundreds of them encircled Epimetheus, and bit and stung him, just as they had done to Pandora. In the unhappy hour that followed, while husband and wife bound soothing herbs on their bruised skin, Pandora told Epimetheus how her fatal curiosity had led her to open the chest and set free the host of evil things.

It was not, however, until later that they realized the extent of Pandora's folly, for the little brown-winged creatures were all the spirits of evil that had never before entered the world. Their names were Sickness and Pain and Sorrow; Envy and Pride and Jealousy; Hunger, Poverty, and Death. All these ills had envious Zeus put into the oak chest, and bound it with only a golden cord. He knew that sooner or later Pandora would open the chest, and then man's life of untroubled happiness would be forever at an end. Never again could the gardens of the earth be places where man might hope to find peace. Evil things had taken up their dwelling there, and they would stay for always and always and always, as long as the world should last.

When Epimetheus and Pandora saw the hateful winged creatures settling down on the leaves and flowers so as to be near at hand to torment them, they wept bitter tears and wished that the gods had never created them. In the midst of her sobbing Pandora had not, however, forgotten about the chest, and she was still wondering what else might be inside it, for she was sure that those mothlike things could never have wholly filled it. Suddenly she heard a wee soft whisper coming from within the chest, and it said: "Open, Pandora, please, please open and let me out."

Pandora stared in surprise, for she had thought that all the evil sprites had rushed out in that moment when she raised the lid. Was there, then, another host of tormenting things still there; and if so, should she let them out to add to her misery and pain?

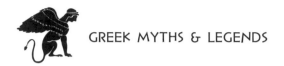

Again the little soft voice cried: "Open, Pandora, please, please open and let me out."

Pandora now called to Epimetheus, and together they listened to the pleading voice which was so very soft and sweet that they were sure it could not belong to any evil thing. Still Epimetheus was unwilling to risk bringing any more trouble into the world; but in spite of her remorse, Pandora was curious to see what it was that was begging so plaintively for freedom. So with Epimetheus's consent she opened the lid once more, and out fluttered a tiny little creature with beautiful gauzy wings. She flew straight to Pandora, then to Epimetheus, and at her touch all their hurts were healed and all their pain forgotten.

The name of this gentle messenger was Hope; and she had been hidden in the chest secretly by one of the pitying gods, who grieved that Zeus was sending so many ills to fret mankind. The host of evil beings, once set free, could never again be shut up in their narrow prison; but wherever they flew – even to the remotest corner of the earth – Hope followed them and brought healing in her wings; and when the world grew wicked, as it did in the days that came after, so that men neglected the altars of the gods, Hope was still remembered with votive offerings and her shrines kept garlanded with flowers.

3

THE DELUGE

The children of Epimetheus and Pandora wandered in the gardens of the earth just as their parents had done; and the generations that followed them lived peacefully and were happy, in spite of the brown-winged sprites that went about doing mischief. Men helped each other to cultivate the fruitful soil, and offered sacrifices to the gods in return for a bountiful harvest.

This golden age of the world's history might have lasted forever if men had continued to reverence the gods; but after a time they ceased to offer prayers for health and safety, and boasted proudly of their own strength. They looked no more to high Olympus for help, but each man trusted to his own right arm. Then strife and discord arose, and fierce wars were fought among all the peoples of the earth. Brother killed brother, and fathers strove with their own sons. Every man's hand was against his fellow, and he knew no law but that of his own will. Seldom now were the fires kindled on the neglected altars, and the smell of burnt offerings dear to the gods no longer mingled with the smoke that rose up to the white clouds around Olympus. The sacred vessels mouldered in forsaken temples; around the shrines of the gods the snakes crawled lazily; and the bat and owl dwelt undisturbed among the pillars of the temples.

For a time the gods sat patient, believing that this state of things could not last; but seeing that mankind was growing worse instead of better, year by year, they determined to put an end to godlessness and to destroy the whole race of man. Then Zeus called a council of the gods to decide on the most effective way of wiping out every vestige of human life so completely that not one soul would be left to tell to his children the story of those evil days, when men neglected to worship the immortal gods and allowed their temples to decay.

The most terrible punishment to visit upon man would be to set the whole world on fire, to make of it one great sacrificial altar on which human victims, and not the garlanded ox, would burn night and day, and from which the smoke would rise up into the heavens so thickly that it would shut out the sight of a blackened and smouldering earth. The one objection to carrying out this plan was the fear lest the flames would leap so high that they would reach even to lofty Olympus, and so endanger the sacred throne of Zeus. Though the fire might not utterly destroy it, the gods could not bear to think of its burnished red-gold base being touched by any flame from earth's unholy fires.

The only other effective method of destruction was water, and this the gods decided to employ. So on a certain day when men were everywhere feasting, and singing songs, and boasting of their victories in battle, Zeus rent the heavens with a mighty thunderbolt, whose crashing drowned all sounds of merriment, and made men turn pale with fear. The skies opened, and the rain poured down in torrents; the rivers became swollen and flooded their banks; the waves of the sea, rising higher and higher, swept in great fury over the land, washing everything before them like so much chaff. Aeolus, god of the storm, opened the cave where he kept the winds securely bound, and let them loose to work havoc on the earth. Soon all the lowland was covered with water; not a dry spot remained anywhere but on the hills, and thither the terrified people rushed in the vain hope that the flood would subside before the mountains were submerged. But the waves rose higher and higher; and the winds, rejoicing in their freedom, beat up the water until it almost touched the clouds. The frail boats to which men had at first desperately clung were shattered to pieces in the fury of the storm, and on the crest of the waves the bodies of the dead were tossed like playthings. Higher and higher rose the water, until at length the mountain tops were covered, and all dry land had disappeared. So were the gods avenged.

There was one spot, however, that was not yet hidden under the waters, and this was the top of Mount Parnassus, the highest hill of Greece. To this place of refuge had fled Deucalion and his wife Pyrrha, two virtuous souls who alone, of all the people on the earth, had lived uprightly and worshipped the gods. When Zeus saw them standing on the top of Mount Parnassus and weeping over the universal destruction, he remembered their piety and decreed that their lives should be spared. So he gave commands that the rains and the floods and the winds should cease, and the dry land appear. Then Aeolus brought the winds back from their mad wanderings and bound them again in the cave. Poseidon blew upon his conch-shell, and the angry waves returned again to the sea. Little by little the tree-tops showed above the water, and the green earth smiled again under the warm rays of the sun.

But it was upon a desolate and unpeopled world that the eyes of Deucalion and Pyrrha rested, and in their utter loneliness they almost wished that they had perished with their friends. They went slowly down the mountain side, not knowing where to go, being led blindly by the will of the gods to the temple at Delphi – the only building that was not destroyed. To this sacred spot men had been wont to come in the old, god-fearing days to consult the wishes of

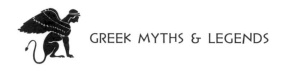

the gods and to learn their own destinies. Here was the divine oracle that not even the most daring mortal would refuse to obey.

When Deucalion and Pyrrha found themselves at the temple of Delphi, they made haste to consult the oracle, for they wished to repeople the land before another morning's sun could look down upon a lifeless earth. To their surprise the oracle returned them this answer:

"Depart from here with veiled heads and throw your mother's bones behind you."

This command seemed impossible to obey; for they could never hope to find any grave, when all landmarks had been washed away; and, even could they do so, it was an unheard-of sacrilege to disturb the bones of the dead. Deucalion sought, therefore, to explain the strange words of the oracle in some other way; and at length he guessed the meaning of the god's answer. It was no human remains that he was commanded to desecrate; the bones referred to were those of Mother Earth. So husband and wife left the temple with veiled heads; and as they went they gathered up the stones at their feet and threw these behind them. All the stones that fell from the hands of Deucalion turned into men, and those that Pyrrha dropped became women.

Thus it was that through the kindness and wisdom of the immortals the earth was repeopled with a new race of men that feared evil, and reverenced piety, and walked humbly before the gods. Never again was Zeus forced to send a deluge on the earth, for men no longer let the altar-fires burn low, nor did they neglect to offer sacrifices because of forgotten prayers.

4

ATHENA

I

Although the brown-winged spirits of evil were kept busy flying up and down the earth, their mischief-making never reached those immortal ones who dwelt above the cloud-wrapped summit of Olympus. It was, therefore, a most unheard-of happening when the father of the gods complained one day of a terrible pain in his head. Some of the gods were skilled in the art of healing; but no one could relieve Zeus's suffering, nor tell what might be the cause of his pain. The trouble grew worse and worse until it was too severe for even a god to endure; so Zeus bade his son Hephaestus take an axe and split open his head. Not daring to thwart the divine will, Hephaestus tremblingly obeyed; and at the first blow a marvellous thing occurred, for out of Zeus's head sprang a maiden clad in armour and bearing a spear in her hand. This was Athena, goddess of wisdom, so called because she came full-grown from the mighty brain of Zeus. So wise did the ruler of the gods find this child of his to be, that he kept her constantly near him, and sought her counsel in dealing with the affairs of men, while Hera, his stately wife, stood jealously by, envying the warrior-maiden her place at Zeus's side.

Being born equipped for battle, Athena delighted in war, and had no feminine shrinking from the noise of clashing steel or the cries of struggling men. No Trojan hero gloried in the war more exultingly than she, as she carried aloft the terrible shield of Zeus – "the Aegis" – and bore in her hand the mighty spear, "heavy and huge and strong". When armies met in battle, the goddess was never far away from the fighting hosts; and ofttimes a dying soldier, turning his eyes for a last look at his comrades, saw the glint of her spear or the flash of her shield as she led the favoured ones on to victory.

But the azure-eyed Athena was not always on the battle-field, for in spite of her warlike appearance she had many very feminine tastes, and among them was a love of weaving. Often would white-armed Hera taunt Athena with her unwomanly fondness for warfare; but when the goddess took up her weaving, even jealous Hera could not withhold her praise, for the hand that could wield a spear like a man had also the delicate touch of a woman.

Now there lived on the earth a maiden named Arachne, who was very proud of her skill in weaving, and boasted that in the whole length and breadth of the land there was no one to equal her in this art. Whenever people spoke with her, she could talk of nothing else but her work; and if a stranger stopped to rest at her door, she would be sure to show him her weaving and to ask him whether in all his wanderings he had seen anything to surpass it. Soon she grew so conceited that she dared to compare herself with the goddess Athena, and boasted that her own work was as beautiful as anything that hung in the halls of Olympus. Her friends grew frightened at her rash speech, and begged her not to let her foolish pride go too far, lest some whisper of her boasting should reach Athena's ears. But Arachne only grew bolder, and said openly that she would not be afraid to challenge the goddess to a contest. These words were overheard by Apollo's raven, who flew quickly back to Olympus to tell what he had seen and heard.

Athena had known for some time of Arachne's boasting, but she had not deigned to notice it. Now, however, when she learned that a mortal maiden had dared to claim superiority to a goddess, she grew very angry and determined to punish such presumption. So she cast off her glittering armour and laid aside her long spear, and went down to earth in the disguise of an old woman. She found Arachne seated on the doorstep, weaving; and as she stopped to admire the girl's work, even Athena was forced to admit that the weaving was beautifully done. Soon Arachne began to boast proudly of her skill and told the pretended old woman that she hoped some day to challenge the goddess Athena to a contest. The listener seemed shocked at these daring words, and begged the maiden to be more humble and not to presume too far; but Arachne only tossed her head and laughed, saying that she wished the goddess would hear her and accept the challenge.

At these bold words Athena's anger broke out, and throwing off her disguise she commanded the astonished girl to fetch two looms and set them up in the doorway. Then she bade Arachne make good her boast. For hours they worked in silence, each weaving with practised fingers an exquisite design in the tapestry; and neither one turning her head to watch her rival's progress. When the last thread was tied and the work finished, Arachne looked anxiously at the goddess's loom, and one glance was sufficient to assure her of her own failure. Never in all her life had she seen work so faultlessly done, and the beauty of it was like that of visions in a dream.

Humiliated at her defeat, and too proud to endure the taunts that she felt awaited her from those who had heard her boast, the unhappy maiden tried to hang herself. But Athena would not let the world so easily forget how a mortal had dared to challenge a goddess; so when she saw Arachne's body hanging by a rope, she quickly changed her into a spider, and bade her spin and spin as long

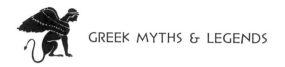
as she lived. Thus when strangers came from all the country round to see the maiden whose skill in weaving had been noised far and wide, there she hung – an ugly black spider in the midst of her dusty web – a warning to all mortals who presume.

II

Many, many years had passed since Epimetheus and Pandora wandered in the gardens of the earth; and many, many generations of men had come and gone since the day when Deucalion and Pyrrha looked down from Mount Parnassus upon an unpeopled land. Cities had been built, with marble palaces and costly temples. Towns had sprung up on river-banks and by the sea. Everywhere man was making for himself a home, and journeying into strange and distant lands. The gods, seated in the council-hall of Zeus, watched the changes taking place upon the earth; and as each new city was built and the flames of its altar-fires rose up toward the white clouds around Olympus, they smiled upon the work of man's hand and made it prosper. Nowhere was the worship of the gods forgotten, but in each undertaking the protection of some deity was sought and a sacrifice offered that success might be assured. Scattered throughout the land, in town or by the wayside, were shrines where the farmer laid his offering of doves in return for a rich harvest, or a soldier hung some trophy of victory upon his safe return from the war or a sailor, starting on some uncertain voyage, burned spices and incense that the gods might grant favouring winds to all those who go down to the sea in ships.

But in every city there was one temple more beautiful than the rest, and this was dedicated to that particular deity who had named the city and was its especial protector; and as city after city was built throughout the fair land of Greece, each of the gods wished to have the naming of it that he might thereby receive added worship and honour. There was much jealousy among them on this score, and they watched eagerly each thriving inland town or seaport, knowing that in a few years it would become a great city, building costly temples and erecting statues to the god whom it delighted to honour.

So once, when a certain town on the coast of Greece began to grow into a large and prosperous city, there was much dispute in the council hall of Zeus as to who should have the privilege of naming it. Perhaps the gods were looking far into the future and saw what this city was destined to become; but however that may be, the gods and goddesses argued so fiercely over the matter that Zeus was obliged to interfere, lest some murmur of this unusual discord should reach the earth. Then one by one the various contestants withdrew until only Poseidon and Athena were left to dispute over their respective rights to the naming of the city. There being no ground for either's claim, Zeus at length decided to give the much-coveted honour to whichever of these two should present the most useful gift to the people of the city.

Poseidon then struck the ground with his trident, and where the earth opened there sprang out a horse with snow-white mane and arching neck and a splendid body on which a king might be proud to ride. The gods and goddesses who had assembled to witness the contest were delighted with Poseidon's gift, and waited impatiently to see what better thing Athena would be able to offer. Surprise, amusement, and contempt were written on the faces of the spectators when the goddess stepped forward, holding in her hand an olive branch. But Zeus, wisest of them all, did not smile, for he was listening while Athena told of the great value her gift would have for the people of the new city. She described all the uses to which its leaves, its fruit, and even its bark could be put, adding that the olive branch was to be a sign of peace among all nations, and was therefore of more true service to man than a war-horse, which would bring upon him only bloodshed and disaster. To these wise words the gods were forced to agree, so too Athena was granted the privilege of naming the city; and she named the place Athens, which it is called to this very day. Before many years passed a splendid marble temple was built on the hill just above the city, and this was dedicated to Athena, whose colossal statue, carved by the famous sculptor Phidias, adorned the interior. They called this temple the Parthenon, and from the ruins that still remain we know that the hand of man has never built anything to equal it in beauty.

5

APOLLO AND KING ADMETUS

There would have been but little trouble between Zeus and his stately wife if no one but Athena ever gave the watchful Hera cause for jealousy; but other goddesses, and even mortal maidens, found favour in the eyes of Zeus, and for their sake he often left her side. From his throne in the high heavens the ruler of the world saw not only the goddesses, with their glory of immortal youth, but also the daughters of men endowed with that same beauty and grace which the gods themselves had bestowed upon the first woman. Though Hera "of the snow-white arms" alone enjoyed the title of queen of heaven, she knew that she had many rivals for the love of Zeus; and it was this jealousy of all loveliness in woman that made her ever watchful and revengeful. Perhaps it was the cause, too, of the very changeable temper that her husband accused her of possessing.

Whoever won the affections of Zeus was sure to be persecuted by "cruel Hera's unrelenting hate", as the poet Virgil says; but this did not hinder the ruler of the gods from leaving very often the marble halls of Olympus to wander, in some disguise, about the earth. It was after such an absence that the watchful Hera learned of Zeus's love for fair-haired Leto, goddess of dark nights. As this new rival was not a mortal maiden who could be punished with death, the wrathful queen was forced to be content with banishing the goddess forever from Olympus, and compelling her to live upon the earth. Not satisfied with this, she decreed that any one who took pity on the unhappy goddess, or gave her any help, would incur the lasting displeasure of Hera.

For days and nights Leto wandered, not daring to ask for food or shelter, since all men knew of Hera's decree. She slept at night in some spot where the trees offered protection from wind and rain, and her only food was the scanty store that she could gather by the way – berries, nuts, wild honey, and sometimes bits of bread dropped by children in their play. One day, being very thirsty, she stopped beside a clear pool to drink; but some reapers who were passing by saw her, and hoping to gain favour with Hera they stepped into the pool and stirred up the water into such muddiness that poor Leto could not drink. Angered by such uncalled-for cruelty, the goddess prayed to Zeus that these wicked men might never leave the spot where they were standing. Zeus from his throne in the high heavens heard her prayer, and in answer he turned the reapers into ugly green frogs and bade them stay forever in the muddy pool. And ever afterward when men came upon slimy ponds, where rank weeds grew and the water oozed from muddy banks, there they found the blinking frogs – even as Zeus had willed.

After wandering some miles further Leto came at last to the seashore and here she begged Poseidon, "the god who shakes the shores", to come to her aid, for she knew that Hera's power did not extend to the ruler of the sea. Seeing her distress, and pitying the poor persecuted goddess, Poseidon sent her a dolphin, who took her on his back and swam with her to the floating island of Delos, which the kindly sea-god had caused to appear out of the depth of the ocean. Here Leto landed, and was for a time content; but the rocking of the island soon grew unbearable, and she begged the aid of Poseidon a second time. He obligingly chained the island to the bottom of the Aegean Sea, and Leto had no further cause for complaint. On this island were born her two children: Apollo, god of the sun, and Artemis, goddess of the moon.

When the children were grown, Zeus took them to Olympus, though not without much protest from the ever-jealous Hera. The young Apollo's beauty and his skill in music gained him great favour among the gods, and found him worshippers in every town and city throughout the land of Greece. So conscious of his power did Apollo become, that he sometimes dared to assert his authority, unmindful of the will of Zeus; and on one occasion he so angered his divine parent that he was banished to the earth, and made to serve Admetus, king of Thessaly.

In spite of his disgrace, Apollo managed to cheer his lonely hours of labour with his music; and as his work was no more difficult than to care for the king's sheep, he had abundant leisure to play upon his lyre while his flocks grazed on the sunny hillsides. As soon as he touched the strings, all the wild things in the forest crept out to hear. The fox came slinking from his hole among the rocks, and the timid deer drew close to the player and stayed beside him, listening. The strains of the wonderful music were carried across the meadows, and the mowers stopped their work, wondering where the player might be. One day they brought word to the king that some god must be among them, for no mortal could produce such music as they had heard. So Admetus sent for the shepherd, and when the youth stood before him, he marvelled at his great beauty, and still more at the golden lyre that Apollo held in his hand. Then when the young musician, in obedience to the king's command, began to play, all those who heard him were filled with wonder, and felt sure that a god had come to dwell among them. But Admetus asked no questions, only made the youth his head shepherd and treated him with all kindness.

Though a god, and no true shepherd, Apollo served the king faithfully, and when, at last, his time of service was over and Zeus called him back to Olympus, Apollo, wishing to show some favour in return for the king's kindness, begged for Admetus the gift of immortality. This request the wise Zeus granted, but only on the condition that when the time came for the king to die, some one could be found to take his place. Apollo agreed to these terms, and Admetus, knowing the conditions on which the gift was made, accepted his immortality gladly. For a time all went well; but the inevitable hour came when the Fates decreed that Admetus's life was ended, and that he must go the way of all mortals unless some one would die in his stead. The king was much beloved by his people; but no one's devotion to his sovereign was great enough to inspire him to make the needed sacrifice.

Then Alcestis, the beautiful wife of Admetus, learned of the price that must be paid for her husband's immortality and gladly offered her life in exchange for the king's. So, in all her young grace and beauty, she went down into the dark region of Hades, where no sunlight ever came and where her joyous laughter was forever hushed in the silence that reigns among the dead. Thus Admetus gained immortality; but his happiness was too dearly bought, for as the days went by he mourned more and more for his beautiful young wife, and in his dreams he saw her walking like a shadow among the grim shapes that move noiselessly in the silent halls of death. Bitterly he repented of his selfishness in accepting the sacrifice of her life, and his immortality grew hateful to him since each day only added to his sorrow. So he prayed to Apollo to recall his gift, and to give him back his wife Alcestis. It was not in the power of that god to change a decree of Zeus's; but the ruler of all things looked down from heaven, and, seeing the great grief and remorse of Admetus, he withdrew the gift that had cost the king so dear, and sent Heracles to the kingdom of Hades with commands to let Alcestis go. Very gladly the god carried this message to the gloomy realm of Hades, where amid the myriad shadow-shapes he sought and found Alcestis; and out of the dreadful darkness in which she walked alone, Heracles led her back to earth again.

6

APOLLO THE MUSICIAN

I

When Apollo left King Admetus and returned to the halls of Olympus, he had not rested there long before he found that there was further service for him to render on the earth. Among the many noted deeds that he performed, the most famous was his slaying of a monstrous serpent called the Python, which was born of the slime that remained on the surface of the earth after the Deluge. Apollo killed the creature with his golden arrows, and then went to the help of Poseidon, who, though a powerful deity in his own realm, was often obliged to ask help of the other gods when he wished to accomplish anything on land. Hearing that Poseidon wished to build a great wall around the city of Troy, and remembering the aid that the sea-god had given his mother Leto in her great need, Apollo went down to the sea and offered his services to Poseidon. Of course no son of Zeus could be expected to do the work of a slave, but this was not necessary, even in the building of a wall; for Apollo sat down on a grassy bank near by, and, with his lyre in his hand, began to play such exquisite music that the very stones were bewitched, and rising from the ground of their own accord took their places in the wall. Still under the spell of Apollo's music, others followed in quick succession, and the wall rose higher and higher, until before nightfall the whole work was finished. When the last stone had dropped into place, Apollo stopped his playing and returned to the bright halls of Olympus; while Poseidon, shaking the salt spray from his shaggy eyebrows, stared hard at the walls that had risen by magic before his wondering eyes.

II

The story of Arachne's sad fate should have been warning enough to all mortals not to compare themselves with the gods; but such was the pride of a certain youth named Aresyas that he boasted openly of his skill in flute-playing, and dared to proclaim himself the equal of Apollo. Now Aresyas had not always been a musician, for he was by birth a shepherd – some even say a satyr – and had never seen a flute or heard it played until one day, as he sat tending his flock on the bank of a stream, he heard sounds of music coming from some spot near by. He was very curious to see who the musician might be, but he dared not move lest he startle the player and make the beautiful melody cease. So he sat still and waited; and presently there came floating down the stream a flute – something that Aresyas had never seen before. He hurriedly snatched it out of the water, and, no longer hearing the wonderful music, he guessed that it had come from the strange thing he held in his hand. He put the flute to his lips, and lo, the same sweet melody greeted his ears, for the flute was not a common thing such as any man might use – it was a beautiful instrument that belonged to no less a person than Athena. The goddess had hidden herself on the bank of the stream and had been trying her skill as a flute-player; but chancing to look down into the water, she saw her puffed-out cheeks and distorted features and angrily threw the flute into the stream. Thus it had come into Aresyas's possession; and the shepherd, having found such a treasure, never let it leave his hands. He neglected his work and left his flocks unguarded while he spent all his days in the delight of flute-playing.

It was not long before he believed himself to be the greatest musician in all Greece; and then it was only a step further to declare that even Apollo could not equal him in the sweetness of his playing. The god of music allowed this boasting to go for some time unpunished; but at last he grew angry at the presumption of the shepherd boy, and summoned Aresyas to a contest in which the nine Muses were to be judges. Nothing daunted, Aresyas accepted the challenge; and on the morning when the contest took place, a great silence fell over all the earth, as if every living thing had stopped to listen. The playing of Aresyas was wonderfully sweet, and as the soft tones of his flute greeted the listeners' ears they sat as if under a spell until the last sounds died away. Then Apollo took up his golden lyre, and when he struck the first chords, the air was filled with music far sweeter than any melody that had fallen from the lips of Aresyas. The judges, however, found it hard to give a verdict in favour of either musician; so a second time Aresyas began to play, and his music was so strangely wild and sweet that even Apollo listened in delight. But, charmed as he was by the youth's playing, the god of music had no intention of being outdone by a shepherd; so when he took up his golden lyre again, he began to sing, and added the wonder of his voice to the sweetness of his playing. When the singing ended there was no longer any doubt to whom the victory belonged; and Aresyas was forced to admit his defeat. As the price of failure was to be the terrible penalty of being flayed alive, the wretched Aresyas had to submit to this cruel death. Apollo bound him to a tree and slew him with his own hands.

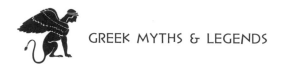
III

When the news of Aresyas's dreadful fate spread abroad, people were careful for many years not to anger any of the deities by presuming to rival them; but in time the memory of that tragic event faded away, and the horror of it was forgotten.

In the halls of King Midas was the noise of great mirth and feasting, and the sound of music filled the spacious room where the king and his court sat at the banquet-table. Beside the king stood Pan, his favourite flute-player, who was no other than the famous sylvan god of shepherds; and as the wine went round and the king grew boastful of his possessions, he exclaimed loudly that not even Apollo himself could produce such exquisite music as fell from the flute of Pan. The guests, remembering the fate of Aresyas, grew pale and begged the king not to let his boast be heard; but Midas laughed scornfully and, raising his drinking cup above his head, called upon Apollo to appear.

To the surprise and dismay of all, the god of music suddenly stood before them, beautiful as the dawn and glowing with divine wrath. Though Pan was himself a deity, he had no desire to challenge Apollo, and looked fearfully at the sun-god's angry frown; but the king, drunk with pride, commanded him to play, and bade the god of music surpass the playing if he could. There was, of course, no question as to which was the better musician, and the guests loudly proclaimed Apollo the victor. One story tells that to prove further the superiority of Apollo's playing the company went to the old mountain-god Tmolus, and let him make the final decision. Tmolus had to clear the trees from his ears to listen; and having done this he bent his head, and all his trees leaned with him. He heard with delight both musicians play; and when the last soft notes fell from Apollo's lyre, the mountain-god awarded him the victory. But Midas at the beginning of the contest had demanded the right to decide on the merits of the players, and he would not accept this verdict. In his mad perversity and fondness for his favourite, he cried out that Pan was the better player, and would therefore be awarded the prize. Angered at this unfair decision, Apollo left the banquet-hall, but not before he had assured Midas that the injustice would be punished.

These words came true in a most unexpected way, for when the king looked into his mirror the next morning, he found a pair of large fuzzy ass's ears growing in the place of his own natural ones. Horrified at his absurd appearance, Midas did not dare show himself to his people; but sent in haste for a barber, and bade him make a wig large enough to cover the monstrous ears. For many hours the barber was closeted with the king, and when the wig was finished, he was allowed to leave the palace, after having sworn never to reveal the king's misfortune under pain of death. For some time the secret was safely kept; but the poor barber found life unbearable, since he lived in constant fear of letting out the truth about the king's ears in spite of his frantic efforts to be silent. Whenever Midas appeared in the city streets, the barber had to rush home and shut himself up lest he should scream out the story of the wig.

One day he thought of a happy solution to his difficulty and one that broke his long seal of silence without endangering his life. He went out into the fields, dug a deep hole, and putting his head down as far as he could he shouted:

"King Midas has ass's ears, King Midas has ass's ears."

Then he went home again, much happier for having told some one of his secret, even though it was only Mother Earth. But the truth once told did not stay hidden even in the earth; for in time the hole was filled again and reeds grew over the spot, and as the wind swayed them back and forth they murmured: "King Midas has ass's ears. King Midas has ass's ears."

It was not long before all the people in the countryside had gathered to hear the strange whispering of the reeds, and then the secret could be kept no longer. But though every one knew the truth King Midas continued to wear his wig, and no one ever saw the real size of his ears.

7

THE LOVE OF APOLLO

I

Like his father, Zeus, the young Apollo was not content to stay always in the shining halls of Olympus, but spent many days wandering over the broad lands of Greece in search of adventure, or for the sake of some maiden's love. There were many fair ones among the daughters of men, and they were wont to look with favour upon the beautiful young god who came down from the high heavens to woo them. Each morning as he drove across the sky the fiery horses that were harnessed to the chariot of the sun, some maiden gazed with longing at the splendour above her, and prayed that the radiant Apollo might look kindly upon her. Seldom did these prayers go unanswered; but sometimes the heart of the god was untouched by the devotion so freely offered, and the maiden pined away over her hopeless love.

Such a one was Clytie, who worshipped the glorious sun-god, and longed in secret for his love; but in spite of her tears and sighing she met with only coldness in return. Each day she rose before the dawn to greet Apollo as soon as his chariot appeared in the heavens, and all day long she watched him until the last rays of light were lost

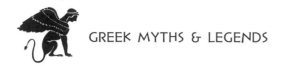

behind the hills. But the young god felt no sympathy for her sorrow, and the unhappy Clytie grew so pale and sick with longing that Zeus in pity changed her into a sunflower, that she might always stand watching the course of the sun, and turn her face forever toward him, no matter where his beams might shine.

II

The great beauty of Apollo usually assured his success whenever he stooped from his high estate to love the maidens of the earth; but once he was repaid for his hard-heartedness to poor Clytie, and failed in his wooing when he sought the love of the beautiful wood-nymph Daphne. He was wandering one day in the forest when he came suddenly upon Daphne as she was gathering flowers, and her beauty and grace so charmed him that he desired her love above everything else in the world. Not wishing to frighten her, he stood still and softly spoke her name. When the nymph heard his voice, she turned quickly and looked at him with the startled eyes of some wild forest-creature. Surprise and fear held her for a moment while Apollo spoke again gently and begged her not to be afraid, for he was no hunter nor even a rude shepherd. But Daphne only shrank away, fearful of his eagerness; and when Apollo grew bolder and ventured to draw near, she turned and fled through the forest. Angered at this rebuff, the god followed her, and though the nymph ran swiftly she could not escape from her pursuer, who was now more than ever determined to win her.

In and out among the trees she darted, hoping to bewilder him into giving up the chase; but Apollo kept close behind, and little by little gained on her flying feet. Wearied but unyielding, Daphne now hurried her steps toward the stream at the edge of the forest, where she knew that she would find her father, the river-god Peneus. As she neared the stream she cried aloud to him for help; and just as Apollo had reached her side and his outstretched hand was on her shoulder, a rough bark began to enclose her soft body in its protecting sheath; green branches sprouted from the ends of her uplifted arms; and her floating hair became only waving leaves under the grasp of the god's eager fingers. Apollo stood dismayed at this transformation, and when he saw a laurel tree rooted in the spot where, but a moment ago, had stood a beautiful living maiden, he repented of his folly in having pursued her and sat for many days beside the river, mourning her loss.

Thus it was that the laurel became the favourite tree of Apollo; and when the god returned sadly to Olympus, he decreed that whenever poet or musician or any victor in the games was to be crowned with a garland of leaves, those leaves were to be taken from the laurel tree in memory of Daphne.

III

In one of the flower-filled meadows of sunny Greece, there played all day a golden-haired boy named Phaëton, who was the pride and delight of his mother Clymene, a stately maiden whom Apollo had once wooed and won. The boy was wilful and headstrong, but beautiful as a young god; and his mother, in her foolish pride, often reminded him how favoured he was above all other children in being the son of Apollo. Each morning she led him to a place where he could see the sun rise, and told him that his father was just then harnessing the fiery steeds to his golden-wheeled car, and would soon be leaving his palace of burnished gold to drive across the heavens, bringing daylight to the darkened earth. She told him of Apollo's great beauty, and of his wonderful music, and of his high position among the gods, because his chariot was nothing less than the glorious sun. Phaëton never tired of hearing these stories, and it was no wonder that he became very proud of his divine parentage, and boasted of it among his playmates. The children only laughed at his wonderful tales, and to convince them he grew more arrogant in his bearing, until they, angered by his continued boasts, bade him give some proof of his claims or else be silent. This Phaëton could not do; so they taunted him with his godlike appearance, and sneered at his pretensions until the boy, roused to action by their repeated insults, ran to his mother, and begged her to tell him whether he might not speak to his wonderful, but unknown father, and obtain from him some proof to silence the children's tongues.

Clymene hesitated to send the child on the long necessary journey, but yielding at last to his entreaties, she showed him the way to his father's palace. It was night when Phaëton set out, and he was obliged to travel quickly if he wished to reach his journey's end before the sun-car left the golden portals of the east. The palace of the sun was marvellously wrought, and the light from its golden columns and glittering jewelled towers so dazzled the eyes of Phaëton that he was afraid to draw near. But remembering the taunts of his playmates, he grew bolder, and sought out his father to beg the boon for which he had travelled so far and wearily. When Apollo, from his ivory throne, saw the boy approaching, he welcomed him kindly and called him by the name of son. Hearing this, Phaëton lost all fear, and told his father how the children had refused to believe Clymene's stories, and had taunted him because he could not prove the truth of his mother's claim.

The lofty brow of Apollo grew cloudy as he listened to Phaëton's words, and he promised to give the boy the proof he desired by granting him any favour he might ask. Instantly Phaëton demanded that he be allowed that very day to drive the sun-chariot; for when those on the earth saw him in that exalted place, they could no longer refuse to believe that he was indeed the favoured child of Apollo. Dismayed at this unexpected request, the sun-god sought to persuade Phaëton to ask some other boon, for he knew that no hand but his own could guide the four winged horses that were harnessed to the golden sun-car. But the boy was determined to carry out his plan; and with all the wilfulness of a conceited child, he refused to heed his father's warnings. As Apollo had sworn by the river Styx – the most terrible of all oaths – to grant Phaëton's request whatever it might be, he was obliged to fulfil his promise; and very reluctantly he led the boy to the portals of the palace, where the impatient horses already stood pawing the ground.

Phaëton gazed at the sun-car in delight, for it was all of gold – except the spokes of the wheel, which were of silver – and the body of the chariot was studded with chrysolites and diamonds that reflected the sun's dazzling brightness. The impatient boy sprang into the chariot and seized the reins in his hands, while his father bound on his head the blazing sun rays; but before the journey was begun, Apollo poured over him a cooling essence, that his skin might not be shrivelled by the burning heat of the sun, and gave him careful instructions how to handle the restless steeds. Phaëton but half listened to these words, and fretted to be off on his triumphant course; so Apollo ordered the gates to be thrown open, and the sun-car dashed out into the heavens.

For a while all went well, for the boy remembered his father's caution about using a whip on the fiery horses; but as the day wore on he became reckless, and forgot everything but his own proud triumph. Faster and faster he drove, flourishing his whip, and never heeding in what direction the maddened horses sped. Soon he lost his way and the chariot came so close to the earth that its fierce heat dried up the rivers and scorched the ground and shrivelled up all vegetation, even turning the natives in that part of the country brown – which colour they are still to this very day. Smoke rose up from the charred and blackened earth, and it so clouded the eyes of the now terrified Phaëton that he could not find his way back to the path of the sun and drove wildly far away from the earth. This caused terrible disaster, for under the sudden cold all growing things withered, and the blight of frost settled over all the land.

Then a great cry arose from the people of the earth when they saw their country laid waste; and though Zeus was fast asleep on his golden couch he heard the cry, and started up in surprise. What *could* be happening on the earth that the sound of human wailing should break in upon the silence of his dreams! One glance was sufficient for him to see the smoke rising from the burnt-up land and to realize the cause of all that useless destruction; for far across the heavens – like a vanishing comet – Phaëton was madly driving the flaming chariot of the sun. Angered at the sight of a mere boy presuming to take upon himself so great a task, Zeus seized one of his deadliest thunderbolts and hurled it at the unhappy youth, whose scorched body was immediately dashed from its lofty seat and sank into the calm waters of the Eridanus River.

Clymene mourned her son's untimely death, and gathered his remains from the river that they might have honourable burial. Phaëton's dearest friend, Cycnus, continued to haunt the river's edge, looking for any relic of his favourite that might chance to rise to the surface of the water. In recognition of this devotion the gods changed him into a swan that might stay forever on the river and plunge his head fearlessly into the clear waters to search for some scattered fragments of his unfortunate friend.

8

ARTEMIS

I

During the childhood of Apollo and Artemis the goddess Leto lived happily on the island of Delos, and forgot all her early misfortunes in the joy of her children. As they grew up she boasted of their strength and beauty to all who came to the shores of Delos, and no village or hamlet – however small – but had heard of Leto's children. When Grecian mothers put their little ones to bed at night, they told wonderful tales of an island far out at sea where a brother and sister lived who were fairer than all the flowers in the meadows; and maidens, sighing for a loveliness greater than their own, wove garlands to adorn the shrines of those two who walked the earth in all their immortal grace.

Leto was proud of her children's fame, and boasted of it far and wide. Few mothers cared to dispute her claim, and these spoke only in whispers; but there was one, bolder than the rest, who openly laughed at the goddess's boast and taunted her with having but *two* such children whom she could praise. This was Niobe, a Grecian princess and the mother of fourteen children – seven sons and seven daughters – all of them fair and strong and godlike in spite of their mortal birth. When Niobe learned that the people in her kingdom were loud in their praises of Leto's children, and were neglecting to honour her own splendid sons and daughters, she was very angry and ordered all the statues of Apollo and Artemis to be destroyed; for the people, in their devotion to beauty, had set up many in the temples and the market place. Then she bade a messenger go tell the goddess what had been done, and show her in what contempt the mother of fourteen children held her who had but two.

When Leto received the message she was so enraged at the insult that her desire for revenge knew no bounds. She called Apollo and Artemis to her side and commanded them to go forth and slay the children of Niobe. It was easy for Apollo to accomplish his part of the cruel task, for he met the seven sons of Niobe hunting, and slew them so quickly that not one of the brothers had time to ask what he had done to merit the god's wrath. The daughters of Niobe were in the palace with their mother; but this did not daunt the young Artemis, who put seven sharp arrows in her quiver, and, bow in hand, went forth to complete Leto's revenge. She found the maidens seated at Niobe's side, weaving, and one by one the remorseless goddess shot them down in spite of their mother's heart-broken cries for mercy. Finding that her entreaties were in vain, and seeing six of her daughters lying dead beside her, the distracted Niobe sought to shield the remaining one with her own body while she prayed wildly to the gods to spare her this one child. But the gods were deaf to her cries, and Artemis, fitting the last arrow to her bow, shot the maiden as she cowered in her mother's arms.

Over her fallen body the wretched Niobe wept so long that the gods at last felt pity for her grief, and changed her into stone. This statue was placed by a running stream, and ever afterward the waters were fed by the tears that continued to course down the cheeks of the stone image; and travellers came from foreign lands to gaze on this marvel of a devoted mother who could not cease from mourning for her children even when turned into stone.

II

Though the goddess Artemis spent most of her daylight hours in hunting, it was not often that she exercised her skill to such cruel purpose as was shown in the case of poor Niobe. Wherever the wild deer roamed, and the pathless forest knew no touch of woodman's axe, there Artemis, fleet-footed and tireless, followed the chase. As soon as the flaming chariot of the sun threw its first streak of light across the hills, the goddess donned her short tunic, and, armed with her golden bow and quiver, set out with her band of nymphs for the day's hunt. At noontide, wearied with the chase, she sought out some secluded spot where the mountain stream ran clear, and where the foliage hung round her like a curtain.

On a certain day, when she and her maidens were enjoying the refreshing coolness of the water, they heard a slight rustle among the trees, and looking around, perceived a young hunter watching them. This was Actaeon, who had himself been following the deer since daybreak, and had been drawn to this spot by the noise of running water. As he neared the stream he heard sounds of girlish laughter, and this so roused his curiosity that he hastily put aside the branches to see who the merrymakers might be. Great was his dismay when he recognized Artemis and her nymphs; but before he could disappear among the bushes the goddess saw him, and catching up some water in her hand, she threw it into his face, crying: "Go now, if you can, and say that you have seen Artemis at her bath."

The moment these words were spoken Actaeon felt a queer change coming over him, and he stared in horror at his hands and feet, which were becoming hoofs, and at his skin, which was rapidly changing into a deer's hide. Antlers grew out of his head, he dropped on all fours, and found himself turned into a stag. Before he quite realized what had befallen him he heard the baying of hounds, and knew that his only safety was in flight. He dashed off through the bushes, but the dogs were on his track. Before he had gone far the pack had overtaken him, since he knew no lore of the wild things by which they elude their enemies, and were snapping and snarling at his throat. Deprived of his human voice he could not cry for help, and in a moment the hounds had torn him into pieces. So was Artemis avenged.

III

There was another young hunter who encountered Artemis and her maidens in the woods, but he met with a kinder fate at the hands of the goddess than did poor Actaeon, whose only fault had been a most natural curiosity.

The fleet-footed Artemis was no more ardent in the chase than was the hunter Orion, who roamed the forest all day with his faithful dog, Sirius. One morning, as he rushed eagerly through the woods in pursuit of a deer, he came suddenly upon the seven Pleiades – nymphs of Artemis – who were resting after a long and arduous hunt begun at daybreak. Charmed with their beauty, Orion drew nearer, but the maidens, terrified at his outstretched arms, fled away through the forest. Undaunted by the remembrance of Actaeon's fate, the hunter pursued the flying nymphs, determined that so much beauty should not escape him. Seeing that he was gaining on them in spite of their swift feet, the maidens called upon Artemis for help, and were at once changed into seven white pigeons which flew up into the heavens before Orion's astonished eyes. Sometime later these same Pleiades became seven bright stars, and were set as a constellation in the sky, where they have remained ever since.

Orion continued to hunt from early dawn until nightfall without any misfortune overtaking him on account of his impetuous love-making. On the contrary his ardour evidently found favour with the goddess Artemis, for one day, when he unexpectedly met her alone in the forest, she smiled graciously upon him and offered to share the day's sport with him. Perhaps it was the beauty of the young hunter as well as his boldness that charmed the goddess; but however that may be, she continued to meet him in the forest, and they hunted together hour after hour until the twilight began to fall. Then Artemis knew that she must leave her lover and mount her silver moon-car.

When Apollo learned of his sister's affection for the young hunter, he was very angry, for Artemis had refused the love of the gods, and had begged of Zeus the right to live unwed. The sun-god determined therefore to put an end to Orion's wooing. So he waited at the shadowy portals of the west until Artemis, her nightly journey over, descended from her silver car and threw the reins on the necks of her wearied steeds. Then Apollo spoke to his sister of her hunting, and praised her skill with the bow. Presently he pointed to a tiny speck that was rising and falling on the crest of the waves a long distance away, and bidding her use this as a target, he challenged her to prove her skill. Artemis, suspecting no treachery, fitted an arrow into her bow and let it fly with unerring aim. Great was her distress when she learned what her brother's trickery had led her to do; for it was no floating log or bit of seaweed that her arrow had pierced, but the body of Orion. Apollo had seen the hunter go each morning to the ocean to bathe, and he thought this an easy way to dispose of the unworthy lover.

Artemis mourned Orion many days; and to keep his memory honoured she placed him and his faithful dog, Sirius, in the sky as constellations.

9

THE STORY OF ENDYMION

The chaste Artemis was not only a famous huntress, but she was goddess of the moon as well. By day she roamed the forest with her band of nymphs, and by night she sailed in her bright moon-car across the star-strewn sky, and looked down at the sleeping earth lying in the shadow except where her soft light fell. As soon as Apollo had driven his tired, foam-flecked horses within the western gates, and twilight had begun to creep over the hills, Artemis mounted her silver car drawn by milk-white steeds, and started on her nightly journey. During the first hours of her ride, the friendly twilight kept a faint glow in the heavens, and the road lay plain before her; but as night came on and the blackness deepened, her horses might have wandered from their accustomed path had not the stars wakened from their day-dreaming and come out in great luminous clusters to light the goddess on her way. Though the journey was always the same, night after night, Artemis never wearied of her course or found the sleeping earth less lovely, as it unfolded hour by hour before her eyes.

One evening as she looked down upon the quiet scene, she saw the form of a shepherd-boy lying upon a grassy hilltop, where the moonlight shone full upon his upturned face. Artemis was not susceptible to love; but when she saw Endymion sleeping, she marvelled at his beauty, and felt a strange longing to be near him. So she stepped softly from her silver car and floated down to the earth – to the spot where the unconscious shepherd lay dreaming. There was perfect stillness all around, and no whisper came but the soft murmur from the pine-trees, which sounded like some great creature sighing in its sleep. For some time the goddess watched the youth in silence, then, stooping, she gently kissed him. Endymion half wakened at her touch, and looked sleepily around, bewildered by the radiance that seemed to be enfolding him in its unearthly light. But in a moment the glory had faded away, and there was only the deep blueness of the night all about him; for Artemis, frightened at her own boldness, had hurried back to her silver car and had sped away into the darkness. Endymion thought then that he had dreamed a dream of some beautiful form that had lingered by his side, and although he waited patiently and hopefully all through the night, he saw no other vision, and only the dawn came to greet his weary eyes.

The next night Artemis drove her milk-white horses impatiently and often at random, until the quiet stars, as they watched her restless course, wondered and felt half afraid. When the clouds wrapped her closely in their white embrace, the goddess drove them angrily aside, lest they shut out from her eyes the sight of the sleeping earth. At last she drew near the hillside where Endymion lay, and, on seeing him there, Artemis glided again from her silver car and stood beside his unconscious form. At her light touch he stirred, and tried to rouse himself from his heavy slumber; but some spell seemed to bind his eyelids, and through sleep-dimmed eyes he saw the radiance fade away. Night after night he felt the presence of that bright being whom his eyes so longed to behold; but only in his dreams could he see her face or touch her floating garments that passed by him like the rustle of the night wind.

Each night Artemis left her restless horses to stand unwatched among the shifting clouds, while she lingered on the earth to gaze upon the sleeping shepherd-boy; and as she stood beside him she wished that he might always be as now – ever beautiful, ever young. So to keep him untouched by sickness or sorrow or death she took him to Mount Latmus, where there was a cave dedicated in her honour which no mortal foot had ever profaned. Here she placed Endymion, and caused an eternal sleep to fall upon him, so that his body in all its youth and beauty might never know decay. And every night when her long journey was ended, and the watchful stars had withdrawn their shining, Artemis hastened to the lonely cave on Mount Latmus, there to linger beside Endymion sleeping, and touch him with a kiss that could not waken.

10

HERMES

I

Hermes was the son of Zeus and Maia, goddess of the plains, and from the day of his birth he was a most remarkable infant, even for a god. When scarcely a day old, he sprang from his mother's arms, and ran some distance off to where a tortoise shell was lying on the ground. Picking this up, he bored holes in its side, stretched strings across it, and began to play. Thus it was that the first lyre was made.

Proud of this beginning to his day's adventures, Hermes ran away again toward evening, when his mother was asleep, and roamed about the fragrant meadows where Apollo kept his herd of cattle. The pasturage was rich and the oxen were fat, and the mischievous young god – only a day old – decided to have some of them for his dinner. He took fifty of the herd and tied branches of leaves to their feet – so that their hoofs might leave no print on the smooth turf – and drove them to a quiet spot far away from the meadow. Here he killed and ate two of the oxen, and kept the rest in hiding for another day's feast. Then he hurried back to his mother who had not yet wakened.

When Apollo found late that evening that fifty of his cattle were gone, he searched but could not find them. As he was about to give them up as lost, he remembered that a son had been lately born to Zeus, whom that divine ruler had appointed to be the god of thieves. Suspecting that his stolen oxen were in the hands of this master-thief, Apollo hastened to where Maia and the babe were sleeping. Rousing the child angrily, the irate god accused him of the theft; but Hermes protested his innocence, and asked, "How could an infant but a day old ever do such an unheard-of thing?" Apollo was unconvinced, however, by this appearance of candour, and feeling sure of the boy's guilt, dragged him off to Olympus, where Hermes found it impossible to pretend any longer that he knew nothing of the missing oxen. He acknowledged his thieving, showed Apollo the hiding place of the stolen cattle, and in return for those that he had eaten gave the sun-god his wonderful new lyre. This gift so delighted Apollo that he presented the day-old prince of thieves with a magic wand, which, when held between any who were quarrelling, would cause all anger and strife to cease. To test the value of the wand Hermes thrust it between two snakes which were struggling over the possession of a wounded bird; and immediately they twined themselves around the staff, and remained coiled together in perfect friendliness. This pleased Hermes so much that he bade them stay there forever as long as the wand should last.

There were two other valuable gifts that the gods gave the young Hermes – a winged cap and a pair of winged sandals – so that, as the messenger of the gods, he might be fleet of foot on his many errands to and from Olympus.

> "Hastily beneath his feet he bound
> The fair ambrosial golden sandals, worn
> To bear him over ocean like the wind
> And o'er the boundless land."

Among the varied duties assigned to Hermes was that of conducting the souls of the dead to Hades; but this did not occupy all the god's time, and he still had many hours in which to go on other missions. In spite of his rather doubtful reputation for honesty, the gods often sought his assistance in their difficulties; and in one very delicate commission he proved himself a competent ally. This was when Zeus went wooing the maiden Io.

The jealous and vengeful Hera was always on the watch whenever her lord took a fancy to go wandering about the earth; so to woo the gentle Io unseen by his wife required some diplomacy on Zeus's part. Accordingly he spread a thick cloud over the meadow where he was wont to meet the maiden, and trusted that its appearance would not arouse Hera's suspicions. He also took the precaution to visit Io at the time when the watchful queen of heaven was accustomed to sleep; but one day Hera awoke sooner than usual, and finding Zeus absent, she at once surmised that he was adventuring again in some love affair. When she looked down at the earth, she saw the thick cloud that hung over the meadow and noticed that it never altered its position, no matter how the winds blew. Feeling sure that this was some trick intended to deceive her, the wrathful goddess glided down to the earth and appeared at the astonished Zeus's side – but not before he had had time to change Io into a heifer.

"Golden-sandalled" Hera walked about the meadow gathering flowers, then she asked her husband why he was lingering there, so far from bright Olympus. Zeus answered that he was amusing himself by creating a heifer. This explanation did not deceive Hera; but she pretended to be satisfied, and praised the beautiful creature's glossy skin and large soft eyes. Then she demanded it of Zeus as a gift, and the ruler of the gods, not knowing how to refuse, consented. The triumphant goddess led away the heifer and put her in charge of Argus. Now Argus had a hundred eyes, and though he often went to sleep, some of his eyes always kept awake; so Hera felt sure that no device of Zeus's could enable Io to escape from the watchful guardian who never wholly slept.

Meanwhile Zeus was in despair over this unhappy ending to his wooing, and sought the help of Hermes, who often lent his ready wits to gods and mortals in distress. Laying aside his cap and sandals and snake-entwined wand, by which he might easily be recognized, Hermes went down to the earth in the disguise of a shepherd. With his pipes in his hand he strolled through the country until he came to the mountain side, where Argus sat watching the heifer; and when he began to play, the music was so sweet that Argus begged him to stop awhile that he might listen longer to the wonderful playing. The wily god consented, and as he piped on, some of the hundred eyes grew drowsy with sleep, but some of them stayed open and watchful.

The droning of the pipes kept on, and to add to the drowsiness of the music, Hermes began to tell stories in a low sing-song tone that cast a kind of spell over the eyes that were still watching. He told of Apollo's affection for the youth Hyacinthus, whom Zephyrus, god of the west wind, also loved; and how, when the sun-god was playing quoits with his friend, Zephyrus in a fit of jealous anger blew aside the missile hurled by Apollo so that it struck Hyacinthus and killed him. But the sun-god would not let the fair youth be forgotten, and changed each drop of his blood into delicate white flowers which were forever to bear his name. Then Hermes told of Aesculapius, son of Apollo and Coronis, who was entrusted to the care of Chiron – most famous of the Centaurs – and was also taught by his divine parent the art of healing. In this he became so skilful that he even restored the dead to life, and so incurred the wrath of Zeus, who, fearing that Aesculapius would receive undue honour, killed him with a thunderbolt. To these stories Hermes added many more that told of the loves of the gods, and at last all the hundred eyes of Argus were closed. Then Hermes, drawing a sharp sword, cut off the great head as it drooped forward, and rolled it down the rocks.

When Hera heard of the death of her faithful servant she was terribly angry, and vowed that she would bring punishment on those who had been the cause of his slaying; but before doing this she commemorated the fidelity of Argus by taking his hundred eyes and putting them in the tail of her favourite bird, the peacock. Then she carried out her revenge by sending an enormous gadfly to torment poor Io, who was still in the form of a heifer. From one country to another the unhappy creature wandered; and once, in a desperate effort to escape her tormentor, she plunged into the sea, which was afterwards called Ionian in her honour. Across this she swam and reached the shore of Africa; but even here the gadfly followed her, and the vengeance of Hera never allowed her a moment's rest. Zeus could do nothing to ease her sufferings by interceding for her to the remorseless queen of heaven; but at last Hera consented to send away the gadfly and to restore Io to her own form if Zeus would promise never to visit her again. Reluctantly the ruler of the gods agreed to this demand, and Io became once more a beautiful maiden.

II

When Zeus went wandering on the earth in search of adventures other than the wooing of some maiden, he often made Hermes his companion, for this slender young god was his favourite among all the dwellers of Olympus. One day both the gods, disguised as travellers, stopped at the hut of an aged couple named Philemon and Baucis; and pretending weariness, they asked to be allowed to rest. The old couple were delighted that strangers had honoured their humble roof, and in order to extend the hospitality still further, Philemon decided to kill the one thing he had that could furnish meat for the guests. This was a large fat goose, who had no mind to be killed and eaten, even to supply a meal for gods; so when the old man tried to catch him, he sought refuge between Zeus's knees. When the ruler of the gods learned that the couple intended to sacrifice their one possession, he was greatly touched by their kindness, but would not allow them to kill the trusting bird that had fled to him for protection.

Then the good wife Baucis set before her guests olives, and cornel berries preserved in vinegar, and cheese, with eggs cooked in the ashes. She laid earthen cups and dishes on the table, which she had already rubbed with sweet-smelling herbs, and placed beside them an earthen pitcher full of their best wine. While the simple meal was going on, and the guests were partaking of a dessert of apples and wild honey, Baucis was so fluttered over her duties as hostess that she did not observe the pitcher; but old Philemon looked on in astonishment at the wine which renewed itself in the pitcher as fast as it was poured out. He whispered to his wife to watch this miracle; and when she, too, saw the never-empty pitcher, she was filled with a vague terror, and looked fearfully at the smiling strangers. So Zeus told the old man and his wife who their guests really were, and bade them ask of him some boon, swearing by the terrible river Styx to grant whatever they might desire. Then Philemon and Baucis begged that they might be allowed to serve the gods as long as they lived; and that when their time of service was over, they might die together. Pleased with the simplicity of this request, Zeus gladly promised that all should be as they wished; and he transformed their humble cottage into a beautiful temple, where they might worship the gods all their days. And when after years of faithful service Philemon and Baucis died, Zeus changed them into lordly oaks, which stood before the pillars of the temple as a monument to their fidelity.

II

APHRODITE

I

Once the stately Hera looked down from high-peaked Olympus and saw Zeus walking in a meadow with a maiden so exquisitely fair that the flowers at her feet looked dull and faded beside her dazzling whiteness. This was Callisto, so famous for her beauty that suitors came from distant lands to woo her; but she cared nothing for their rich gifts, nor would she listen to any vows of love. Then Zeus sought her as she wandered alone in the meadow; and the maiden gladly yielded to the great ruler of the gods the love that no mortal man had been able to win. When white-armed Hera learned how many hours Zeus spent by the side of Callisto, she determined to punish the helpless maiden, and accordingly turned her into a bear. For a long time Zeus sought her in the familiar meadow, but she never came again to meet him. Then one day he found her in the forest with her little son Arcas – both turned into bears by the jealous hate of Hera. Grieved as he was at this misfortune, the ruler of Olympus could not restore them to their human form; but he took them to the heavens, that they might suffer no further harm, and placed them in the sky as the constellations of the Great and Little Bear.

Zeus often assumed the form of a bird or animal so as to escape Hera's watchful eyes. As a swan he won the love of Leda, and their child was the fair-haired Helen whose beauty cost the men of Troy so dear. As a white bull he wooed the gentle maid Europa, who was frightened at his sudden appearance in the meadow where she was playing; but as soon as she saw how tame the beautiful animal was and how anxious to be petted, she lost all her fear. She made a wreath of flowers to hang about his neck, and grew so accustomed to her new playmate that she got upon his back as he bent his lordly head to receive her garlands. The bull then galloped away toward the sea, and before the terrified girl could realize what had happened he plunged with her into the waves. As soon as they were far from the land, the white bull spoke gently to Europa and told her who he really was and how, for love of her, he had assumed this strange disguise. So the maiden was no longer afraid, but allowed herself to be carried to an unknown land that was afterward called Europe in her honour.

It was no wonder that Hera kept watch over the earth as no other goddess needed to do, for she knew that the loveliness that belonged to the daughters of men could easily lure great Zeus from his golden throne. She was therefore very reasonably angry when she looked one day through the white clouds around Olympus and saw – not on the earth, but in the lap of the ever-tossing sea – the most beautiful being that could exist outside of a dream. So wonderfully fair was this maiden upon whom Hera fixed her resentful gaze, that she seemed too perfect to be made of flesh and blood, and the jealous watcher was almost persuaded that it was no real living thing which rested softly on the crest of the waves, but some creature made from the rainbow colours and white mist of the sea. The ocean rocked her lightly on its breast, and Zephyrus, the west wind, bore her gently toward the shore. The sunlight shone on her rosy flesh, and her long hair lay out upon the waves, glistening like spun gold. The sky above her was not more soft or deep than the blueness of her eyes, and the smile upon her perfect lips was of a subtle sweetness more alluring than the breath of spring. As she lay pillowed in the arms of the slow-swinging sea, the west wind bore her to the island of Cyprus; and when her foot touched the warm sand, the goddess rose from the waves, which were so loath to yield her to the waiting earth, and stepped lightly upon the shore. She flung the wet ringlets from her forehead, shook the foam from her breast and shoulders – white as the purest marble – and stood upright in the warm sunshine – the most perfect thing that the wondering old earth had ever looked upon. This was Aphrodite, goddess of love and beauty, born of the foam of the sea, and destined to be the most far-famed of all the dwellers in Olympus.

It was not long before others than the watchful Hera had seen this vision of loveliness, and she was eagerly welcomed by the gods as soon as she appeared among them. The beauty and grace of the new goddess so charmed them that all were eager to yield her homage, and she was immediately sought in marriage – even Zeus himself becoming an enamoured suitor. But "laughter-loving" Aphrodite refused to be wed, and would not listen to any wooing. Then the ruler of the gods, finding his proffered love scorned by the proud goddess, determined to punish her by compelling her to marry Hephaestus, the ugliest and most ill-favoured of deities; and as Zeus's word was law in all the universe, Aphrodite was obliged to obey. But though married, she was by no means a devoted or faithful wife, and she caused poor Hephaestus many unhappy moments; for he saw how his misshapen form repelled her, and he knew that she would soon seek for happiness elsewhere.

The first to win the love of "golden" Aphrodite was Ares, the handsome god of war, who, though delighted at being honoured as the chosen one of beauty, was careful that the goddess's preference should not be known. When he and Aphrodite met in some lovers' bower, they placed Alectryon – the attendant of Ares – on guard, so that no one, not even prying Hera, would come upon them unawares. Things went on happily for some time; but one day Alectryon fell asleep at his post, and slept so soundly that he did not see Apollo, in his golden chariot, driving close to the trysting place of the lovers. When the sun-god realized what was happening, he went straightway to Hephaestus and told him how much his wife was enjoying the society of Ares.

Hephaestus, angry and ashamed, set to work to forge a net of linked steel; and when it was finished, he hurried with it to the spot where Aphrodite and the god of war were still conversing together. Stepping up softly behind them, Hephaestus drew the net over their heads, and thus held them fast. Then he hastened back to Olympus, where he told his story and bade all the gods go look upon the ridiculous and humiliating plight of the imprisoned lovers. When the captured pair were at last set free, Ares rushed off to find Alectryon and to learn why they had not been warned of Apollo's approach. Finding his sentinel peacefully sleeping, unmindful of the disaster that had occurred through his neglect of duty, Ares was so enraged that he changed Alectryon into a cock, and commanded him to rise early every morning and crow to announce the coming of the sun.

II

The next fancy of Aphrodite was for Adonis, a handsome young hunter, who was so fearless in his pursuit of game that the goddess often felt anxious for his safety. She urged him to give up the chase and spend all his day with her; but however much Adonis enjoyed the society of Aphrodite, he also loved to roam the forests, and no entreaties could induce him to give up his favourite sport. One day Adonis was following a wild boar, and believing that the creature was wounded, he boldly drew near, when the boar turned suddenly upon him and drove his long tusks into the youth's side. As he lay dying in the forest, Aphrodite heard of the tragic ending of the day's hunt and hurried to save him. So careless was she of her own hurt that she rushed heedlessly through the rough briers, which tore her soft skin and scattered drops of blood on the white wood flowers. When she reached Adonis, he was already past her help and could not respond to her caresses. Holding his lifeless body in her arms, Aphrodite wept and mourned for her beloved; and her tears, as they fell upon the sympathizing earth, were changed into anemones. Then to hide from her eyes the painful sight of the young hunter's mangled body, the kindly earth again took pity on her grief and turned the drops of blood that came from Adonis's side into red roses. Still the goddess would not be comforted, but sat mourning alone with her dead.

Then Hermes came to lead the soul of Adonis to gloomy Hades; and when the messenger of the gods had departed with his slight burden, Aphrodite went back to Olympus, and throwing herself on the ground before Zeus's throne, she besought him to give Adonis back to her, or else to allow her to stay with him in Hades. Since the world could not well spare the goddess of beauty, Zeus refused to let her go to the sunless realm of Hades; but neither would that dread ruler consent to give up Adonis to her longing arms. Then the gods, touched by the depth of Aphrodite's grief, interceded on her behalf, and reluctantly Hades agreed to allow Adonis to spend six months with the goddess in the warmth and joy of the sunlight if for the rest of the year he would be content to dwell in Hades.

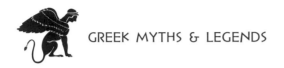

III

Another of the fortunate ones who gained the love of Aphrodite was Anchises, prince of Troy; but though the goddess lavished much affection upon him, she was rather ashamed of her attachment, for Anchises was of only mortal birth. She therefore bade him to keep the matter secret, and for a time Anchises obeyed; but being proud of his relation to the goddess he forgot her instructions, and boasted of his good fortune. This so angered the wilful Aphrodite that she never bestowed her favours on him again; but transferred all her affection to her son Aeneas, who fared better at her hands than his father Anchises. In the many adventures that befell this famous hero, Aphrodite was always a ready protectress, and whenever Aeneas was involved in some apparently hopeless situation, his goddess mother would immediately hide him in a thick mist which was sure to baffle his enemies. Sometimes, as in the Trojan war, she wrapped him in her shining robe and bore him from the battle-field; and if the hero *was* constantly in tears, as the poet Virgil says, it was certainly not the fault of Aphrodite.

As to the ultimate fate of Anchises, some authorities say that the offended goddess borrowed one of Zeus's thunderbolts and disposed of her talkative lover in this fashion; but the most probable story is that he lived to see Aeneas become a famous prince of Troy, and was himself carried from the ruins of that burning city on the shoulders of his devoted son.

12

THE STORY OF EROS AND PSYCHE

Eros, god of love, was the son of Ares and Aphrodite; and though he was always the happiest of children, his mother was distressed because he never grew up, but remained year after year a chubby, dimpled child. When she consulted Themis, the goddess of justice, to find out why Eros was never any older, she was told that "Love cannot grow without Passion." This explanation was at first very mystifying; but later, when Anteros was born, Aphrodite understood the meaning of the strange words. Eros then developed into a tall, slender youth who did not revert to his childish form except in his brother's absence, when he again became a rosy, mischievous child. Though grown larger in stature, the god of love still kept his gauzy wings, and always carried a bow and a quiver full of arrows. No mortal ever saw him, though many knew when he had come and gone; but should any one be touched by a shaft sent carelessly from Eros's golden bow, he was henceforth a slave to the slender, winged god who bore lightly in his hand so much of human happiness and misery.

There was once a king who had three daughters whose beauty was famed far and wide; but the loveliness of the youngest was so great that people called her the goddess of beauty and worshipped her with offerings of flowers. The maiden, Psyche, was troubled over all this adoration, and begged her followers to cease from their mad worship; for she knew that Aphrodite would be sure to punish the one who usurped her title and received the homage due only to an immortal. The people continued, however, to call Psyche the goddess of beauty; and when Aphrodite saw her own temple forsaken and her shrines ungarlanded, she was so incensed at the insult that she vowed to punish poor Psyche, who had been a most unwilling object of all this mistaken devotion. The goddess summoned her son Eros to her presence and bade him go slay the maiden who had presumed to be her rival in beauty.

Believing that his mother's anger was justified, Eros was quite willing to kill the offending mortal with one of his poisoned arrows; and accordingly he went in search of Psyche, whom he found asleep in one of the rooms of her father's palace. It was night, and the moonlight shone through the open window, falling softly upon the couch where the maiden, unconscious of her doom, lay sleeping. One bright beam had lightly touched her forehead just as Eros entered, and he saw with delight the loveliness that his mother had been eager to destroy. As he leaned nearer to the sleeping maiden one of his own arrows grazed his side, and all unknowingly he was wounded. Not wishing to harm the beauty that he was now beginning to love, Eros softly left the room and went back to Olympus.

When Aphrodite found that her rival was not dead, and that Eros refused to hurt a thing so fair, she began to persecute poor Psyche until life grew unbearable for the helpless maiden, and she determined to kill herself. So she stole secretly from the palace and climbed up a high mountain, where there was a ledge of rock overhanging a steep cliff. It was rather fearful to look down into the valley from the rocky ledge, and for a moment Psyche's heart failed her; but then she remembered the daily annoyances that Aphrodite inflicted upon her, and she remembered also the words of the oracle which said that her future husband was to be "no mortal, but a monster whom neither gods nor men can resist". So, summoning all her courage, she threw herself over the cliff, expecting to be dashed to pieces upon the rocks below. But Eros had been watching over her, ever since she began her weary journey up the mountain; and when he realized what she meant to do, he commanded Zephyrus to keep very near and to catch her lightly when she fell. So it was not upon the cruel rocks that Psyche's soft body lay, but in the friendly arms of the west wind who bore her to a distant island, where Eros had already made preparations for her coming.

On the thick grass in the midst of a beautiful garden, Zephyrus laid his slight burden; and when Psyche opened her eyes, she found herself unhurt, though bewildered by her strange journey through the air and by its unexpected ending. She rose from the grass and began to wander about the garden, wondering where she might be and what land lay beyond the blue water whose waves rolled lazily upon the beach that stretched away for miles at the foot of the garden. Then she strolled further inland among the flowers, and soon came to a beautiful palace whose doors were opened wide as if to welcome her. Timidly she entered the stately hall, and saw before her a richly-laden table and a chair placed in readiness for the coming guest. Soon she heard voices speaking to her gently, and they bade her eat and drink, for the feast was spread in her honour. Seeing no one, but reassured by the kindly voices, she ate of the food so generously provided. Then she went again into the garden, but left it soon and hurried down to the sea; for when evening came on, she began to be lonely, and the silence of the garden grew oppressive. On the beach she heard the sound of lapping water and felt herself a part of the life that beats forever in the restless changing sea.

At night she sought the palace where the unseen servitors again ministered to her wants; and in the darkness, Eros came to woo her. He did not reveal his name, but he told how he had rescued her from death and brought her to this island, that she might never again be persecuted by jealous Aphrodite. Everything that she wished for would be hers for the mere asking, and the invisible attendants would always be on hand to do her bidding. He himself would ever be her loyal lover; and would come each night to cheer her solitude. The only thing that he asked in return was that she should never seek to know his name or try to see his face. Psyche listened to the words of Eros, and was won by the soft pleading of his voice. She was content to stay on the unknown island, and to be with her unseen lover, whose name and face must remain forever a mystery. Many happy weeks passed, and Psyche never wished to leave her new home, for though she was often lonely as she walked each day in the rose-garden, she forgot the long hours of solitude when Eros came at night to gladden her with his love and to tell her of his wanderings.

As time went on Psyche began to wonder how things were faring at her father's palace; and she wished very much to see her sisters who must have long since believed her dead. Eros had told her she might ask for anything that she wished save the two forbidden things, so she summoned the west wind and bade him bring her sisters to her. Zephyrus gladly obeyed, and soon Psyche saw her two sisters standing beside her, more astonished than she to find themselves there. For hours they talked together, and Psyche told them of her adventure on the mountain and how she had been rescued by the friendly west wind. She told them of her mysterious lover, of his riches and his great kindness, and regretted that she could not describe his appearance; but, she explained, this was impossible since she herself had never seen him. As the sisters listened to Psyche's story, their hearts were filled with bitter envy that she should be thus favoured above all other maidens; and they planned to rob her of her happiness. They reminded her of the words of the oracle that she should marry a monster; and under the pretence of a loving interest in her welfare, they urged her to break her promise to her lover and to find out whether he was in truth a monster that was only waiting his time to devour her. Psyche at first scorned these malicious suggestions, but by and by they began to make an impression on her troubled mind, and she found herself ready to listen and to believe. Finally she agreed to carry out the plan that her sisters arranged, which was to secrete a sharp knife in her room and use it to kill the monster as he slept.

When Zephyrus had taken the sisters back to their own home, and Psyche was once more alone, she felt ashamed of the promise that she had made them; but at the same time she could not forget the words of the oracle nor cast off the suspicions that now filled her mind. She was anxious, too, to see her lover's face and to be able to confront her sisters with the truth when they should taunt her again. So that night when Eros was fast asleep, she rose softly, and by the light of a tiny lamp which she noiselessly lit, she groped for the knife with which she intended to slay the creature who – her sisters assured her – was so frightful that he dared not show his face. Cautiously she stepped to Eros's side, and held over him the flickering lamp; but how astonished she was to behold – not an ugly monster as she had expected – but a slender youth whose beauty was so great that she felt her heart beat fast with joy. Breathless she gazed at the unconscious form, and dared not move for fear of waking him; but as she bent adoringly over him a drop of oil fell from her lamp on Eros's shoulder, and he awoke.

For a moment he stared with startled eyes at the knife and the lamp held in her trembling hands; then he understood the meaning of it all, and his beautiful face grew sad. In a voice full of pity he spoke to the now remorseful Psyche, and told her that, as she had broken her promise, he must go away from her and never come again. In vain Psyche wept and begged him to forgive her rash deed, confessing that it was her sisters who had tempted her to betray her trust. But Eros gently freed himself from her clinging arms, and spreading his gauzy wings flew out into the night. Psyche, still weeping, went down into the garden, hoping that Love might relent and return in spite of his parting words; but as the hours passed she was still waiting alone, and when the morning came it found her fast asleep, lying wet-eyed among the dew-laden flowers.

When at last Psyche awoke, it was midday; and looking around she found to her surprise that she was in a deep valley with mountains on all sides, and that the palace with its rose-garden had vanished. All day she wandered in the valley, meeting no one who might direct her to her home; and when at length she came to a stately marble temple, she was glad to enter it and rest. Though she did not know to whom the temple was dedicated, Psyche prayed to the gods for help; and Demeter, at whose altar she was kneeling, heard her, and in pity answered her prayers. She told the disheartened maiden that her lover was no other than Eros, the god of love, "whom neither gods nor man can resist", and that if she wished to gain favour in the eyes of his mother – and thereby win her lover back – she would do well to seek the temple of Aphrodite and offer her services to the offended goddess.

Psyche listened to these friendly words, and thanked Demeter for taking pity on her suffering. When she left the temple she walked many miles through the valley, until she came to a shrine on which were hung flowers, fruit, and jewels, which the suppliants of Aphrodite had brought as votive offerings. Before this shrine Psyche knelt very humbly, and implored the goddess of beauty to accept her service and set her some task by which she could prove her fidelity.

Aphrodite was still angry at the memory of Psyche's former honours, and she was not to be placated by any prayers, however sincere. She accepted the maiden's service, but determined to torment her by setting impossible tasks.

She brought Psyche into a granary, where there were thousands of different kinds of seeds all thrown in bewildering and unsorted heaps. Pointing to these, the goddess bade her separate them all, and pile them together so that by nightfall each seed should be in its proper place. Poor Psyche was in despair at ever being able to tell one kind of seed from another; but Eros, hearing her sighs, sent an army of ants who worked silently and swiftly at the enormous heap of seeds, and before twilight came the work was done.

When Aphrodite saw this almost impossible task accomplished, she knew that Psyche had never done the work unaided; so reproving her angrily for her incompetence, she gave the maiden another commission, which was to gather some golden fleece from the sheep that were browsing in a meadow not far from Aphrodite's shrine. Next morning Psyche set about her task, but as she neared the river that must be crossed before she could reach the meadow, the kindly reeds on the water's edge spoke to her, and warned her of the danger of her undertaking. They told her that the rams in the flock were so fierce that they would surely destroy her if she ventured at this hour among them; but that if she waited until noontide, when they grew drowsy and lay down on the grass beside the river, then she could cross in safety, and gather the bits of golden fleece which she would find caught on the bushes. Psyche listened gratefully to this advice; and when the sun was high overhead, and the panting sheep were gathered by the river, lulled to sleep by the drowsy murmur of the reeds, she crossed the water fearlessly, and gathered an armful of golden fleece from the bushes among which the flock had wandered. That night she delivered her precious burden to Aphrodite, who again reproved her angrily, knowing well that it was through Eros's intervention that she had escaped the dangerous rams.

Then the goddess gave her a third errand, and bade her go down to gruesome Hades to beg of Persephone, Hades's queen, a box of her magic ointment, which could restore all fading beauty to its former perfection. In the early morning Psyche set out on her journey, fearful of the dangers that lurked by the way, but eager to gain the favour of her hard-hearted mistress, so that she might thereby win her lover back. When she had walked many hours, not knowing where to find the entrance to remote and unsought Hades, a voice whispered softly in her ear, telling her of a certain cave through which she might enter the dreaded region of the dead. Then the voice directed her how to go unharmed past Cerberus, the three-headed dog, and how to persuade Charon, the silent ferryman, to row her across the black and swiftly-flowing river. Encouraged by this timely help, Psyche was able to secure the desired box, and to come safely out of that dark country from which only the gods are privileged to return.

As she trod wearily up the valley back to the shrine of Aphrodite, it occurred to her to take a little of the magic ointment for herself, for she knew that these days of waiting and working had dimmed the beauty that once charmed Eros's eyes. So she opened the box and out sprang the invincible Spirit of Sleep, who seized upon poor unresisting Psyche and laid her, apparently lifeless, by the roadside. But Eros was watching over his beloved through all the stages of her journey; and when he saw her unconscious on the ground, he flew quickly to her assistance, and fought with the masterful Spirit of Sleep until he conquered it, and compelled it to return to the box from which it had been set free. Then he roused Psyche from her sudden sleep and told her that her troubles were at an end, for henceforth he would always stay beside her. Together they went up to bright Olympus and stood before Zeus's throne, where Eros besought the gods to look with favour upon their love and to grant to Psyche the gift of immortal life. To this great Zeus gladly consented; and Aphrodite, who was now ready to forgive her one-time rival, welcomed her as the fitting wife of Eros – for Psyche is but another name for Soul, and the Soul, to find its true happiness, must dwell forever with Love.

13

FAMOUS LOVERS

I ECHO AND NARCISSUS

Echo was a wood-nymph and a follower of Artemis; and she had the one fault of wanting to talk all the time, especially if she found some one who was willing to listen. One day Hera went down in great haste to the earth, suspecting that Zeus was spending too much time in the society of the nymphs; but before she had gone very far into the forest she met Echo and stopped to speak to her. Now Echo knew that the ruler of the gods was happily engaged with the nymphs, and would not be pleased at his wife's sudden appearance; so she began to talk rapidly to Hera, and to tell her such entertaining stories that the unsuspicious goddess waited to listen. While Echo was thus keeping the jealous queen from seeking for her husband, Zeus – warned of her coming – left the nymphs and returned in haste to Olympus. When, later on, Hera learned that Echo had intentionally kept her listening so that Zeus could make his retreat unseen, she was so angry with the officious nymph that she forbade her ever to speak again, except to repeat the last word of any conversation she might hear. Thus she could never more tell beguiling stories, or interfere on behalf of Zeus.

At first Echo was very miserable over this misfortune; but in spite of it she managed to spend her time happily in the forest, and to hunt with the other nymphs of Artemis. One evening as she stopped at a brookside to drink, she met a handsome youth named Narcissus, and at once fell in love with him; but unfortunately she could not tell him of her affection except by languishing looks and sighs. Narcissus was not at all pleased by her evident interest in him, for many maidens had loved him, and he had turned coldly from their advances, preferring to roam the forest alone. Sometime later Narcissus was hunting with a companion, and, having rushed away in pursuit of a stag, he found that his friend was no longer in sight. He called to him, but no one answered except the devoted Echo who was always trailing his footsteps. When Narcissus called "Are you here?" Echo replied, "Here." "Come!" cried the youth, and Echo answered, "Come." Then she appeared before the young hunter and mutely begged for his love; but Narcissus scornfully turned from her, exclaiming, "You shall never have me." "Have me," cried the unhappy maiden; but her frank offer was repulsed, and the hard-hearted youth turned away. Echo made no further attempt to win his love, but went into the mountains to live out her sad life alone. No one ever saw her again, and in time she pined away and died; but her voice remained to whisper among the hills, and to give back the last word to any one who sought to call her.

As for Narcissus, his scorn of love brought its just punishment, for Aphrodite decreed that he should suffer even as poor Echo had done. One day when he was hunting in a remote part of the forest, he came upon a beautiful deep pool in which all objects were reflected as clearly as in a mirror. No wild things had ever come to drink of the cool stream; no feet of beasts had ever trampled the grass on its margin or muddied its pure waters; not even a floating leaf had ruffled its calm surface.

When Narcissus knelt on the lush grass at the pool's edge and looked down into the clear water, he was surprised to see a beautiful face gazing up at him from the depth of the pool. He leaned nearer, and the face did not withdraw, but seemed to approach his own. Then he put out his arms to the water-nymph who, he believed, was returning his advances, and he was delighted to see two white arms stretched out as if to clasp him in their embrace. But as soon as he attempted to grasp them, there was only the cool water in his hands, and the nymph had vanished. When the surface of the pool had grown clear again, and Narcissus leaned anxiously over it to see what had become of this baffling maiden, there she was still, gazing at him with her beautiful eyes. Again and again Narcissus strove to embrace her, but she eluded his eager arms, and each time he clasped only the unsubstantial water. Maddened by these repeated defeats, he spoke reproachfully to the water-nymph, and asked her why she thus tormented him; but though the lovely mouth so near his own seemed to move as if framing words, no answer came to his appeal.

Each day Narcissus sought the forest pool, and each day he found the nymph ready to return his smiles and fond looks, but always escaping from his touch. By and by he spent all his time beside her, and cared for nothing else than to gaze beseechingly into the lovely eyes that looked into his own with the same fever of longing. Absorbed in the adoration of this strange being who seemed so responsive to his passion and yet so unwilling to allow him near, he forgot to eat or sleep, and became only a wan shadow of his former self. The nymph, too, was pining away with hopeless love, for her face grew pale and thin, and the deep-shadowed eyes were full of sadness. Sometimes Narcissus slept from sheer exhaustion; but when the moonlight fell on the calm water, he would wake with a start and look anxiously to see whether the nymph was sharing his weary vigil. And always he found her waiting there in the cool depths of the pool. Finally he grew so sick with longing that he died of his hopeless love without ever knowing that it was no water-nymph whom he adored, but only his own reflection. The gods, believing that such devotion should not go unrecognized, changed him into a white flower which bears his name; and this is usually found blooming beside some clear lake or tiny crystal pool.

II PYRAMUS AND THISBE

In far-off Babylon there dwelt a youth and maiden whose families lived in adjoining houses with a party-wall between the two estates. As the heads of these households were sworn enemies, in spite of their proximity, the wall was made so high that no one could climb over it, much less see what was on the other side. The maiden Thisbe, as she walked in her garden, often wondered who it was whose feet she could hear pacing up and down along the wall; and one day she was delighted to find a small crack in the masonry which enabled her to peep into the adjoining garden. About this time young Pyramus was planning some way to scale the wall, when he, too, discovered the same chink; and when he peered cautiously through it, he found to his great joy that there was a sweet-faced maiden standing near, who hastened to assure him that she did not share in the family feud. This acquaintance soon ripened into friendship, and Pyramus and Thisbe spent many hours standing patiently by the chink in the wall, which was the only way in which they could exchange confidences. Soon they grew dissatisfied with this meagre allowance of space in which to see each other, for by this time they had become so much in love that the tender whispers breathed through the broken wall only made them long to be together without this cruel barrier between them.

So they planned to steal away from their watchful parents on a certain night, and meet just outside the city walls at Ninus's tomb, where a great white mulberry tree would hide them in its protecting shadow. Accordingly, at the appointed hour, the trembling Thisbe wrapped herself closely in her veil and crept out of the house. Finding that she had come first to the trysting-place, she waited under the mulberry tree, and idly watched the moonlight shining on a broad pool that lay close to Ninus's tomb. Suddenly a lioness stole out of the bushes, her mouth bloody with the recent gorging of oxen, and slunk down to the pool to drink. Thisbe, terrified at the sight of the creature's dripping jaws, fled into a near-by cave for refuge; but in her fright she let fall her silken veil, and it dropped on the ground near the tree.

The lioness having drunk her fill walked over to the tree and sniffed curiously at the bit of silk, then worried at it with her bloody teeth, as a dog plays with a rag. Just as the lioness departed, Pyramus came hurrying to the trysting-place, and seeing Thisbe's torn and blood-stained veil and the print of the lioness's feet on the ground, he was beside himself with remorse and horror. Being certain that his beloved had been torn to pieces by some wild beast, he cursed his own carelessness in letting her come first to a spot so full of dangers. Then he drew his sword, exclaiming that he no longer wished to live now that Thisbe was dead. He called upon the mulberry tree to bear witness to his oath of undying devotion, and then fell heroically upon his sword, uttering the name of Thisbe with his last breath. As his blood gushed out upon the ground at the foot of the tree, the earth absorbed it so quickly that the white fruit of the tree turned a deep purple, and its juice became like drops of crimson blood.

All this time Thisbe was hiding safely in the cave, and when she at length ventured out, she gazed fearfully around to be sure that no lioness was lying in wait to devour her. When she reached the spot where she hoped to meet her lover, what was her terror and dismay to find him stretched dead upon the ground with her veil held close to his parted lips. Realizing what had happened, and that it was too late now to convince him of his terrible mistake, Thisbe knelt down beside him and vainly strove to bring him back to life. Finding this useless, she seized Pyramus's sword and plunged it into her heart, determined to die with him. As she sank forward on her lover's lifeless body, she prayed to the gods to have pity on her great love and to allow her to be buried in the same tomb with her beloved Pyramus. The gods heard her dying prayer and answered it by making the hard hearts of the parents relent so far that they consented to bury the lovers together. A costly tomb was erected over them as a fitting monument to these two unfortunates whom life so cruelly divided.

III HERO AND LEANDER

In the town of Sestus on the Hellespont lived a beautiful maiden named Hero, who was a priestess in the temple of Aphrodite. Most of her time was spent in the service of the goddess; but when these hours of attendance were over, and she was free to leave the temple, Hero was glad to seek her own dwelling-place, which was a lonely tower on the cliffs overlooking the sea. Here the maiden loved to sit, watching the white-winged gulls as they skimmed over the waves, or listening to the breakers as they dashed angrily against the rocks at the foot of her tower. The beauty of Hero was famed throughout the countryside; and many a youth sought the temple of Aphrodite at festival time under the pretext of honouring the goddess, but really to gaze upon the lovely young priestess. Among those most eager to see the maiden was Leander, a youth who lived in a town just across the Hellespont and within sight of Hero's tower. When he joined the solemn procession that came to do homage to Aphrodite, he saw the beautiful priestess and determined to win her in spite of the many restrictions that forbade even an acquaintance with one dedicated to the temple. Ignoring the thought of the inevitable punishment that would be meted out to him if his rash presumption were known, Leander managed to find an opportunity to speak with Hero and to tell her of his love.

At first she would not listen to his pleading; but at last she was won by the sincerity of his words, and consented to disregard her sacred vows by receiving him in her tower. Leander did not dare to visit her until nightfall; and as he would have to swim across the Hellespont in the darkness, Hero promised to put a light in her tower so that he might have some beacon to guide him as he breasted the uncertain sea. When night came and Leander stood impatiently on the shore, waiting for the promised signal, suddenly a torch blazed in the distance, and he knew that Hero was awaiting him in her lonely tower. He plunged fearlessly into the waves; and though the current was swift, he struck out boldly and was carried out of its dangerous grip. Now and then he looked up to where the light was still burning, and his heart beat fast with hope when he saw it grow larger and brighter as he neared the land. At last he reached the rocks at the foot of the tower and was soon standing beside the trembling Hero, who had feared each moment to see him sink beneath the waves.

The lovers were so happy in being together that each night Leander swam across the treacherous sea, and Hero placed her torch in the tower to light him on his perilous journey. All summer they lived in this idyllic happiness, but when winter came with its storms and its icy hand, Hero feared for her lover's safety and begged him not to venture into the sea. Leander laughed however at her fears and continued to brave the narrow stretch of water that lay between his home and Hero's tower. The wind often beat him out of his path, and the icy water numbed his limbs; but he kept bravely on, with his eyes fixed on the welcoming light. One morning a fierce storm broke over the sea, and increased in fury through the day, so that by night the waves were lashing themselves madly against the rocks, and the wind beat the sea-gulls back to land. Hero dreaded the approach of that hour when Leander would start on his nightly journey, for she knew that he would not hesitate to risk his life in the maddened sea for the sake of being beside her.

When the time came for her to light the torch, she did so reluctantly, hoping that Leander would not come. On the opposite shore stood the impatient lover, waiting for the accustomed signal, and when it blazed out into the night, he plunged boldly into the waves. But now the sea was too strong even for his experienced arms, and the huge waves tossed him about as though he were so much foam. The wind and rain beat upon his defenceless body, and the cold sea gripped him in its deadly embrace. He struggled bravely to make some headway, and called upon the gods for help; but his cries were drowned in the howling of the storm. His strength began to fail as he fought desperately with the current – grown terrible in its swiftness – but now and then he lifted his head weakly above the waves to see whether Hero's torch was still burning. Just as he was making a last heroic effort to reach the land, a sudden gust of wind blew out the light; and seeing this, Leander with a despairing cry, gave up his unequal battle and sank down into the sea. The next morning when Hero, anxious and fearful, stood on the rocks at the foot of the tower, she saw Leander's body, which had been tossed there in wanton cruelty by the waves. Unable to endure this sight, and not wishing to live any longer now that her lover had perished, Hero threw herself into the sea; and when the tardy fishermen came to launch their boats on the furious waves, they found the white-robed body of the young priestess lying dead beside her faithful Leander.

IV PYGMALION AND GALATEA

Pygmalion, king of Cyprus, was a sworn bachelor, and had shunned the society of women for many years. He was also a famous sculptor, and spent all his leisure hours carving wonderful things out of marble and ivory. Though he would not deign to admire any living woman, he had lofty ideals of feminine beauty, and loved to carve statues whose perfection of form and exquisite grace surpassed any charms that could be claimed for a flesh-and-blood maiden. Once Pygmalion made a beautiful ivory statue that was such a marvel of loveliness that even the sculptor himself became enamoured of it, and lavished upon it a devotion that was hardly consistent with his supposed indifference to love. This perfect creation he called Galatea, and he treated her with all the extravagant fondness that a lover bestows upon his mistress. He brought her presents of quaint seashells and delicately perfumed flowers, beads, pearls, and the rarest of jewels, and even gayly coloured birds. Sometimes he hung a string of precious stones about her neck, and draped her white body in softest silks, treating her in every way as a maiden reluctant to be wooed.

When the festival of Aphrodite was being celebrated, Pygmalion joined in the procession and placed a rich offering on the goddess's shrine. As he did so he looked up toward high Olympus and prayed to Aphrodite to grant him a wife like his peerless Galatea. The goddess heard his prayer, and as the patroness of all true lovers, she inclined with favour to his wish; so when Pygmalion returned to his home and hastened into the presence of his adored statue, he was bewildered at the change that seemed to be coming over it. A beam of sunset light that was streaming in through the open window had touched the ivory coldness of the statue and warmed it with a rosy glow that made it look wonderfully soft and yielding. But this was not all, for as the astonished sculptor stood wondering at this unexpected answer to his prayer, the beautiful face of Galatea turned toward him, and the perfect lips parted as if to speak. Breathlessly Pygmalion watched the statue gradually warming into life, and when he was at last assured that it was no longer a piece of unresponsive ivory, but a breathing, blushing maiden, he knelt adoringly at her feet and besought her to be his queen.

14

THE STORY OF ORPHEUS AND EURYDICE

The deeds of the immortal gods were told and sung at every fireside in Greece; and among these hero-tales there was none more popular than the story of how Apollo built for Poseidon the famous wall of Troy. Many musicians would have been glad to perform a similar service for the mere fame that it would bring them, but they feared that the attempt to imitate Apollo would only result in failure and ridicule. So no mortal ever presumed to say that he could make rocks and stones obedient to the spell of his music. There was, however, one musician, Amphion, king of Thebes, who was anxious to prove that his playing was equal to Apollo's, but knowing how unwise it was to vie with an immortal, he determined not to test his skill publicly, but to carry out his cherished plan at night, when men were dreaming in their beds. He was eager to build a high wall around Thebes, and to build it as Apollo did the wall of Troy; so when the sun set, and darkness crept over the earth, Amphion stood just outside the city gates and began to play on his lyre. Immediately the stones rose from the ground and moved rhythmically into their places in the wall, which soon rose strong and high – a firmer defence than any that could be built by men's hands.

Another famous musician was Arion, who won not only praise for his great skill in playing, but also much wealth. Whenever a contest was held in which a prize of money was given, Arion was usually a competitor; and, as his music was really finer than that of most players, he easily won the reward. Once he was returning from a festival in Sicily whither many musicians had gone on account of the rich prize; and as he had come off victor, he was leaving the foreign shores well-laden with gold. Unfortunately he happened to embark on a ship owned by pirates who had heard of his great wealth, and were plotting to seize whatever part of it he had on board. As the easiest way to do this was to kill him, the pirates began to bind him with ropes that he might not be able to struggle when thrown overboard. Arion calmly accepted his fate, but begged the brutal crew to allow him to play once upon his lyre before going to his death. To this the pirates consented, and when the wonderful music filled the air, a school of dolphins swam toward the ship and kept close beside it, charmed by Arion's playing. Feeling sure that there was some magic in the music, the pirates hastened to throw the player and his lyre into the sea without waiting to bind him; but Arion did not drown as they had expected, for a friendly dolphin caught him on its back and swam with him to the shore, where he landed in safety. When in the course of time Arion died, the gods placed him, together with his lyre and the kindly dolphin, in the sky as constellations.

The most famous of all musicians, except the one who played in the shining halls of Olympus, was Orpheus, son of Apollo and of the muse Calliope. When he was a mere child, his father gave him a lyre and taught him to play upon it; but Orpheus needed very little instruction, for as soon as he laid his hand upon the strings the wild beasts crept out of their lairs to crouch beside him; the trees on the mountainside moved nearer so that they might listen; and the flowers sprang up in clusters all around him, unwilling to remain any longer asleep in the earth.

When Orpheus sought in marriage the golden-haired Eurydice, there were other suitors for her hand, but though they brought rich gifts, gathered out of many lands, they could not win the maiden's love, and she turned from them to bestow her hand upon Orpheus who had no way to woo her but with his music. On the wedding day there was the usual mirth and feasting, but one event occurred that cast a gloom over the happiness of the newly-married pair. When Hymen, god of marriage, came with his torch to bless the nuptial feast, the light that should have burned clear and pure began to smoke ominously, as if predicting future disaster.

This evil omen was fulfilled all too soon, for one day when Eurydice was walking in the meadow, she met the youth Aristaeus, who was so charmed with her beauty that he insisted upon staying beside her to pour his ardent speeches into her unwilling ears. To escape from these troublesome attentions, Eurydice started to run away, and as she ran she stepped on a poisonous snake, which quickly turned and bit her. She had barely time to reach her home before the poison had done its work, and Orpheus heard the sad story from her dying lips. As soon as Hermes had led away the soul of Eurydice, the bereaved husband hastened to the shining halls of Olympus, and throwing himself down before Zeus's golden throne, he implored that great ruler of gods and men to give him back his wife. There was always pity in the hearts of the gods for those who die in flowering time, so Zeus gave permission to Orpheus to go down into Hades, and beg of Hades the boon he craved.

It was a steep and perilous journey to the kingdom of the dead, and the road was one that no mortal foot had ever trod; but through his love for Eurydice Orpheus forgot the dangers of the way, and when he spoke her name, the terrors of the darkness vanished. In his hand he held his lyre, and when he arrived at the gate of Hades, where the fierce three-headed dog Cerberus refused to let him pass, Orpheus stood still in the uncertain darkness and began to play. And as he played the snarling of the dog ceased and the noise of its harsh breathing grew faint. Then Orpheus went on his way undisturbed, but still he played softly on his lyre, and the sounds floated far into the dismal interior of Hades, where the souls of the condemned labour forever at their tasks. Tantalus heard the music, and ceased to strive for a drop of the forbidden water; Ixion rested a moment beside his ever-revolving wheel; and Sisyphus stood listening, while the rock which he must roll through all eternity fell from his wearied arms. The daughters of Danaüs laid down their urns beside the sieve into which they were forever pouring water, and as the mournful wailing of Orpheus's lyre told the story of his lost love, they wept then for a sorrow not their own. So plaintive, indeed, was the music, that all the shadowy forms that flitted endlessly by shed tears of sympathy for the player's grief, and even the cheeks of the Furies were wet.

When Orpheus came before the throne of Hades, that relentless monarch repulsed him angrily as he attempted to plead his cause, and commanded him to depart. Then the son of Apollo began to play upon his lyre, and through his music he told the story of his loss, and besought the ruler of these myriad souls to give him the single one he craved. So wonderfully did Orpheus play that the hard heart of Hades was touched with pity, and he consented to restore Eurydice to her husband on condition that as they went out together from the loathed country of the dead he should not once turn his head to look upon her. To this strange decree Orpheus gladly promised obedience; so Eurydice was summoned from among the million shadow-shapes that throng the silent halls of death. Hades told her the condition on which her freedom was to be won, and then bade her follow her husband.

During all the wearisome journey back to earth, Orpheus never forgot the promise he had made, though he often longed to give just a hurried glance at the face of Eurydice to see whether it had lost its sadness. As they neared the spot where the first faint glimmerings of light filtered down into the impenetrable darkness, Orpheus thought he heard his wife calling, and he looked quickly around to find whether she was still following him. At that moment the slight form close behind him began to fade away, and a mournful voice – seemingly far in the distance – called to him a sad farewell.

He knew that no second chance would be given him to win his wife from Hades's hold, even if he could again charm the three-headed Cerberus or persuade Charon, the grim ferryman, to take him across the river. So he went forlornly back to earth and lived in a forest cave far from the companionship of men. At first there was only his lyre to share his solitude, but soon the forest creatures came to live beside him, and often sat listening to his music, looking exceedingly wise and sorrowful. Even in his sleepless hours, when he fancied he heard Eurydice calling, he was never quite alone, for the bat and owl and the things that love the darkness flitted about him, and he saw the glow-worms creep toward him out of the night-cold grass.

One day a party of maenads found him seated outside the cave, playing the mournful music that told of his lost love, and they bade him change the sad notes to something gay so that they might dance. But Orpheus was too wrapped up in his sorrow to play any strain of cheerful music, and he refused to do as they asked. The maenads were half maddened by their festival days of drinking, and this refusal so enraged them that they fell upon the luckless musician and tore him to pieces. Then they threw his mangled body into the river, and as the head of Orpheus drifted down the stream, his lips murmured again and again "Eurydice", until the hills echoed

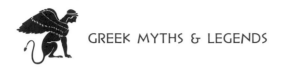

the beloved name, and the rocks and trees and rivers repeated it in mournful chorus. Later on, the Muses gathered up his remains to give them honourable burial; and it is said that over Orpheus's grave the nightingale sings more sweetly than in any other spot in Greece.

15

ARES AND HEPHAESTUS

I

The three children of Zeus and Hera were Hebe, Ares, and Hephaestus. Hebe, goddess of youth, was cupbearer at the feasts of Olympus and poured from golden flagons the sparkling, ruby-tinted nectar. Many times were the brimming cups emptied and filled again, for the gods loved long draughts of the life-giving nectar that kept off all sickness and decay. No wine of earth's yielding ever appeared at these royal banquets, nor were there seen here the heaped-up platters of food such as mortals crave; for the gods ate only of the divine ambrosia which ensured to them eternal youth and beauty.

For so long a time had fair-haired Hebe served at the feasts of Olympus that the gods never thought that she could be deprived of her office; but once, as she was handing Zeus a well-filled cup, she stumbled and fell, and the ruler of gods and men was so angry that he vowed that she should never again be cupbearer. Since no one among the gods was willing to fill this humble position, Zeus was obliged to seek over the earth for some mortal to take the place of poor disgraced Hebe. To make the journey as speedily as possible he assumed the form of an eagle, and spent many days soaring over the land before he found the youth whose slender grace made him feel assured that its possessor would be able to serve the gods less awkwardly than Hebe. On the sunny slopes of Mount Ida he saw a group of youths playing games, and among them was one whom Zeus determined to bear away at once to Olympus. This was Ganymede, a prince of Troy; and the fact that he was no common mortal, but a king's son, did not deter Zeus from swooping down upon the astonished youth, and carrying him aloft on his wings. Whether Ganymede was happy in Olympus we do not know; but the story goes that he remained forever at Zeus's side, and the city of Troy never saw him again, nor did the king his father ever know the reason for his strange disappearance.

II

Ares was the god of war; and though he was the least loved of all the deities in Olympus, he was the one most feared by the people of every land. As he was always a hater of peace, and would stir up strife among men for the mere delight of fighting and bloodshed, the poet Homer calls him "the slayer of men, one steeped in blood, the destroyer of walled towns". His shrines were never wreathed with flowers, nor were children often found among the people grouped about his altars. Instead of the yearling ox with gilded horns, men sacrificed a savage bull to the god who took no pleasure in the tame shedding of blood. Sometimes Enyo, goddess of war, accompanied Ares in his chariot to watch over his safety; and since she was equally eager to urge men on to bloody fighting, their appearance together on the battle-field brought terror to the bravest heart. Seldom were prayers addressed to these two deities, except those of vengeance upon enemies; and there was little hope of peace for the nation when men thronged the temples where Ares and Enyo were jointly worshipped. The fiercest passions were kindled at their shrines, and their altars were the only ones that were ever defiled by human sacrifices.

Though so fierce in warfare, Ares was as susceptible to love as were all the immortals; for he was not only the chosen one of golden-haired Aphrodite, but was also the devoted lover of the vestal Rhea Silvia. This maiden, being dedicated to the goddess Hestia, did not dare to listen to any words of love until her time of service in the temple was over; for the penalty of breaking her solemn vows would be the terrible one of being buried alive. But Ares was not to be denied; so at last the vestal yielded, but kept her marriage secret and continued to live in the temple until the birth of her twin sons Romulus and Remus. When her parents learned that she had failed to keep the sacred promise made at the altar-fire of Hestia, they demanded that she should suffer the prescribed punishment. She was therefore taken at night into an underground room of the temple and enclosed in the wall which had been built to allow for just such a tragic event. As her children were declared outcasts, they were taken into the forest and left to perish by the teeth of wild beasts. Romulus and Remus did not die, however; for a she-wolf carried them to her lair and reared them with her own cubs. Later on they were found by a kindly shepherd who took care of them until they grew to manhood. Then they left him, and went out into the world to seek adventures, which soon ended in Romulus killing his brother Remus and himself becoming the founder of Rome.

When this new city was well established, Ares was made its patron deity and protector; and before an army set out on any military campaign the leader would first go into the temple where the sacred shield – the Ancile – hung; and touching it fearfully would pray, "Oh, Ares, watch over us." This shield was carefully guarded in Rome, for upon it depended the safety of the city. It was a special token sent by the god of war to show that the people of Rome were under his protection; for once when a plague was raging among them and the dead were numbered by thousands, the Romans fled to the temple of Ares and begged him to help them. As they were praying, a shield fell from the skies into their midst, and a voice told them that as long as this – the sacred Ancile – was with them, no harm could come to Rome. That day the plague ceased, and ever afterward the shield was jealously guarded. To ensure its safety, eleven other shields were made so like the Ancile that no one but the Salii, the priests of the temple, knew which it was. These were carried in the streets during the festivals in honour of Ares which were held in March – the month that bears his name; and as the priests bore aloft the shields they sang war songs and performed rude war dances. Sometimes the shields were displayed on the broad grounds where the soldiers and youths of the city held their exercises. This place was dedicated to the god of war, and was called the Campus Martius, or Field of Ares.

During the war between the gods and giants, Ares was so eager to prove his skill in warfare that he engaged in a fierce battle with Otus and Ephialtes. These two giants were only nine years old; but they were already of immense size, as they increased in height at the rate of nine inches every month. The young giants were very proud of having conquered the god of war, and carried him off the battle-field in triumph. They bound Ares with iron chains, and kept a careful guard over him so that none of the gods could set him free. Whenever Ares attempted to escape at night, believing that the giants were asleep, the rattle of the chains woke his guardians, and all hope of rescuing him was over. In this disgraceful bondage the unhappy Ares lingered for fifteen months until Hermes, the prince of thieves, unfastened the chains and restored the god to freedom.

When Cadmus went on his search for his sister Europa, whom Zeus, in the form of a white bull, had carried off to a distant land, the devoted brother was at last bidden to give up his hopeless quest, to settle in the country, later called Boeotia, and to found a city there. Cadmus was glad to rest after his long march, and he sent some of his men in search of a spring. When they did not come back, he sent others to look for them, and when these did not return, he went himself to see what had caused all this delay. He carried his sword in his hand, and also a long spear, for he guessed that some disaster had overtaken his men. He wandered some time before he discovered any trace of them, and then at the edge of a forest he came upon the lifeless body of one of those who had first set out to find the spring. As he went farther into the forest he found others of his men, all of them lifeless, and soon he came to a large cave, at the entrance of which bubbled a fountain of purest water.

Not knowing that this was a grove sacred to Ares, and a fountain that had never been polluted by mortal touch, Cadmus stooped to drink, when suddenly, out of the deep shadows of the cave, rushed a huge dragon with crested head and glittering scales and a triple tongue vibrating between triple rows of teeth. This monster, twisting his body into a huge coil, darted toward Cadmus with gleaming fangs; but the young prince dealt his assailant a terrific blow that pierced the dragon in a vital spot, and it rolled over dead upon the floor of the cave. Then Cadmus heard a voice telling him to take out the dragon's teeth and to sow them in the ground where he wished to build his future city of Thebes. As soon as the teeth were sown, a crop of giants in glittering armour sprang up out of the ground, and when they were about to turn their spears upon Cadmus, he again heard the voice – this time bidding him throw a stone into the midst of the armed men. This caused a terrific battle to begin among the giants themselves, and soon they were all killed except five who laid down their weapons and offered their services to Cadmus.

As a punishment for the desecration of his grove and the slaying of its sacred guardian, Ares compelled Cadmus to serve him for eight years. At the end of this time the prince was made ruler of the new city of Thebes, and Ares so far forgave the sacrilege of his grove as to give Cadmus his daughter Harmonia in marriage. The career of the new king was very prosperous at first, and Cadmus was supposed to have contributed a great boon to his people by the invention of the alphabet. Later on he incurred the wrath of the gods by forgetting to offer them suitable sacrifices, and both he and his wife Harmonia were changed into serpents.

Just above the city of Athens was a hill called the Areopagus (from the Greek word meaning Ares Hill), which received its name from a famous trial that took place there. Poseidon's son had carried off the daughter of Ares; and when the god of war learned of the abduction, he hurried after the daring youth and killed him. Then Poseidon demanded that Ares should be punished for his deed of blood; and to decide the matter, both were summoned to appear before a court of justice, which was held on the hill above Athens. As it was the custom for all important cases to be tried at night, so that the judges might not be prejudiced by the favourable appearance of either party, the court assembled in the darkness, and Ares told the story of his daughter's capture and his own subsequent revenge. In spite of Poseidon's objections to what he considered an unfair verdict, the judges decided in favour of Ares, and he was therefore acquitted. The hill was afterwards called by his name, and the judges of the principal court of justice were always termed *areopagitæ*.

III

Hephaestus, god of fire and the forge, was not often seen in the halls of Olympus, for he knew that the gods despised him for his ungainly appearance, and he preferred to stay in his own sooty workshop. He had also no desire for the society of his divine parents, since his mother had never shown anything but indifference toward him, and his father had been the cause of his deformity. Zeus was once so angry with Hera for interfering in his love affairs that he fastened her to the end of a strong chain, and hung her out of heaven. Hephaestus, seeing his mother in this sad plight, dragged at the chain and finally succeeded in drawing Hera into safety. Full of wrath at this defiance of his wishes, Zeus kicked his son out of heaven; and as the distance of the fall was so great, it was a whole day and night before Hephaestus reached the earth. Had he been a mortal, there would have been nothing left to tell the story of his meteor-like descent; but being a god, he still lived and had only a slight deformity and lameness as the result of his fall. When he learned that Hera was so unconcerned over his fate that she had never even enquired whether he was badly hurt, he would not go back to Olympus, but shut himself up in the heart of Mount Etna, where he established a mighty forge that poured out fire and smoke for many years after.

Hephaestus did not forget about his mother's heartless indifference; but none of the gods suspected him of harbouring any revenge, until one day a beautiful golden throne arrived in Olympus as a present to Hera from her son. The goddess admired the exquisite designs carved on its polished surface, and seated herself in it proudly. Now Hephaestus had contrived to hide some springs in the interior of the throne, and these were so skilfully arranged that the moment a person was seated, the entire structure quickly contracted and held the occupant prisoner. So in a moment proud Hera found herself securely caught, and no assistance that the gods could render her was of the least avail. Then Zeus sent Hermes to the grimy abode of Hephaestus to beg politely that the god of fire would honour, with his presence, the feast that was that day to be held in Olympus; but Hephaestus was not to be moved by any flattery, for he well knew why he was so much desired at this particular time. So Hermes returned alone to Olympus, and Zeus was obliged to think of some other device for luring Hephaestus from his forge. This time he sent Dionysus, god of wine; and when the scowling deity of Etna saw Dionysus's jolly red face and heard his hearty laugh, he welcomed the jovial visitor and drank freely of the wine that Dionysus poured. The roisterous god of revels, who dearly loved to see good wine flowing, beguiled Hephaestus into taking draught after draught of the choice vintage that he had purposely brought, until the sullen master of the forge was unable to tell what was happening, and allowed himself to be led unresistingly to Olympus. Once there the gods persuaded him to release the repentant Hera, and to allow himself to be reinstated in Zeus's favour.

Though Hephaestus grudgingly complied with these requests, he would not consent to live in Olympus, but returned to his workshop in Mount Etna. There he made many things out of gold and precious stones and gave them to the gods as evidence that he no longer bore them any ill will. Their golden thrones were made by Hephaestus's crafty hands, and the wonderful palaces, with all their costly furnishings, were the best result of his skill. He also forged Zeus's thunderbolts and fashioned the weapons that the gods used in battle. He made Apollo's marvellous sun-chariot, and even deigned to use his skill in shaping the arrows that Eros used in his golden bow.

When Zeus decreed that laughter-loving Aphrodite should wed his misshapen son, Hephaestus took his reluctant wife to the smoky workshop in Mount Etna, and for a while Aphrodite was amused at the unusual sights and sounds that greeted her in her new home; but she soon wearied of the dirt and darkness, and left the society of her surly husband to return to Olympus, where there was plenty to delight her pleasure-loving soul.

16

THE STORY OF PERSEPHONE

When Zeus made himself ruler of the world, he imprisoned some of the warring giants under Mount Etna in Sicily, much to the disgust of Hades, who was always fearing that when the giants got restless and turned over and over underground (thus causing earthquakes), they would some day make such a large crack in the earth that daylight would be let into Hades. So Hades often went up out of his sunless land to look carefully over the island, and to be sure that no new fissure was being made in the earth's surface. One day, as he was driving his four coal-black horses through the vale of Enna, he saw a group of maidens gathering violets on the hillside; and among them was one so exquisitely fair that Hades determined to take her for his wife. This was Persephone, daughter of Demeter, the goddess of agriculture, a maiden who had ever shunned the thought of marriage and preferred to spend her life playing games, and dancing in the beautiful plain of Enna, where there is never any frost or snow, but springtime lasts through all the year.

Hades had often tried to gain a wife by gentle means, but no one would consent to share his gruesome home; so, knowing that this maiden he desired would never listen to soft words of love, he determined to take her by force. Driving his fiery horses at full speed, he rushed toward the group of laughing girls, who scattered and fled at his approach. Persephone alone stood still, and stared, frightened and wondering, at the grim figure confronting her, while the flowers she had gathered dropped from her trembling hands. In a moment Hades had seized her in his strong arms; and, trampling all her violets under his ruthless feet, he sprang into the chariot and urged his horses to their full speed, hoping to reach Hades before the maiden's cries brought Demeter to the rescue.

As he neared the Cyane River the waters, wishing to befriend Persephone, began to rise higher and higher, and with tossing waves opposed the madly-rushing steeds. Fearing to risk the chariot in the angry waters, Hades struck the ground with his terrible two-pronged fork, and a great chasm opened before him, into which the ruler of Hades hurriedly plunged. Then the earth closed again over him and the captured maiden. During the dreadful moments when Persephone felt herself held a prisoner in the arms of this bold wooer, she called wildly to her mother for help; but soon she realized that her cries would never reach Demeter's ears, and that she must find some other way to let the goddess know of her unhappy fate. So she summoned enough strength to struggle in her captor's embrace until she freed one arm from his hold, and with it loosened her girdle, which she flung into the Cyane River just before the yawning earth hid her so completely that no traces were left to tell where she had gone.

When Demeter came that evening into the vale of Enna and found that her daughter was not playing as usual with the other maidens, she questioned them, and learned their tearful story of the chariot with its four black horses and terrible driver. Just what had become of Persephone no one could tell her; so the distracted mother began her search, not knowing whether she might at any moment come upon her daughter's body mangled by the chariot wheels. For days and days she wandered, never stopping to rest except for a few hours at night when it was too dark for her to see her way. Rosy-fingered Aurora, when she left her soft couch to open the gates of the morning, and Hesperus, when he led out the stars at evening, saw her still searching for the lost Persephone. Sometimes she was so weary that she sank down by the roadside and let the night-dew drench her aching limbs. Sometimes she rested under the trees when a storm broke over her head; but even here the rain beat down upon her, and the wind blew its cold breath in her face. Kindly people gave her food whenever she stopped to ask for it, and though none knew that she was a goddess, they sympathized with her grief when she told them that she was seeking her lost child. Only once did she meet with unkindness. She was sitting at a cottage door eating gruel from a bowl, and a lad – Stellio by name – laughed insolently at her enjoyment of the meal. To punish him for his rudeness the goddess threw some of the gruel in his face, and immediately he was changed into a lizard.

One day Demeter found herself near the city of Eleusis, and to avoid being recognized as a goddess, she disguised herself as an old beggar woman. She sat for a long time on a stone by the roadside, mourning her lost Persephone, until a little girl came by, driving some goats. Seeing the old woman's tearful face, the child stopped to ask her her trouble, but before Demeter could answer, the girl's father joined her and together they begged the stranger to come to their cottage and rest. The goddess yielded at last to their kindly insistence, and as she walked beside the old man, whose name was Celeus, he told her that at home he had a sick boy who had lately grown so ill that to-day they believed he would surely die. Demeter listened to his pathetic story, and for a moment forgot her own grief. Seeing a chance to return the old man's kindness, she followed him into the cottage; but first stopped by the meadow to gather a handful of poppies. When the parents led her to the sick child's bedside, she stooped and kissed the pale little face and immediately it became rosy with health. The boy sprang up well and strong again, to the great astonishment of his delighted family.

As they sat at the simple evening meal, the goddess put some poppy-juice in the glass of milk set out for the boy; and that night, when he was in a heavy sleep, she rubbed his body with oil, murmured over him a solemn charm, and was about to lay him on the red-hot ashes in the fire – that his mortal parts might be consumed and he himself be made immortal – when his mother chanced to enter the room, and springing forward with a cry of horror, snatched the boy from the fire. Before the excited mother could vent her wrath on the old woman, Demeter assumed her goddess form and quietly reproved the intruder; for her interference had not averted a harm, but had prevented a great gift from being conferred upon the unconscious child.

When Demeter left the cottage of Celeus, she continued her wanderings over the earth, and finally returned, discouraged and heartbroken, to Sicily. Chancing to be near the river Cyane, she went down to the water's edge to drink, and happily discovered the girdle that Persephone had dropped there in her flight. This made her hopeful of finding further traces of her lost daughter, so she lingered by the river bank, eagerly scanning the overflowing stream. As she stood there holding the recovered girdle in her hand, she heard a low murmuring sound as if some one were speaking in whispers. The goddess listened, wondering from what place the voice came; and soon she found that the soft tones proceeded from a fountain which was so close to her that its lightly-tossed spray fell on her hand. The murmur was often indistinct, but Demeter understood enough to realize that the words were addressed to her, and that the fountain was trying to tell her how Hades had come up from Hades and carried off Persephone to be his wife.

While the goddess was musing over this painful revelation, the fountain went on to say that it had not always been a stream in sunny Sicily, but was once a maiden named Arethusa and a native of the country of Elis. As a follower of Artemis she had roamed the wooded hills; and one day, being wearied from the chase, she sought refreshment in the forest stream. The drooping willows hung protectingly over the water, and here the nymph bathed fearlessly, believing herself alone. But Alpheus, the river-god, heard the splashing of the water, and rose from his grassy bed to see who was disturbing his noon-day rest. At the sight of Arethusa he was so delighted that he ventured to approach her; but she fled terrified through the forest, calling on Artemis for help. The goddess, hearing her cries, changed her into a fountain; and to further baffle the pursuing Alpheus, she wrapped it in a thick mist. As the river-god could no longer see the nymph, he was about to give up the chase, when Zephyrus maliciously blew away the cloud, and Alpheus saw the bubbling fountain. Suspecting that this was Arethusa, the god changed himself into a rushing torrent, and was preparing to mingle his impetuous waves with the waters of the fountain, when the nymph again called on Artemis to protect her. The goddess came to her rescue by opening a crevice in the earth, and here the shivering waters of the fountain found a speedy refuge. To keep far out of the reach of Alpheus it continued to flow underground for many miles, and even crept beneath the sea until it reached Sicily, where Artemis again cleft the earth and allowed the fountain to come up into the sunlight. During her journey through the dark underworld, Arethusa said that she had seen Persephone sitting, tearful and sad, on a throne beside the grim ruler of the dead.

When she heard this story, Demeter was no longer in doubt where her lost daughter could be found; but the knowledge gave her little comfort, for she was aware how useless it would be to ask Hades to give up the wife he had so daringly won. Seeing no hope of regaining her child, Demeter retired to a cave in the hills, and paid no heed to the waiting earth that had suffered so long from her neglect. There was drought in the land, and the crops were failing for want of water. The fruit trees were drying up, and the flowers were withering on the parched hillsides. Everything cried out for the protecting care of Demeter; but the goddess stayed her hand, and in the solitude of the cave mourned unceasingly for Persephone. Famine spread over the land, but the people, in spite of their dire need of food, burned sacrifices of sheep and oxen on the altars of Demeter, while they importuned her with their prayers. Zeus heard their cries and besought the goddess to take the earth again under her wise care; but Demeter refused to listen, for she was indifferent now to the welfare of men, and no longer delighted in the ripening harvest.

When sickness and death followed hard upon the famine, Zeus saw that he must save the sorely-stricken land, so he promised the goddess that her daughter should be restored to her if she had eaten nothing during all her sojourn in Hades's realm. Hermes was sent to lead Persephone out of Hades; but when he reached there, he found that Hades had already given his wife some pomegranate seeds, hoping that she would thereby stay forever in his keeping. Dismayed at this unexpected downfall of her hopes, Demeter was about to shut herself up again in the cave, when Zeus, on behalf of the suffering earth, made a compromise with Hades whereby Persephone was to spend half her time with her mother in the land of sunshine and flowers, and the rest with her husband in cold and cheerless Hades. Each spring Hermes was sent to lead Persephone up from the underworld lest her eyes, grown accustomed only to shadows, should be dazzled by the blinding sunlight, and she herself should lose the way. All things awaited her coming; and as soon as her foot touched the winter-saddened earth the flowers bloomed to delight her eyes, the grass sprang up to carpet her way with greenness, the birds sang to cheer her long-depressed spirit, and above her the sun shone brilliantly in the blue Sicilian sky.

Demeter no longer mourned, nor did she again suffer a great famine to afflict the land. The patient old earth smiled again on Persephone's return, for then her mother gave the blighted vegetation a redoubled care. But her happiness did not make the goddess forget the kindly old man who had given her food and shelter at Eleusis, for she returned there and taught the boy Triptolemus all the secrets of agriculture. She also gave him her chariot, and bade him journey everywhere, teaching the people how to plough and sow and reap, and care for their harvests. Triptolemus carried out all her instructions; and as he travelled over the country he was eagerly welcomed alike by prince and peasant until he came to Scythia, where the cruel King Lyncus would have killed him, in a fit of jealous wrath, had not Demeter interfered with timely aid and changed the treacherous monarch into a lynx.

17

HADES AND THE
UNDERWORLD

In the beginning of the world, before the gods came to dwell in Olympus, all the universe was in the hands of the Titans; and among these the greatest was Cronus – or Cronos – who wedded his sister Rhea (also called Cybele) and became the father of three sons and three daughters, Zeus, Hades, Poseidon, Demeter, Hestia, and Hera. For many ages Cronus and Rhea, having subdued all the opposing Titans, ruled over heaven and earth; but when the cruelty of Cronus drove his children into rebellion, there arose a mighty war in the universe, in which the sons and daughters of Cronus leagued against their father, who had called upon the other Titans for aid. After years of combat the six brothers and sisters, helped by the Cyclops, defeated the allied Titans and imprisoned them in the black abyss of Tartarus – all except a few who had not joined in the war against the children of Cronus. Among those who were wise enough to accept the new sovereignty were Mnemosyne (Memory) and Themis, goddess of justice. Those descendants of the Titans who refused to acknowledge the supremacy of Zeus were consigned to the centre of Mount Etna, and were the giants who constantly turned over and over, making Hades fear for the safety of his realm. A few of the giants were spared: Atlas, whose punishment was to hold the heavens on his shoulders, and Prometheus and Epimetheus who had espoused the cause of Zeus and so escaped the fate of the conquered Titans. When the children of Cronus found themselves masters of the world, they agreed to accept Zeus as their ruler, on condition that the two other brothers be given a share in the universe. So a division was made whereby Hades became king of the underworld – or Hades; Poseidon took the dominion of the sea; and Zeus, having married his sister, Hera, established his dwelling in Olympus as lord of heaven and earth.

The kingdom of Hades was dreaded by all mortals, and its ruler inspired men with great fear. Though Hades was known to visit the earth from time to time, no one wished to see his face, and each man dreaded the moment when he should be obliged to appear before the grim monarch of Hades, and be assigned a place among the innumerable dead. No temples were dedicated to Hades, though altars were sometimes erected on which men burned sacrifices to this inexorable god while petitioning him to be merciful to the souls of the departed. The festivals held in his honour were celebrated only once in a hundred years, and on these occasions none but black animals were killed for the sacrifice.

The underworld, over which Hades reigned, was deep in the heart of the earth; but there were several entrances to it, one being near Lake Avernus, where the mist rising from the waters was so foul that no bird could fly over it. The lake itself was in an extinct volcano near Vesuvius. It was very deep, and was surrounded by high banks covered with a thick forest. The first descent into Hades could be easily accomplished (*facilis descensus Averno*, says the poet Virgil); but no mortal was daring enough to venture far into the black depths, lest he should never again see the light of day.

At the portals of Hades sits the fierce three-headed dog Cerberus, who keeps all living things from entering the gate, and allows no spirit that has once been admitted to pass out again. From here a long dark pathway leads deeper into Hades, and is finally lost in the rivers that flow around Hades's throne. The waters of the river Cocytus are salt, as they are made of the tears that stream forever from the eyes of those unhappy souls who are condemned to labour in Tartarus – that part of Hades that is the exclusive abode of the wicked. The Phlegethon River, which is always on fire, separates Tartarus from the rest of Hades, and wretched indeed is the soul that is forced to cross its seething waters. On the banks of the Acheron, a black and turbid river, stand the souls who come fresh from the sunlit earth; for all must pass this river and be brought before the judgment-throne of Hades. There is no bridge over the murky stream, and the current is so swift that the boldest swimmer would not trust himself to its treacherous waters. The only way to cross is by the leaky, worm-eaten boat rowed by Charon, an aged ferryman who has plied his oar ever since the day that the curse of death first came upon the earth.

No spirit is allowed to enter the leaky craft until he has first paid Charon the fee of a small coin called the obolus. (During the funeral services, before the body is committed for burial, this coin is laid on the tongue of the dead, that the soul may have no trouble in passing to the throne of Hades.) If any spirits cannot furnish the necessary money, they are ruthlessly pushed aside by the mercenary boatman and are required to wait a hundred years. At the end of this time Charon grudgingly ferries them over the river free of charge. As the unstable boat can hold but few, there is always an eager group of spirits on the further bank, clamouring to be taken across the river; but Charon is never in a hurry, and repulses, sometimes with his oar, the pitiful crowd that waits his grim pleasure.

There is also in Hades the river Styx, by whose sacred waters the gods swear the most terrible of all oaths, and on the other side of Hades's throne is the softly flowing Lethe, of which only those souls can drink who are to spend endless days of happiness in the Elysian Fields. As soon as those blessed spirits have tasted of the waters of Lethe, all regrets for friends that mourn completely vanish, and the joy and grief, and pleasure and pain of the soul's life on earth are forgotten. In the Elysian Fields there is no darkness such as fills the rest of Hades with its thick gloom; but a soft light spreads over the meadows where the spirits of the thrice-blessed wander. There are willows here, and stately silver poplars, and the "meads of Asphodel" breathe out a faint perfume from their pale flowers.

"There do men lead easiest lives.
No snow, no bitter cold, no beating rains are there."

The sighs and groans that rise by night and day from the black abyss of Tartarus do not reach the ears of those who dwell at peace in the Elysian Fields, and the sight of its painful torments is hid forever from their eyes.

Beside Hades's throne sit the three Fates (also called *Moirae*), those deathless sisters who hold the threads of life and death in their hands. Clotho, the youngest, spins the thread; Lachesis, the second, twines into it the joys and sorrows, hopes and fears that make up human experience; and Atropos, the eldest sister, sits by with huge shears in her hand, waiting for the time when she may cut the slender thread.

Hades and his queen Persephone are seated side by side on a sable throne, ruling over the myriad souls that compose the vast kingdom of the dead. Perched on the back of the throne is the blinking owl, who loves this eternal darkness, and the black-winged raven that was once a bird of snowy plumage and the favourite messenger of Apollo. The raven fell from his high estate on account of some unwelcome tidings that he once brought to Apollo when that god was an ardent lover of the fair-haired Coronis. Believing that no one could supplant him in the maiden's affections, Apollo was happy in the thought of being beloved by so beautiful a mortal; but one day his snow-white raven flew in haste to Olympus to tell him that the maiden was listening to the wooing of another lover. Enraged at this duplicity, Apollo seized his bow and shot the faithless Coronis; but the moment that he saw her lying dead, he repented of his rash deed and vainly sought to restore her to life. Though skilled in the art of healing, Apollo could not save the maiden; and in his frenzied grief he cursed the unfortunate raven that had brought the evil tidings, and banished it forever from his sight.

> "Then he turned upon the Raven,
> 'Wanton babbler! see thy fate!
> Messenger of mine no longer,
> Go to Hades with thy prate!
>
> 'Weary Hades with thy tattle!
> Hither, monster, come not back;
> And – to match thy disposition –
> Henceforth be thy plumage black.'"

Near Hades's throne are seated the three judges of Hades (Minos, Rhadamanthus, and Aeacus) who question all souls that are brought across the river. When they have learned every detail of the newcomer's past life, they deliver the cowering spirit into the hands of Themis, the blindfolded goddess of justice, who weighs impartially the good and bad deeds in her unerring scales. If the good outweighs the evil, the soul is led gently to the Elysian Fields; but if the bad overbalances the good, then the wretched spirit is driven to Tartarus, there to suffer for all its wrongdoings in the fires that burn forever and ever behind the brazen gates. To these gates the guilty one is urged by the three Furies, whose snaky hair shakes hideously as they ply their lashes to goad the shrinking soul to its place of torment. Sometimes they are joined by Nemesis, goddess of revenge, who hurries the doomed spirit over the fiery waters of the Phlegethon with her merciless whip, and sees that it follows no path but the one leading to the brazen gates of Tartarus.

As soon as the gates close on the newly-admitted soul, there is a renewed clamour of voices, while heart-breaking sighs and groans mingle with the curses of those who in their misery dare to defy the gods. And beneath all the awful sounds that greet the listener's ears, there is an undertone of pitiful wailing like the sea's "melancholy, long-withdrawing roar" that seems to come from millions of throats too feeble to utter a loud cry. The deepest sighs proceed from the Danaïdes – the beautiful daughters of Danaüs, king of Argos – who must forever strive to fill a bottomless cask with water. They form a sad procession as, with their urns on their arms, they go down to the stream to begin their hopeless task, and then climb wearily up the steep bank to pour the water into the ever-empty cask. If they pause a moment, exhausted with fatigue, the whips of some avenging attendants of Hades lash them again into action. Their punishment is severe, but the crime for which they are suffering was a dreadful one. The fifty daughters of Danaüs were once pledged in marriage to the fifty sons of Aegyptus, brother of Danaüs; but when the wedding was being celebrated, their father remembered the words of an ancient prophecy that said that he would die by the hand of his son-in-law. Fearing for his life, he confided to his daughters what the oracle had foretold, and gave them each a dagger, bidding them slay their husbands. On the evening of the wedding, when the sons of Aegyptus were heavy with wine, the new-made wives stole in upon them and killed them as they slept. Danaüs then believed himself safe, until he learned that one of his daughters had spared her husband out of love for him. This son-in-law was eager to avenge his brothers' murder, and having sought out the wicked Danaüs, fulfilled the prophecy by killing the king with the very dagger intended for his own death. The gods punished the cruel daughters – except Hypermnestra, who had saved her husband – by condemning them to labour in Tartarus at their impossible task.

Near the Danaïdes stands Tantalus, the father of Niobe, who on earth was a most inhuman and brutal king. He ill-treated his subjects, defied the gods, and dared to make his own will the religion of his kingdom. He boasted that the gods were not so omniscient as people were led to believe; and insulted the immortals by offering them at a banquet the flesh of his own son Pelops, believing that they would never learn the truth of this loathsome feast. But the gods were not deceived, and left the meal untouched – all except poor Demeter, who, still mourning over her daughter's detention in Hades, did not realize what was happening and bit off some of the lad's shoulder. When the gods restored Pelops to life, Demeter was very sorry for her carelessness and gave him a shoulder of ivory. The inhuman Tantalus was condemned to the torments of Tartarus, where he stands up to his chin in a clear stream. Though frenzied with thirst he can never drink of the water, for whenever he bends his head the stream recedes from his parched lips. Above him hangs a branch of delicious fruit; but when, tormented with hunger, he strives to grasp it, the branch eludes his eager fingers. Thus he stays, always "tantalized" by the sight of food and drink he never can secure.

Not far from Tantalus is Salmoneus, also a king, who dared to challenge the gods by impersonating Zeus. He made a huge bridge of brass, and drove heavily over it while he threw lighted torches among the people who were waiting below, hoping thus to frighten them into believing that he was the very ruler of the heavens who hurls the mighty thunderbolts. This insult to his divinity so angered Zeus that he seized a real thunderbolt and soon dispatched the arrogant king. When Salmoneus came before the throne of Hades, his fate was quickly decided, and he was driven to terrible Tartarus, where he sits under a huge rock that threatens every moment to fall and crush him beneath its weight.

Another unhappy king is Sisyphus, who, when ruler of Corinth, became a famous robber, and in the pride of his great wealth dared to set the gods at naught. Therefore he was consigned to Tartarus, and his punishment is to roll an immense stone to the top of a steep hill. As soon as he reaches the summit, the rock slips from his aching arms and tumbles to the foot of the hill, and he must at once start on the hopeless task of pushing it up the long ascent again.

"With many a weary step, and many a groan,
Up the high hill he heaves a huge round stone."

Beyond Sisyphus lies Tityus, a giant whose huge body covers nine acres of ground. He was condemned to the blackness of Tartarus because he dared to affront a goddess with his addresses, and so was doomed to suffer, like Prometheus, by being chained to a rock, while a vulture tears at his liver. Near him is Ixion, who was promised the hand of a certain maiden in marriage, on condition that he would give her father a large sum of money. Ixion agreed, but when the maiden became his wife, he refused to give the stipulated sum, in spite of her father's clamorous demands. At length, wearied by the old man's insistence, Ixion slew him; but the deed did not go unpunished, for the gods summoned him to appear before them and answer for his cruelty. Ixion pleaded his cause so well that Zeus was about to dismiss him, when he saw the presumptuous mortal making love to Hera. This offence could not be overlooked, so Ixion was sent to Tartarus, where he was bound to an ever-revolving wheel of fire.

If any one could follow the course of the gentle Lethe River, it would lead beyond the sunless realm of Hades to a quiet and far-distant valley, where, in a soundless cave, live Hypnos, the god of sleep, and his twin brother Mors, god of death. "Here the sun, whether rising or in his mid course, or setting, can never come; and fogs, mingled with the dimness, form a strange twilight. No wakeful bird calls forth the morn, nor do watchful dogs disturb the brooding silence. No sound of wild beast or cattle, nor any noise of creaking bough, nor human voice, breaks in upon the perfect stillness, where mute Rest has her abode. Before the cave bloom abundant poppies and other sleep-producing herbs, which Night gathers, that she may distil their juice and scatter slumbers on the darkened earth. Within the cave is no door that could creak on rusty hinges, and no porter stands at the entrance of that inner room where, on a downy couch made of black ebony and draped with sable curtains, over which black plumes wave, lies Hypnos, the god of sleep – Sleep, the repose of all things, gentlest of the deities from whom all care flies, the peace of mind who can soothe the hearts of men wearied with the toils of the day, and can refit them for labour."

Near Hypnos sits Morpheus, one of his many sons, who watches over his slumbers and sees that no one shall break in upon his sleep. This god holds a vase in one hand, and with the other he shakes the nodding poppies that bring drowsiness and sleep. Sometimes he assumes varied forms in which he appears to men at night, and always he flies through the darkness with wings that make no noise. Around the couch of Hypnos hover shadowy forms, the Dreams, which are as numerous as the forest leaves or the sands upon the seashore. In a distant corner of the room lurk the horrid Nightmares, which creep out of the cave to visit sleeping mortals, but are never led to earth by Hermes, as are the welcomed Dreams. Two gates lead out of the valley of sleep, one of horn and one of ivory.

> "Of dreams, O stranger, some are meaningless
> And idle, and can never be fulfilled.
> Two portals are there for their shadowy shapes,
> Of ivory one, and one of horn. The dreams
> That come through the carved ivory deceive
> With promises that never are made good;
> But those which pass the doors of polished horn,
> And are beheld of men, are ever true."

Homer's Odyssey, Book XIX

Thanatos, god of death, occupies one of the rooms in the cave of sleep. He is a fearful-looking deity, cadaverous as a skeleton, and wrapped in a winding sheet. He holds an hourglass in one hand, and a sharp scythe in the other; and stands watching the sand run out of his glass that he may know when a human life is nearing its end. Then, as the last grains fall, he glides from the valley of sleep and stalks silently and unseen upon the earth, where he cuts down the unhappy mortal, who cannot even hear the rustle of his garments as he approaches. It is nothing to him whether the life he takes belongs to childhood or youth, for he mows them down as relentlessly as he does tottering old age. And to the rich he is as unsparing as to the poor.

The divinities who dwelt in the Cave of Sleep were distrusted by the ancients, and Thanatos was held in universal dread. No homage was ever offered to him, and no temples were dedicated in his honour; though sacrifices were sometimes made to ward off his dreaded coming. He was never represented in art except in a pleasing aspect, for although they believed him to have in reality the fearful appearance that tradition ascribed to him, yet the beauty-loving Greeks refused to have this kind of horror embodied in marble. So when Death appears in sculpture, it is usually with his brother Sleep, and both are represented as sleeping youths, whose heads are crowned with poppies or amaranths, and who hold inverted torches in their listless hands.

18

POSEIDON AND
THE SEA-GODS

I

In the days when the Titans ruled the universe, Oceanus, with his wife Tethys, controlled all the lakes, rivers, and seas; but when the Titans were overthrown, Poseidon took possession of this great kingdom, and old Oceanus reluctantly gave up his dominion over the waters of the earth. Though anxious to assert his supreme authority, Poseidon allowed some of the descendants of the Titans to keep their small kingdoms, on condition that they own allegiance to him as their ruler. Among these was Nereus, son of Oceanus, who was celebrated for his vast knowledge, his gift of prophecy, and his love of truth and justice. He and his wife Doris (also a child of Oceanus) had fifty daughters called Nereids, and they were so beautiful that Poseidon chose one of them, named Amphitrite, for his wife. There were two others of the Nereids who became famous: Galatea, beloved by the Cyclops Polyphemus, and Thetis, the mother of Achilles; but none of them equalled Amphitrite in beauty.

When Poseidon first went wooing the Nereid, she was frightened by his formidable appearance, for he drove in a chariot drawn by huge sea-horses with brazen hoofs and golden manes; and the god himself carried his terrible trident, or three-pronged spear, with which he shatters rocks, and commands the storms, and shakes the shores of earth. None knew better than Amphitrite the extent of Poseidon's power, for she had often watched him, when a storm was at its height, raise his all-compelling trident, and immediately the waves would cease raging and there would be a great calm. Sometimes she saw a ship, doomed by the sea-god to disaster, gliding confidently in quiet waters, when all at once a fierce storm would break over its head; and the hapless sailors, as they breasted the angry waves, would pray vainly to Poseidon for the help that would never come. Many a good ship had nearly gained her port when

> "He spake and round about him called the clouds
> And roused the ocean – wielding in his hand
> The trident – summoned all the hurricanes
> Of all the winds, and covered earth and sky
> At once with mists, while from above the night
> Fell suddenly."

Odyssey, Book V, line 348.

When Amphitrite saw this imposing-looking god driving toward her, she was frightened by so much splendour, though she could not help admiring Poseidon himself with his sea-green beard, and his long flowing hair crowned with shells and seaweed. Since the enamoured god could never come near enough to plead his suit, he sent one of his dolphins to do the wooing; and this was so successful that the fair Nereid was persuaded to become Poseidon's wife, and share his golden throne in the heart of the sea. To reward the dolphin for its skill in having won for him his much-desired bride, Poseidon placed it in the sky, where it forms a well-known constellation.

Though Poseidon had undisputed control over all the waters of the earth, and over all that moves through the paths of the sea, he once aspired to greater power, and even plotted to dethrone Zeus. But the ruler of gods and men discovered his wicked plans, and to punish him deprived him of his kingdom for some years, during which time he was obliged to submit to the humiliation of serving Laomedon, king of Troy. It was while he was in service here that he sought Apollo's help in building the wall of Troy, whose stones fell into place under the spell of the sun-god's music. Laomedon had promised Poseidon a large reward if the wall was built within a certain time; but when it was finished, he refused to pay the sum agreed upon. Though angered at this treachery, Poseidon had to endure the king's injustice until his years of service were over; but as soon as he was restored to his former power, he created a terrible sea-monster, which spread terror and death over all the land. Not knowing how to meet this calamity, the Trojans consulted an oracle, and were advised to sacrifice to the monster a beautiful maiden each year; and so prevent the wrath of Poseidon from overwhelming the whole country in disaster.

Reluctantly the sorrowing people prepared to obey the oracle; and a victim was chosen by lot, and led by the priest to a large rock on the seashore, where she was securely chained. Then the hideous sea-beast glided out of its cave in the slimy rocks and devoured her. Each year this terrible ceremony was repeated, and at last the lot fell upon Hesione, the king's only daughter. Laomedon tried in vain to save her, but the lot was cast, and nothing could avert the appointed sacrifice. In despair, the wretched father saw the fatal hour approaching; and when the day drew near when Hesione was to be led down to the sea, he forgot his avarice and proclaimed throughout the land that a great reward would be given to any one who could slay the monster. Heracles appeared just in time to save the doomed maiden, and killed the monster with his oaken club as it was dragging Hesione into its cave. The king was overjoyed at his daughter's rescue, and told Heracles that he might claim the reward; but even when he saw the hero come with the beast's head as a proof that he had slain it, he refused to part with his much-loved gold. So Heracles returned home, but he did not forget Laomedon's perfidy; and when later on he came again to Troy, he killed the king and took his children captive to Greece.

Poseidon, like all the immortals, loved more than once; and among those who shared his affections was a maiden named Theophane, who had so many suitors that it kept the jealous sea-god in constant fear lest she should prefer some earthly lover. So he took her to the island of Crumissa, and there changed her into a sheep, while he carried on his wooing in the form of a ram. The offspring of this marriage was the famous golden-fleeced ram, whose pelt was the object of that ill-fated expedition made by Jason and his fellow Argonauts.

Poseidon also loved the goddess Demeter, and followed her during the long time that she spent in search of her daughter Persephone. Demeter was angered by the sea-god's persistent wooing, and hoping to escape from him, she took the form of a mare; but Poseidon was not so easily discouraged, for he changed himself into a horse and contentedly trotted after her. The child of this strange pair was Arion, a wonderful winged steed that had the power of speech, and was of such incredible swiftness that nothing could ever equal it in speed.

The most famous children of Poseidon and Amphitrite were Triton and Proteus. Triton was his father's trumpeter, and at Poseidon's command he blew upon his conch-shell to calm the restless sea. His body was half man and half fish, and he gave the name of Tritons to all his male descendants, who, with the Nereids and Oceanides (daughters of Oceanus), followed the chariot of Poseidon when he went abroad to view his kingdom. Proteus had charge of the great flock of sea-calves which fed on the soft seaweed and basked in the warm sands near his cave. He was celebrated for his wisdom and for the truth of the answers that he gave to those fortunate enough to make him speak. Homer calls him "the Ancient of the Deep whose words are ever true"; but his knowledge was not easy to obtain, for he had the extraordinary power of assuming any shape he pleased, and only those mortals gained his advice who persistently clung to him through his many bewildering changes.

> "When the climbing sun has reached
> The middle heaven, the Ancient of the Deep,
> Who ne'er deceives, emerges from the waves,
> And, covered with the dark scum of the sea,
> Walks forth, and in a cavern vault lies down.
> The sea-calves from the hoary ocean throng,
> Rank with the bitter odour of the brine,
> And slumber near him. Then ye must exert.
> Your utmost strength to hold him there, although
> He strive and struggle to escape your hands;
> For he will try all stratagems, and take
> The form of every reptile on the earth,
> And turn to water and to raging flame.
>
> * * * * *
>
> But hold him fast, until the aged seer
> Is wearied out in spite of all his wiles,
> Then question him."
>
> Homer's *Odyssey*, Book IV.

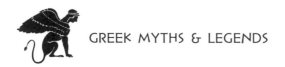

II

Aristaeus was the son of Apollo, and the water-nymph, Cyrene. Beside tending his flocks and herds, he took care of the olive trees and vineyards, and was a famous keeper of bees. He was very proud of his hives, and the swarm of bees increased each year under the guidance of his skilful hands; but one day he found hundreds of the bees lying lifeless beside the hives, and on the morrow there were still more among the dead. Not knowing how to account for this disaster, Aristaeus hurried to his mother to ask her help in saving the few bees that remained. Cyrene lived under a mountain stream; and, hearing that her son wished to speak to her, she commanded the river to divide and form a wall on either side, so that Aristaeus might walk in dry places. When the youth told her of the tragedy befalling his hives, she could not help him, but bade him go to old Proteus, for he alone could tell what the trouble was and find a remedy. She warned Aristaeus of the difficulty in holding the Ancient of the Deep when he tried to bewilder and terrify the stranger by rapidly assuming different forms; and she bade him remember that he must keep the sea-god fast bound if he would receive the wished-for answers. Then she led him to the cave of Proteus and hid him there, exhorting him to be bold and fearless.

At noon the Wizard of the Deep came up out of the sea, followed by his herd of sea-calves; and while they lay stretched out on the warm sands, the god sought the retreat of his cave and soon was in a deep slumber. When Aristaeus saw Proteus fast asleep, he stepped cautiously up to him and bound him with strong fetters. The god woke with a start, and tried to shake himself free of his chains; but on finding that he was a prisoner, he resorted to all the trickery that he could command. He became a fire, a flood, a wild beast, a horrible serpent, and many other forms calculated to terrify the beholder.

But Aristaeus was not afraid, and soon the old wizard realized that he must submit; so he assumed his own shape, and asked the youth what it was that he wished to know. The son of Cyrene told him of the death of his bees, and begged for some remedy. Then Proteus reminded him of how he had been the real cause of Eurydice's death, by making her flee from him in such haste that she did not see the snake at her feet. The wood-nymphs, who were Eurydice's companions, had therefore wished to punish Aristaeus, and had sent this destruction to his hives. It was necessary to appease the wrath of the nymphs; and to do this Proteus bade the youth build four altars, and sacrifice on them four bulls and four cows of perfect form and size. This burnt offering was to placate the nymphs, and when it was made, he must pay funeral honours to Orpheus and Eurydice to pacify their anger against him. At the end of nine days he was to return to the grove where he had made the sacrifices.

Aristaeus thanked the Ancient of the Deep for his wise words, and after releasing him from the fetters, hurried away to do as Proteus had advised. The sacrifices were made, and suitable honours paid to the dead; and then, after waiting impatiently for nine days, Aristaeus went back to the grove. To his great joy he found that a swarm of bees had taken possession of the carcasses, and that he was now the owner of a much larger number than he had ever had before.

III

One of the many sea-gods who ruled under Poseidon was Glaucus, who was once a poor fisherman, and earned his living by selling the fish that he caught each day. One morning he had an extra large haul; and when he threw the fish on the ground beside him, he noticed that they were eagerly nibbling the grass that grew very thickly in the spot where he had flung his net. As he stood watching them, the fish suddenly leaped up from the ground; and having flopped back into the water, swam away. Curious to see whether it was the grass that gave them this extraordinary power, Glaucus chewed a bit of it himself, and immediately he felt an irresistible desire to plunge into the sea. Fearlessly he dived beneath the waves, and soon found no difficulty in keeping under water, for the ocean seemed now to be his native element. He saw his beard turning a lovely sea-green; and he found that his hair, grown suddenly long and green, was trailing out behind him. His arms were azure-coloured, and his legs became a fish's tail; but he felt no regrets over losing his human form, and stayed contentedly in the ocean. In time Poseidon made him one of the lesser gods, and took him into the friendly fraternity of the sea.

As Glaucus was swimming one day near the shore, he saw a beautiful maiden named Scylla; and fell so much in love with her that he forgot he was half fish, and begged her to be his wife. Scylla stared at his green hair and blue skin, but this did not frighten her, nor did she wonder at his fish's tail; for she had often played with the sea-nymphs, and was accustomed to their strange appearance. Glaucus felt encouraged by her behaviour, and begged her to listen to the story of his life. He told her how he had suffered a sea change, and now occupied the lofty position of a god. The maiden was interested in this recital, but she had no desire to marry a merman, even if he were a god; so when Glaucus ventured to come nearer to her, she turned and fled. Discouraged but still determined, the young god sought the aid of the enchantress Circe, and begged her to give him some love-potion by which he might win the unwilling Scylla. Circe was so well pleased with the handsome sea-god that she urged him to accept her love, and forget the maiden who scorned him; but Glaucus would not yield to the persuasions of the enchantress, and kept pleading for the desired love-potion.

Seeing that she could not gain his affections, Circe determined that at least no one else should enjoy his love; so she refused to make the potion, and sent Glaucus angrily away. When she saw him go sorrowfully from her palace, she mixed a magic liquid, brewed from poisonous plants and deadly weeds, and this she poured over the waters where Scylla was wont to bathe. The maiden, suspecting no treachery, sought the ocean at her accustomed hour, and as soon as the poisoned waves touched her body she became a horrible monster with six heads – each having three rows of sharp teeth. She saw all around her serpents and barking dogs that were part of her own body, which had suddenly become rooted to the spot where she stood. She never regained her human form, but stayed in this place forever to terrify all mariners, and to devour the hapless sailors that came within her reach. Opposite her was the den of Charybdis, who three times a day swallowed the waters of the sea, and three times threw them up again. On the rock above the den was an immense fir-tree, and all ships that passed that way watched eagerly for this signal of danger, and prayed that they might safely steer between the double horrors of Scylla and Charybdis.

> "There Scylla dwells,
> And fills the air with fearful yells; her voice
> The cry of whelps just littered, but herself
> A frightful prodigy – a sight which none
> Would care to look on, though he were a god.
> Twelve feet are hers, all shapeless, six long necks,
> A hideous head on each, and triple rows
> Of teeth, close set and many, threatening death.
> And forth from the dark gulf her heads are thrust,
> To look abroad upon the rocks for prey –
> …. No mariner can boast

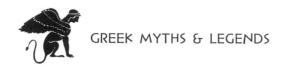
That he has passed by Scylla with a crew
Unharmed."

Homer's *Odyssey*, Book XII

IV

Two other minor deities of the sea were Leucothea and Palaemon.
They were not born of the ocean-nymphs or any water-god, but were
once mortals, named Ino and Melicertes. Ino was the wife of King
Athamas, whom cruel Hera goaded into madness; and through fear
of him Ino fled from the palace with her little son, Melicertes, in her
arms. She hoped to reach some place of safety; but imagining herself
pursued, in her frenzy she plunged from a cliff's edge into the sea.
Neither she nor her son perished, however, for the gods, in pity for
her sufferings, changed them both into ocean deities under the names
of Leucothea and Palaemon. They were widely worshipped by all
who had business in great waters, and their protection was invoked
against the danger of shipwreck. A famous altar to Palaemon was
built on the shores of Corinth, and in his honour were instituted the
celebrated Isthmian games.

V

Poseidon was not only willing to befriend a goddess in distress, as he
did when he raised the island out of the sea for Leto, but was equally
ready to assist mortals – especially in their love affairs. Once he lent
his chariot to a youth named Idas when he wished to elope with
the maiden Marpessa, whose father had refused to allow the lovers

to wed. They were overjoyed at Poseidon's kindly offer of assistance; and on the day arranged for their flight, the happy pair mounted the chariot, and the swift steeds carried them far out of reach of Marpessa's angry father. When he discovered that his daughter had eloped with her lover, he started in pursuit; but finding it impossible to overtake Poseidon's splendid horses, he flew into such a rage that he flung himself into a river and drowned. (The river was afterwards called by his name – Evenus.)

Knowing themselves out of reach of the irate father, the lovers continued their journey very happily, and believed that no misfortune could overtake them, when suddenly Apollo appeared before them, and, declaring himself in love with Marpessa, offered to fight Idas then and there for the possession of the maiden. Poor Idas felt that his chances for happiness were indeed ended, for how could a mortal contend with an omnipotent god? Suddenly a thunderbolt fell from the blue sky, and a voice declared that Marpessa herself should choose between her two suitors. The maiden looked at the glorious sun-god, and her heart beat fast at the thought of being loved by one so beautiful and young; but when she turned to Idas, she remembered that he was a mortal like herself, who would grow old as she grew old, and would, therefore, not cast her aside when her youthful charm was gone, as Apollo would be sure to do as soon as her beauty waned. So she held out her hand to Idas, and refused the sun-god's love. This choice was approved by Zeus, and the lovers, happy once more, urged Poseidon's swift horses over the mirror-like sea, which the kindly god had made calm as a forest pool on the softest summer day. In time they reached a pleasant land far from their native country, and here they lived happily ever afterward. The chariot, no longer needed, was sent back to Poseidon with many thanks for his timely aid; and each year Idas and Marpessa burned as sacrifices to their protector a white bull, a white ram, and a white boar, which was the kind of offering most pleasing to Poseidon.

19

DIONYSUS

Among all the maidens whom Zeus honoured with his love, none was more beautiful than Semele, daughter of Cadmus and Harmonia. Cadmus was the brother of Europa, whom Zeus, in the form of a white bull, carried on his back across the sea. The maiden's three brothers had been with her in the meadow, and had witnessed her strange departure, but knowing that it would be useless to attempt to catch the fleet animal, they hurried to their father, Agenor, and told him of the manner in which his favourite daughter had been spirited away. The old man was frenzied with grief, and bade his three sons to go in search of Europa and not return until they had found her. The youths set out, accompanied by their mother, Telephassa, and spent many weary days in a fruitless search for the stolen maiden. At last Phoenix refused to go any farther, and, not daring to return to his father, he remained in a land that was afterwards called in his honour – Phoenicia. Cilix, the second brother, grew weary of the hopeless quest and settled in a country named from him – Cilicia; and finally Telephassa, exhausted by fatigue and grief, died, and Cadmus was left to continue the search alone. He kept doggedly on for many days, and when he reached the town of Delphi, he consulted the oracle, hoping to find some clue to help him. To his surprise the oracle gave this ambiguous answer: "Follow the cow and settle where she rests." Cadmus left the temple, and before he had journeyed far he saw a cow walking leisurely in front of him. Judging this to be the animal intended to guide him, he followed her, and on the way was joined by a curious crowd who were eager to see where the absurd procession would finally stop. Some hoped that by accompanying the hero on his march they might meet with new adventures. The cow at last lay down in Boeotia, and here Cadmus founded the city of Thebes.

To reward Cadmus for his loving search for Europa, Zeus gave him in marriage the fair Harmonia, daughter of Ares and Aphrodite. The child of this union was Semele, whom Zeus wooed in the disguise of a mortal; but such was the maiden's pride that she would not listen to his pleading until he told her who he really was. Then her love was easily won, for no pride could be above yielding to the ruler of Olympus. Zeus was very happy in the society of Semele, and went down to earth many times to visit her, but it was inevitable that Hera should notice his frequent absences, and should set about finding out where the charm lay that lured him so often to the earth. When she discovered her beautiful rival, she decided upon an ingenious method of punishing her, and accordingly took the form of Semele's old nurse, Beroë. By feigning a loving solicitude for her charge's welfare, she soon won the confidence of the unsuspecting maiden, and listened with well-concealed anger while Semele talked of her lover and showed her pride in having won the affections of the greatest of gods.

The nurse was evidently delighted at Semele's happiness, but seemed worried over the new suitor's identity, and now and then expressed a doubt as to whether he really was the great Zeus. On questioning the maiden more closely, she assumed a virtuous indignation when Semele admitted that her lover always visited her in the disguise of a mortal, and that she had only his word as proof of his divinity. Hearing this, the old woman urged Semele to make sure that it was no impostor who was playing on her credulity, and pricked the girl's pride by asking her why it was that Zeus – if it were indeed he – should not honour her as he did the stately Hera by appearing before her in all his splendid majesty. Then the imposter nurse described the glory of Zeus as it was seen by the dwellers in Olympus, and finally so worked upon Semele's pride and curiosity that the unsuspicious maiden promised to put her lover to the test. So when Zeus came again, she begged him to grant her a favour, and the ruler of the gods, not knowing of Hera's wiles, readily promised to grant any request Semele might make. To further bind himself, he swore by the river Styx – the most terrible of all oaths. Then the maiden bade him return to Olympus, clothe himself in all his regal apparel – omitting no part of his terrible splendour, not even the dreaded thunderbolts – and having done this, return to her, that she might know he was indeed the awful Thunderer.

Zeus was dismayed at this request, for he knew that no mortal could endure the greatness of his glory. He begged Semele to ask another boon; but the maiden was obstinate, and insisted upon her request being granted. Sorrowfully Zeus returned to Olympus, and after robing himself in his fearful majesty, he dimmed the radiance wherever he could, wrapped about him the mildest lightning, and took in his hand the feeblest thunderbolt.

> "To keep his promise he ascends, and shrouds
> His awful brow in whirlwinds and in clouds;
> Whilst all around, in terrible array,
> His thunders rattle, and his lightnings play.

* * * * *

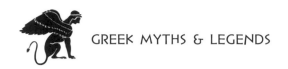

Thus dreadfully adorned with horror bright
The illustrous god, descending from his height,
Came rushing on her in a storm of light."

Ovid, *Metamorphoses*, Book III.

But in spite of his attempt to lessen his splendour, even this mild glory so overwhelmed poor Semele that when Zeus appeared before her, she dropped dead at his feet. In trying vainly to bring her back to life, Zeus did not notice what havoc the lightning, that played about his head, was making in the palace. In a short time the whole place was reduced to ashes, and in the smouldering ruins the body of Semele was consumed. The only person who escaped uninjured was the infant son of Zeus and Semele, the golden-haired Dionysus.

Having rescued his son from the burning palace, Zeus first entrusted him to his aunt Ino, who cared for him as tenderly as if he were her own child. But the jealous hatred of Hera was not satisfied with the death of Semele, and she tried to extend her vengeance to Dionysus by sending the fury Tisiphone to goad Athamas, the husband of Ino, into madness. As king of Thebes, Athamas had always been a kind ruler, but when the frenzy, inspired by cruel Hera, took possession of him, he imagined that his wife and children were wild beasts, and attempted to kill them. He did succeed in slaying Learchus, but Ino and her other son, Melicertes, escaped from his murderous fury, and afterwards became deities of the ocean.

Not daring to leave the infant Dionysus in such a household, and fearing the further persecutions of Hera, Zeus took the boy to Mount Nysa, where the nymphs – the Nysiades – guarded him faithfully. During his youth, Dionysus was made god of wine and revels, and was entrusted to the tutorship of Silenus, one of the most famous of the satyrs. This jovial old man had a bald head, pointed ears, a fat red face, and a body that was half man and half goat. As he carried a wine bag with him wherever he went, he was generally tipsy, and would have broken his neck long before reaching old age if he had tried to walk unsupported; but some of Dionysus's chosen band of followers always held him up on either side; or, when they themselves were unsteady, set him on an ass's back. Thus protected, he roamed about with Dionysus, and taught him all the craft of wine-growing and the making of choicest wine. The young god soon became a master of revels, and had a large train of followers composed of men and women, nymphs, fauns, and satyrs. They were usually crowned with ivy leaves, and were always drinking wine, eating grapes, singing, and dancing. The most unruly among them were the maenads, who, though women, were often so crazed with wine and the excitement of their dancing that they committed such inhuman crimes as tearing the musician Orpheus to pieces. Wherever Dionysus travelled – and it was far and wide – he taught the people the art of cultivating grapes and making wine. He was always welcomed, and when they knew he was approaching, men, women, and children flocked to meet him and his merry company.

Hera tried hard to check his triumphant progress, but she did not dare take his life for fear of Zeus's wrath; so she afflicted him with a kind of madness that drove him forth a wanderer alone over the earth. He had many adventures during this unhappy period, and finally landed in Phrygia, where the goddess Rhea cured him and taught him her religious rites. After this he wandered in Asia and India, teaching the people the wonderful new art of making wine. When he returned to Greece, he was welcomed everywhere, until he reached his native city of Thebes, where his cousin Pentheus was king. When Pentheus heard that the people were flocking out of the gates to meet Dionysus and his revellers, he tried to stop the excited crowds and force them to return. In vain he pleaded, commanded, threatened. Men and women, and even children, were eager to join in the revels, and would not turn back. Then Pentheus sent some of his servants to seize Dionysus and bring him a prisoner to the city. Soon the messengers returned, but they had not succeeded in getting near the god – so great was the crowd that pressed eagerly around him. They had, however, captured one of his followers; and when they dragged their prisoner before the king, he stood in the presence of the angry monarch without any sign of fear in his calm face. Pentheus commanded the man to tell what sort of revelry and rites were performed under the leadership of Dionysus; and threatened to put him instantly to death if he did not tell the truth. The prisoner smiled at the king's anger, and seemed quite undisturbed by the threats against his life. He refused to tell anything of the ceremonies attending the worship of Dionysus, but began calmly to relate his own story.

He said that his name was Acetes of Mæonia, and that he was a poor fisherman by birth, but had himself learned the pilot's art of steering by the stars. He had thus become master of a cruising vessel; and once, when he was near the island of Dia, he sent some of his men to shore for fresh water. They soon returned, bringing with them a youth whom they had found asleep in the forest, and had captured, hoping to obtain a large ransom for him, as the lad was surely some king's son – so haughty and regal was his bearing. When Acetes saw the youth, he begged his men not to force him on board the ship, for the pilot felt convinced that it was no mere mortal who stood so proudly before them. But the sailors would not listen to his advice, and thrust the youth roughly on board. Then Acetes refused to steer the ship; but the men only laughed and declared that they could pilot the craft as well as he. An angry discussion took place on the decks, and soon the quarrelling grew so loud that the captured youth, who had been gazing listlessly over the sea, turned to the wrangling crew and asked in what direction the ship was sailing.

"We will steer wherever you wish to go," replied one of the men with a wink at his companions.

"Then sail back to Naxeos, for that is my home," said the youth. The sailors promised to do so, but turned the ship toward Egypt, where they hoped to sell their prize for a large sum in gold. Acetes made several brave attempts to get possession of the helm and steer for Naxeos, but the sailors struck him down, and threatened to throw him overboard if he interfered in their plans.

Soon the lad seemed to notice that the familiar shores were receding, and anxiously enquired if they were really sailing toward Naxeos. He begged them not to ill-treat a friendless boy; but to let him return home in safety. Then the crew, weary of their pretence, told him brutally that he was being taken to Egypt to be sold as a slave; and that he could try his pretty speeches on his future master. The youth did not reply to these taunts, but looked calmly at the jeering sailors, and raised his hand above his head. Immediately the ship stopped as if it had been suddenly rooted to the sea; and though the men pulled frantically at the oars, not an inch could the vessel move. Then, as in a dream, they saw ivy twining rapidly about the sails, and wrapping the oars in its strong tendrils. A vine with its heavy clusters of grapes clung to the mast and the sides of the ship. There was the delicious smell of crushed fruit in the air, and the fragrance of new-made wine.

The sailors stared at the transformed ship and at the captured youth, who now shook off his mask of simplicity and appeared before them in all his godlike beauty – for it was no other than the divine Dionysus whom they had derided and had hoped to sell as a slave. The sound of flutes was heard all around him, and the shrill notes of the pipes. At the feet of Dionysus crouched tigers, lynxes, and panthers, and the god himself bore in his hand a staff wreathed with ivy. Then terror seized the trembling sailors, and they sprang madly over the side of the ship; but as soon as they touched the water they were changed into dolphins. Only Acetes was left standing on the deck before the smiling Dionysus, who bade him have no fear, but take the helm and steer straight for Naxeos. The pilot gladly obeyed, and soon reached the desired port, where he left his ship and became a follower of the god of wine.

When Acetes finished this remarkable story, King Pentheus swore that not a word of it was true, and ordered his prisoner to be taken away at once and executed. The soldiers threw Acetes into a dungeon; but while the preparations for his execution were being made, his chains suddenly dropped off and his prison doors flew open. When the jailers came to lead him to his death, he was nowhere to be found. Meanwhile the king had learned that the people were thronging around Dionysus on the Cithæron mountain, just outside the city, and were eagerly joining in all the joyous rites that attended the worship of the god of wine. The shouts of the Bacchanals filled the air, and in spite of his anger against them, Pentheus was curious to see what these ceremonies were that occasioned such roisterous mirth. So he disguised himself as a beggar, and joined the shouting crowd that surrounded Dionysus and his followers. The noisiest of the revellers were the maenads, who danced and sang in a very frenzy of excitement as they tossed their ivy wreaths into the air and poured the red wine recklessly upon the ground. When this group, flushed with wine and half clad, whirled madly toward him, the king was astonished to see among them his own mother Agave. As he leaned nearer to the shouting dancers, wondering how his mother came to join in such orgies, she suddenly saw him, and pointing a finger at his shrinking figure cried:

"There is the monster who prowls in our woods. Come on, sisters. I will be the first to strike the wild boar." Blinded by the madness that Dionysus had purposely inspired, she rushed upon the terrified king, followed by the crowd of half-crazed maenads. In vain did Pentheus cry out that he was her son. Agave and her companions trampled him down in their fierce onslaught, and in a moment tore him to pieces. Thus was the worship of Dionysus established in Greece.

The spot that the god of wine loved best was the island of Naxeos; and here he spent much of his time when he was not wandering over the earth to teach the art of making wine. One day Dionysus was walking on the seashore with his ivy-crowned company, who followed him singing and dancing to the music of their shrill pipes. As they neared a spot where the rocks rise like a cliff above the water's edge, they discovered a maiden sitting on the white sand. This was Ariadne, who had been deserted by her lover, Theseus, and left to pine away alone on the island. For days Ariadne had sat looking mournfully out over the sea; and now when Dionysus, with his joyous group of revellers, suddenly broke in upon the silence of her solitude, she was frightened by the sight of so many strangers. Dionysus soothed her fears, and in a short time so won the maiden's confidence that he persuaded her to become his wife. Ariadne was quite content to stay on the island with such a merry company, and if she ever felt any regret over the faithless Theseus, it was soon forgotten in the joy of the wedding celebrations, which lasted for several days. As a marriage gift, Dionysus placed on Ariadne's white forehead a crown adorned with seven glittering stars; but wonderful as it was, it did not eclipse the beauty of the wearer. The happiness of the newly-wedded pair did not last long, however, for in a few months Ariadne sickened and died. After her death Dionysus left the island, and did not return there for many years; but before he set sail he took Ariadne's crown and threw it up into the sky, where it forms a brilliant constellation known as Corona.

One day Silenus fell asleep in the forest, and his companions, believing him safe for a while, went away and left him propped up against a tree with his wine-bag at his side. Here he was found by some peasants, who were subjects of Midas, king of Lydia. The rustics watched the sleeping Silenus for a long time, wondering who he might be. At length the old man woke up, and after rubbing his eyes, asked the staring peasants where he was. As he received no answer to his question, Silenus motioned to the rustics to help him up, and then started to hunt for Dionysus and his lost companions. Seeing him unable to walk the men led him to the court of King Midas who, as soon as he saw the wanderer's jolly red face and his body – half goat and half man – knew at once that it was Silenus, the tutor of Dionysus. This Midas was the same king who had challenged Apollo to compete in the musical contest with Pan; and, because of his unfair decision, had been cursed with ass's ears by the offended god. The fact that Silenus had ears unlike the average mortal may have made King Midas feel a bit more sympathy for the old man's distress; but whatever the reason might be, he entertained Silenus royally for ten days, and then led him back to his pupil, who had been wondering at his long absence.

Delighted to have Silenus returned to him unharmed, Dionysus promised to give the king any reward he might name; and Midas, being very avaricious, asked the god to grant that all that he touched should turn into gold. Dionysus had hoped that Midas would desire a better gift than this; but having made a promise, the god was ready to fulfil it, and he therefore assured the king that his wish was granted. Midas, overjoyed at his good fortune, hastened back to his palace, and on the way he hesitatingly tried his new power. He touched some leaves that hung from the trees near by, and immediately they became golden. He took up a stone from the roadway, and it turned into gold in his hand. He plucked an apple, and in a moment it looked like one of the golden fruit from the garden of the Hesperides. Midas was almost beside himself with joy; and as soon as he reached his palace he began at once to turn all its furnishings into gold. He was so delighted with his wonderful gift that he felt no desire to eat or drink or rest; but at last he grew a little weary of turning things into gold, and, being hungry, sat down at his well-filled table.

He took great pleasure in seeing the cloth and the cups and the plates change as everything else had done at his touch; but to his great amazement and horror, he also found that the bread he took in his hand, the food that touched his lips, turned into hard, unyielding gold. He tried to drink from the shining cups, but the wine in his mouth became melted gold. Then Midas knew the real meaning of his magic touch, and realized sorrowfully that until it was taken away, he would slowly starve in the midst of his great wealth. Already he hated his gift, and longed for some way to divest himself of his ill-fated power. He cried aloud to Dionysus for help, but no answer came to his prayers. Again he besought the god, and this time acknowledged his avarice, and lamented the greed that had led him to ask for the gift of the golden touch. Dionysus heard his prayers, and, believing him truly repentant, commanded him to go to the river Pactolus, trace the stream to its source, and plunge his head and body into the purifying water. In this way he could cleanse himself of his fault and its punishment. Midas did as he was instructed, and came away from the river a wiser and happier, though a poorer man. If at any time he was ever tempted to regret his lost gift, he had only to look into the river at the glittering golden sand on the bed of the stream; for where the king had stood, the sand was changed into gold, and so it has remained to this very day.

20

PAN AND THE NYMPHS

Pan, the god of woods and fields, god of the flocks and herds, and patron deity of all shepherds, was said to be the son of Hermes. It is apparently not known who his mother was, but she must have had some sylvan blood in her veins, for the youthful Pan showed every evidence of having been born of woodland creatures, as he had the pointed ears of the fauns, and the horns and goat's legs of the satyrs. The story goes that his mother – whichever nymph it was of the many reputed to have borne him – was disgusted with his absurd appearance, and refused to own him for her child; but Hermes was delighted with his son's grotesque figure, and took him to Olympus to amuse the gods.

Pan's favourite dwelling place was Arcadia; and here he wandered over the hills and among the rocks, or roamed through the fertile valleys. He delighted in hunting, and amused himself with various pastimes – his especial pleasure being to lead in the dances with the nymphs. He was devoted to music, and was usually seen playing on the syrinx – or shepherd's pipes – which he himself invented and named from a nymph whom he unsuccessfully wooed. The maiden Syrinx was a follower of Artemis; and one day, as she was returning from the chase, she met Pan, who immediately fell in love with her beauty, and begged her to be his wife. The nymph had always scorned to listen to any lover, and Pan's appearance did not tend to soften her objections; so while he was praising her many charms and pleading for her love, she turned and ran away. The woodland god was not to be put off so lightly, however; and he promptly gave chase to the fleeing maiden, who, finding that her pursuer was gaining on her, called wildly on the river-nymphs for help. She had by this time reached the water's edge; and just as Pan's arms were about to enfold her, the kindly nymphs changed her into a cluster of reeds. The god was much chagrined at the failure of his hopes; but since he could not have the living maiden, he determined to take whatever remained of the beautiful thing that had charmed him. So he gathered a bunch of the reeds, and after cutting them into unequal lengths, bound them together into a sort of shepherd's pipes. When he put the reeds to his lips, they gave forth the softest and most plaintive tones, and Pan called them the syrinx in honour of the nymph.

Before inventing this new instrument, Pan had played upon the flute, and it was his skill in this direction that made King Midas dare to affront Apollo by declaring Pan to be the better musician. The god of woods and fields was not, however, a frequenter of palaces, but made his home in grottoes and piped to the murmuring trees. He loved to prowl by night in lonesome places, and lurk among the shadows where some belated traveller, startled by the weird hoot of an owl, would see his grotesque form and rush away, filled with that unreasoning terror called a "panic". Pan's partners in the sylvan dance were the wood-nymphs, who always welcomed him and his followers. When his days were spent among the mountain solitudes, the Oreads, or mountain nymphs, danced with him in the moonlight; and when he preferred to live in the valleys, the Dryads, or nymphs of vegetation, joined in the revels led by Pan and his company of fauns and satyrs. The Naides, the beautiful water-nymphs who dwelt in the clear depths of the fountains, did not come out of their quiet haunts to take part in the merriment; nor did the shy Hamadryads leave the safe shelter of their trees to mingle in the joyous dance. Among these latter nymphs each had her particular tree, and lived and died with the one entrusted to her care. It was held, therefore, to be an act of wanton cruelty to destroy or even mar a tree, lest the Hamadryad who inhabited it should be hurt and possibly killed. It was unwise to break off a flower recklessly, or to pull it rudely from the earth, for in this humble form might be lodged the spirit of some woodland creature.

Such a sad mistake did Dryope once make, and suffered for her carelessness by being changed from a mortal into a Hamadryad. Dryope was a beautiful young princess, the wife of Andraemon, and the mother of a golden-haired boy. Every day she carried her child to a small lake near the palace, and let him gather the gayly-coloured flowers that grew on the water's edge. One day, as she wandered by the lake, Dryope saw a lotus blossom and pointed it out to her little son, who immediately tried to pluck it. As it was much beyond his reach, his mother leaned over the water and broke it off the stem. To her surprise, she saw drops of blood slowly oozing from the stem; and as the boy eagerly grasped the lovely flower in his chubby hand, a crimson stream trickled through his clasped fingers. He dropped the blossom with a frightened cry, and ran screaming to the palace, while Dryope stood looking down, bewildered, at the bleeding flower. Just then she heard a voice telling her that she had killed the nymph Lotis, who, to escape from the arms of the hateful god Priapus, had taken the form of a lotus.

When Dryope realized the dreadful thing that she had unknowingly done, she turned pale with fright, and would have hurried away from the unlucky spot; but when she tried to turn from the sight of the dying flower, she found that she could not move. Her feet seemed rooted to the ground; and, as she looked down, she was horrified to see that a rough bark was beginning to enclose her limbs. With dreadful rapidity it spread upward, and soon encircled her whole body, while her arms changed into twisted branches and her hands into green leaves. In vain she called to her husband and her friends for help. When they arrived, there was nothing left of the fair Dryope but her tear-stained face, which was covered all too soon by the cruel bark. Just before she disappeared completely from their sight, she begged that her little son might be taught to play beneath her branches; and when, in all the after days, the boy sat willingly beside the tree and listened to the soft rustling of its leaves, the passers-by would say: "Dryope is whispering to her child."

The danger of recklessly destroying any tree is shown by the story of Erysichthon, who dared to defy the goddess Demeter, and so received a fitting punishment. There was a certain grove of trees sacred to Demeter, and among them was a lofty oak on which votive tablets were often hung, and around which the nymphs and Dryads danced hand in hand. Erysichthon ordered his servants to cut down this venerable oak; and when they hesitated, telling him that it was a tree beloved by Demeter and should not suffer such a sacrilege, he seized the axe himself and made a deep gash in the trunk. To the great horror of those who stood by, blood began to flow from the wound; and as Erysichthon was about to deal the tree another blow, one of his servants caught at his arm, imploring him not to touch the oak again, for the blood showed that a Hamadryad was being wounded. Maddened at this interference, and determined to carry out his brutal will, Erysichthon declared that he would cut down the tree if by so doing he killed a dozen Dryads. He lifted his axe for a mighty stroke, and as the servant again sought to stay his arm, he turned fiercely and killed the man with one swift blow. Then he proceeded to fell the tree, and soon it was lying, bruised and bleeding, on the ground.

The nymphs rushed to Demeter, and begged her to punish this wicked violation of her grove. The goddess promised that Erysichthon's deed should not go unpunished, and sent an Oread to the remote part of Scythia, where the ice lies thick on the dreary soil and the land is always desolate. "Here dwell drowsy Cold and Paleness and Shuddering and dreadful Famine." When the Oread drew near this barren country, she saw far off the gaunt form of Famine pulling up with her teeth and claws the scant bits of vegetation that could be found here and there in the frozen earth. The nymph did not want to linger near the dreadful form of Famine, lest the hag should reach out her lean finger and touch the maiden's robes; so she hurriedly delivered the message of Demeter, and sped quickly back to her own fair land of Thessaly.

Not daring to disobey the goddess's command, Famine left her dreary country and sought out the home of Erysichthon. She found him asleep; and as he slept she enfolded him with her wings, and breathed into his nostrils her deadly breath. Then she returned to her frantic digging in the unyielding soil. When Erysichthon awoke, he was at once consumed with a fierce desire for food; but, however much he ate, the terrible craving never ceased. All day long he devoured things greedily, but at night his hunger was still unsatisfied. His servants piled up food in enormous quantities before him, but the gnawing pangs of hunger never left him. He spent all his wealth in a vain attempt to buy enough food to appease the insatiable monster within him; but, though he at last sold all that he had, even to his house and his clothing, it was not enough to buy him the food he craved. There was nothing left him now but his daughter; and frenzied by his hunger, he offered to sell her to a slave-dealer.

The girl pitied her father's sufferings and would have done anything to help him; but she resented his baseness in selling her, for she came of a noble race. While her purchaser was disputing with her father over the price, the maiden, who was standing on the seashore, a short distance away from her new master, implored Poseidon to save her from the disgrace of being sold as a slave. The kindly sea-god heard her cry, and changed her into an old fisherwoman. When the bargain between Erysichthon and the dealer was settled, the man looked around for his new purchase, but she was nowhere to be seen. The only person on the seashore, beside the brutal bargainers, was an old woman who sat mending her net. The irate owner searched in vain for his slave and even asked the fisherwoman if she had seen a weeping maiden. Unable to find the girl, he at last went away, concluding that Erysichthon's daughter had tried to escape and so had been drowned in the sea. The maiden was rejoiced at her deliverance; but her cruel father, on seeing her regain her own form, decided that this was an easy way of making the money he desperately needed. So he sold his daughter again and again, and each time she sought the help of Poseidon, who obligingly turned her into many different shapes. At last even this device failed to bring to Erysichthon enough money to meet the ever-increasing demands of his hunger. In despair over the lack of food he began to eat his own flesh; and in a short time he had devoured so much of his body that death came to end his torment. So was Demeter avenged.

The Hamadryads were seldom seen by men, but people knew them to be both gentle and beautiful. That they could repay a kindness is well shown by the story of Rhoecus, who gained the love of one of the shyest of these nymphs. One day the youth happened to see an oak-tree bent so far down by the wind that some of its branches were already broken. He propped up the tree, and gently bound up the broken limbs; then as he turned to go, he heard a soft voice calling him. It was the Hamadryad who had expected to die with her stricken tree, and was now so grateful to Rhoecus that she bade him ask of her any reward he wished. The youth boldly asked for her love, and the nymph reluctantly yielded to his wish, promising to meet him at the oak-tree each day just before sunset. To keep him mindful of the hour set for the tryst, she told him that she would send him a messenger – a bee – which would also guide him to the spot where she was waiting.

Rhoecus was very happy with the Hamadryad; and never failed to follow the flight of the bee that came each day at sunset to lead him to the trysting-place. One morning, however, he began to play at dice with his friends, and the game continued through the long summer afternoon. As it drew toward sunset, Rhoecus forgot that it was his hour to meet the Dryad, and continued his game, even though he noticed vaguely that a bee was buzzing near him. Soon the bee came close to his face, and buzzed so persistently that Rhoecus brushed it angrily away. Each time he tried to shake it off it came buzzing back, and at last he struck at it so viciously that it fell to the ground. Then in a flash Rhoecus remembered his promise to the Dryad, and throwing away his dice, he hurried to the trysting-place. He called to the nymph and begged her to come to him once more; but no sweet face appeared though a voice spoke from the heart of the oak-tree bidding him a sad farewell. Rhoecus had already repented bitterly of his forgetfulness; but nothing could restore him to favour. He sat all night beside the oak-tree, but the Dryad never came to him again.

21

THE VESTALS

Hestia was the oldest child of Cronus and Rhea, and was the goddess of the family hearth. As the hearth was the basis of all domestic ties, Hestia was considered the guardian of family happiness, and her worship was an essential part of the family life. The hearth in ancient days had a much greater significance than in modern times, for it was the centre of the household, around which the family gathered for their common meal and common worship. On the hearth, as an altar-fire, the head of the household offered prayers and sacrifices; and it made a bond of union so generally recognized that he who partook of food there, or who shared in the family worship, could ever afterward lay claim to the master's hospitality. If a suppliant was seeking protection from any danger, it was to a man's hearth that he came as a sure place of refuge. The flames that burned on this family altar were sacred to the goddess Hestia, and prayers for domestic happiness and the household's welfare were usually offered to her. Thus the fire burning on the hearth of each dwelling was a perpetual worship of the beneficent Hestia, and even the sacrifices made to other gods were partly in her honour; for whenever the flames were rekindled, a prayer was offered to the goddess of the family fireside.

Every dwelling was, therefore, in some sense, a temple of Hestia; but there was also in each city a stately edifice where all the citizens worshipped at her sacred fire, and were thus bound together in one great family. In Rome, where the worship of Hestia was most celebrated, a beautiful circular temple, dedicated to the goddess, stood in the Forum. It was not necessary to place a statue of Hestia here, for the eternal fire that glowed on her altar was her living symbol, and through this she was worshipped. This fire was supposed to have been brought to Italy by Aeneas when he fled from burning Troy and carried with him out of the city two valuable possessions, *i.e.* the fire of Hestia and his own household gods – or Penates. When a colony was sent out from any city, the emigrants took some of the fire from the temple of Hestia in the mother town, and guarded it during their voyages, that they might use its flames to light the fires that were to burn on the hearths of the new homes. Each city cherished carefully the fire that was sacred to Hestia, and never allowed it to burn out, for that was an evil omen sure to presage disaster. If by any chance it was allowed to become extinct, it was never relit from any ordinary fire, but was kindled with a spark produced by friction, or by drawing fire from the sun's rays through a glass.

The temple at Rome was the most famous of those dedicated to Hestia, for here was the school of the Vestal Virgins whose duty it was to tend her ever-living fire. As any neglect on their part might bring some public calamity upon Rome, this altar was jealously guarded; and when, as it sometimes happened, enemies threatened the city, the Vestals carried the fire of Hestia down the Tiber and kept it in concealment until the danger was over. Since so much depended on the watchfulness and fidelity of the Vestals, the office of priestess to the temple was held in high honour, and the maidens were chosen from the noblest families of Rome. They entered the service at the very youthful age of six, and spent thirty years in the temple. The first ten years were devoted to learning their important duties; the next decade was the period for filling the office of priestess, and performing all the solemn rites that belonged to the worship of Hestia; the last ten years were given to instructing the novices. When the thirty years of service were over, the Vestals could continue in the temple, or leave it and marry if they desired; but so holy were the Virgins thought to become through their long residence in the temple, that it was held a sort of sacrilege for any man to marry them. Therefore the priestesses usually died, as they had lived, in the service of the goddess.

The chief duty of the Vestals was to watch in turns, by night and day, the sacred fire of Hestia, and to see that the flames never grew dim. During their entire period of service, they were obliged to keep the strictest vows of chastity, under penalty of being buried alive in a vaulted room, built especially for this purpose by the king, Numa Pompilius. The Vestals were, however, so true to all the vows made at the great altar-fire, that in a thousand years only eighteen failed in their promises and thus suffered punishment. The story is told that the Vestal Tuccia was accused of having broken her vow, but was able to prove her purity, by being given the miraculous power to carry water in a sieve from the Tiber to the temple.

Though the restrictions placed upon the Vestals were severe, and the rules of their order were pitilessly enforced, yet the privileges that they enjoyed were such as to raise them in dignity above the other women of Rome. They were entirely released from all parental authority; they had conspicuous places at the theatres and gladiatorial shows, and occupied seats of honour at all public festivals. Treaties and important state documents were entrusted to their care as in a place inviolable; and their persons were held so holy that, when they died, they were buried within the city limits – a privilege granted to but few. When they went abroad, each was preceded by a lictor; and consuls, prætors, and even tribunes made way for them, while if any one passed under their litter, he was put to death. If they chanced to meet a criminal on his way to punishment, they could demand his release, provided that it could be proved that the meeting was accidental. The Vestals wore a robe of pure white linen with a wide purple border, and over their shoulders was a purple mantle. When the festivals of Hestia, the Vestalia, were held, the priestesses marched in a procession through the streets, carrying their sacred fire, while the Roman matrons followed them barefooted, chanting hymns in praise of Hestia. During these ceremonies all work was suspended in the city, the houses were decked with flowers, and the beasts used in the procession were wreathed in garlands; banquets were set out before the houses, and the people gave themselves up to a gala-day.

II

When Aeneas fled from burning Troy, and took with him some of the fire from the temple of Hestia, as the thing most necessary in the founding of a new city, he also brought to the shores of Italy his own household gods – or Penates – who presided over the daily affairs of the household, and were the guardians of each member of the family on whose hearth they held the place of honour. The statues of the Penates were of clay, wax, ivory, silver or gold according to the master's wealth, and were always carried to the new home when the family changed its dwelling place. When the common meal was served, a small portion of it was set aside for the Penates, and a libation of wine was poured to them on the hearth. In return for this daily deference, the Penates blessed the household with happiness and prosperity.

22

MINOR DEITIES

I AEOLUS

Not far from sunny Sicily and the deep crater of Etna, in which Hephaestus built his glowing forge, were the Aeolian Islands – now called Lipari Islands – where Aeolus, god of the winds and storms, kept his turbulent children. He never allowed them to roam at will, but held them securely bound in a great cave, and let them loose one at a time when they needed exercise or when the gods demanded their release. Only once were they allowed to give free play to their boisterous feelings, and rush over the waters, making havoc everywhere, and this was when Zeus sent a deluge upon the impious earth. Since that time the winds have never roamed at large, though they always chafe at being restrained in their narrow prison and long to break free.

Aeolus wooed and married the dainty Aurora, goddess of the morning, who bore him his sons, *i.e.* Boreas, the north wind; Notus, the south wind; Eurus, the east wind; and Zephyrus, the soft and gentle west wind. Sometimes Aurora sought the services of her children, but they were entirely under the control of their father Aeolus who ruled them with a strict hand. Sometimes when the stately Hera sought his assistance, he let the winds sweep over the calm sea until the waves rose mountain high, for he was reputed to have received his royal status as a god from Hera's hands, and so was ever anxious to serve her. Once, at her request, he let loose the fiercest winds to destroy the ships of Aeneas – that unfortunate hero who was always being pursued by "cruel Hera's unrelenting hate". The goddess was so eager for his destruction that she went herself to the cave of the winds, and begged Aeolus to shatter the Trojan ships. So a terrible storm broke over the sea, and the winds drove the vessels of Aeneas far out of their course, scattering them here and there, until no two could see each other amid the fury of the tempest. When Poseidon realized what was happening, he lifted his head above the white-capped waves and saw the Trojan ships tossed about and beaten out of their course. As he himself had given no commands for such a storm, he knew it was the never-ending hatred of Hera for the Trojans that had brought about the disaster. But the sea, and all that therein is, was Poseidon's to control, and he was justly angry with Hera's interference; so he recalled the winds from their mad race and bade the storm cease.

Quite differently did Aeolus treat another famous hero, Odysseus, whose ships, on the long homeward journey, touched at the Lipari Islands. Here the wanderer was hospitably entertained by Aeolus, and when he set sail again, the kindly god sent the west wind to blow the ships gently over the sea, while he shut up the blustering winds in a leather bag and tied it with a silver string. This bag he gave to Odysseus, "the sagacious", and bade him keep it closed until the journey was over. For nine days and nights the hero stood at the helm watching, while the west wind bore the ships along without the help of oars. At last, exhausted by his long vigil, Odysseus fell asleep; and the sailors, believing that the bag contained treasure that King Aeolus had generously given, untied the string and freed the roistering winds. The ships were now driven hither and thither by the madly-rushing winds, and were tossed over the sea far away from the longed-for Ithaca. Finally they were blown back to the Lipari Islands, where Aeolus received them but coldly, and refused to help them further. So they turned their prows once more toward home, and worked wearily against wind and weather by the slow pull of the oars.

The Athenians built a temple to Aeolus, which is still extant, and is generally known as the Tower of the Winds, or the Temple of Aeolus. The structure is hexagonal, and on each side there is a flying figure of one of the winds. Notus (or Auster), the south wind, was usually represented by an old man with dusky wings. He is clad in a black robe, and his head is covered with clouds, for he sends the rains and sudden showers. Eurus, the east wind, was a young man full of impetuous and lively motion. Corus, the northwest wind, drove clouds of snow before him, and Boreas was a figure rough and shivering. Zephyrus had a lapful of flowers, and was the one wind sent to play among children. Boreas was the bringer of hail and tempests, and when he wooed the nymph Orithyia, he sought in vain to approach her gently, and to breathe his love softly. But he could not sigh, and his lightest whisper frightened the maiden by its harshness; so Boreas gave up attempting to win her by gentle means and boldly carried her off to his home in the midst of snow and ice. Their children were Zetes and Calais – winged warriors who accompanied the Argonauts on their famous expedition, and performed a valuable service in driving away the Harpies.

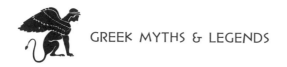

II IRIS AND AURORA

Iris was the special attendant of Hera, and was often employed as a messenger by both Hera and Zeus. In the *Iliad* she is the swift servant of the gods; but in the *Odyssey* it is Hermes who is the messenger to and from Olympus, and Iris is never mentioned. Sometimes Iris is described as the rainbow itself; sometimes the rainbow is only the road over which she travels, and which therefore vanishes when it is no longer needed. When Hera sends Iris to the Cave of Sleep "she assumes her garments of a thousand colours, and spans the heavens with her curving arch". As the personification of the rainbow – that brilliant phenomenon that vanishes as quickly as it appears – Iris might easily be considered the swift messenger of the gods.

* * * * *

Aurora, rosy-fingered goddess of the dawn, opened the gates of the morning for the impatient horses of the sun, who chafed at being held behind the golden bars until Apollo was ready to start forth on his daily course, attended by the faithful Hours. Though Aurora was the wife of Aeolus and mother of the winds, she had the usual weakness of the deities of Olympus for falling in love with mortals who won her favour. Thus she became enamoured of the young hunter Cephalus, but was unable to gain his love, as he himself had already wedded the fair Procris, one of Artemis's nymphs. The happiness of these lovers was a maddening sight to the jealous Aurora, and she determined to find some way to end it. Procris had brought to her husband as a dowry a hunting dog named Lelaps, who could outrun the swiftest deer, and a javelin that never missed its mark. So all day long Cephalus hunted in the forest, and his long absences gave the malicious Aurora an excuse for whispering to the young wife that her husband spent his time in the society of a wood-nymph. For some time Procris resisted these suggestions of the goddess; but at last, overcome by jealousy, she followed Cephalus to the forest to see who the maiden was that charmed him. At noonday the weary hunter sought his accustomed resting place; and as he lay beneath a wide-spreading tree, he called to the breeze to come and refresh him. Believing that he referred to some wood-nymph, Procris sank down among the bushes in a swoon; and her husband, hearing the leaves rustle suddenly behind him, hurled his javelin into the thicket, supposing that some wild beast was crouching near him ready to spring. To his horror he discovered the body of Procris; and though he did all that he could to staunch the wound made by his unerring spear, his wife died in his arms – but not before an explanation had been given.

Though Aurora had succeeded in separating the lovers forever, she did not thereby gain the affections of Cephalus, but was obliged to console herself with the Trojan prince, Tithonus. She begged Zeus to confer upon him the boon of immortal life; but forgetting that he would sometime grow old, she neglected to ask for him the greater gift of eternal youth. For a while she was very happy with her lover, but as soon as he lost the attractions of youth she wearied of his company and wished to get rid of him. She shut him up in a room of her palace, where his feeble voice could often be heard; and then, knowing that he would never die, she cruelly changed him into a grasshopper.

The son of Aurora and Tithonus was Memnon, who became king of the Ethiopians, and went with a band of warriors to help his kindred in the Trojan war. He fought bravely, but at length met his death at the hands of Achilles. When he fell on the battle-field, Aurora commanded her sons, the winds, to carry his body to the banks of the river Aesepus in Asia Minor, where a tomb was erected to his memory. To honour him further, Zeus caused the sparks and cinders from his funeral pyre to be changed into birds, which divided into two flocks and fought until they fell into the flames. Every year, on the anniversary of Memnon's death, the birds returned to celebrate the funeral rites in this same strange way. When the flames from the funeral pyre had burned out, Aurora sat by the ashes of her son, weeping and mourning his loss; and the many tears that she shed turned into glistening dewdrops. In Egypt there were two colossal statues, one of which was said to be the statue of Memnon; and tradition tells that when the first rays of morning fell upon it, it gave forth a sound like the snapping of harp strings.

23

HERACLES

PART I

Heracles was the son of Zeus and Alcmene – a lovely princess, the granddaughter of Perseus and Andromeda. Hera hated her as she did all her mortal rivals, and sought to bring misery and suffering on the unoffending maiden. When she learned that Heracles, the son of Alcmene, was born, she sent two immense serpents with poisonous fangs to attack the child while he slept. The baby happened to waken just as the creatures were twining themselves about him; and grasping their necks in each of his tiny hands, he strangled them, thus showing from his birth the wonderful strength that was later to make him a famous hero. The education of Heracles was entrusted to Chiron, the most renowned of the centaurs, who had himself been instructed by Apollo and Artemis in hunting, medicine, music, and the art of prophecy. The idea of a creature half man and half horse was not repulsive to the ancients, who were too fond of a horse to consider man's union with him degrading. When Heracles left the kindly tutelage of Chiron, he set out on his own adventures, and before he had travelled far he met two beautiful women, each of whom offered to guide him on his journey. Kakia (Vice) told him that if he followed her, he would gain love, riches, and ease; and Arete (Virtue) promised him honour, bought at the price of hardship, poverty, and endless toil. For a while the youthful hero deliberated over the two very different rewards offered him, and at last he gave his choice to Arete, who henceforth led him through many perils, and into labours such as no man had ever yet performed.

Like most heroes, Heracles was a great wanderer; and on one of his journeys he came to the city of Thebes, where Creon, the king, entertained him and showed him so much favour that when Heracles asked for the hand of Creon's daughter Megara in marriage, the king gladly gave his consent. The hero then rested from his wanderings, and spent many happy years in the society of his wife and children; but Hera had not forgotten her old hatred of Alcmene's offspring, and she determined to end this happiness. So she afflicted Heracles with a sudden madness; and in his delirium he killed his wife, and threw his children into the fire. When at last he recovered his senses, he suffered terribly over the thought of the crimes that he had unwittingly committed, and would have gone off to the mountains to spend his days in sorrow and remorse, had not Hera demanded that he should expiate his deeds of bloodshed. Accordingly she sent Hermes to lead him from his solitude among the hills and to take him to his cousin Eurystheus, king of Argos, whom he was compelled to serve for a whole year. During this time he performed the twelve great labours that have made his name famous as the doer of mighty deeds.

The first task that Eurystheus gave the hero was to procure the skin of a monstrous lion that inhabited the Nemean forest. This creature's frequent attacks had brought terror to all the countryside, for it was not content with carrying off cattle and sheep, but had killed the children at play, and mangled shepherds who were watching with their flocks. When the people heard that Heracles was setting out to fight the lion, they tried to persuade him to give up the adventure; but he, who had strangled two huge serpents in his infancy, was not afraid of a lion, however fierce and strong it might be. So he boldly entered the forest, and having tracked the great brute to its den, he attacked it fearlessly and killed it with his bare hands. Then, throwing the body of the lion over his shoulder, he started back to the palace of Eurystheus; but when the king saw Heracles approaching, he begged him to leave his burden outside the city gates. So the hero skinned the lion, and took the shaggy pelt to be henceforth his favourite covering.

Heracles's second labour was to kill the Hydra, a nine-headed monster that infested the Areshes of Lerna. With the blows of his great oak club the hero was able to strike off eight of the heads, but the central one was immortal and could not be destroyed. Further to complicate the difficulty, Heracles found that as soon as he struck off one head, two others sprang up in its place. To prevent this discouraging miracle from continuing, the hero bade his friend Iolaus, who had accompanied him, take a lighted brand and sear the wounds as soon as they were made. Through this wise precaution the Hydra was finally killed, and its one immortal head was buried under a huge rock. While this difficult struggle was going on, Hera, always eager to thwart the hero, sent a large crab to pinch Heracles's feet as he wrestled with the Hydra. He succeeded in crushing it with his club; but Hera did not leave its body on the trampled and blood-stained ground. In recognition of its services to her, she placed it in the sky as the constellation of Cancer (the Crab). Before Heracles left the dead Hydra he dipped some arrows in its venomous blood, knowing that any wound received from their poisoned tips would surely be fatal. These arrows were later of great service to Heracles, and only once did he regret their deadly quality.

The next task that Eurystheus set was the capture of the golden-horned and brazen-hoofed stag of Cerynea, which ran so swiftly that it did not seem to touch the ground. Heracles pursued the stag for many miles, but was unable to overtake it until he drove it into the cold regions of the north, where its fleetness was hindered by the great drifts and the ice-covered ground. Finally the stag ran into a deep snow bank, and so Heracles captured it and took it home in triumph.

The fourth labour to which Heracles lent his great strength was the killing of a wild boar that haunted Mount Erymanthus in Arcadia. While on this expedition, the hero was attacked by the centaurs, and when he shot at them with his poisoned arrows, one of the deadly missiles flew far and struck his loved tutor Chiron, who was galloping toward the combatants, hoping to settle the quarrel peaceably. When Heracles saw Chiron fall, he rushed to his side and tried to staunch the fatal wound; but the dying centaur knew that his end had come, and sorrowfully bade the hero farewell. To reward Chiron for his long service, the gods transferred him to the heavens as the constellation Sagittarius.

Heracles was next sent to kill the flock of fierce birds whose cruel beaks and sharp talons made havoc in the country around Lake Stymphalus. The foul mist that rose from the stagnant water over which the birds hovered was so deadly to breathe that Heracles could hardly approach the lake; but with the help of his poisoned arrows he was able to wound the birds at a distance. After hours spent in this pestilent atmosphere he killed the entire flock and returned to the court of Eurystheus to report his success.

The most unpleasant of all Heracles's labours was the cleaning of the stables where Augeas, king of Elis, kept his herd of a thousand oxen. These stables had not been cleaned for thirty years; and when Heracles caught one glimpse of the filth within them, he felt that this was too degrading a task for him to undertake. But the work had to be done; and since he could not put his hand to anything so foul, he looked about for some other means to accomplish the labour. Not far from the stables flowed two rivers, the Peneus and Alpheus, and these Heracles turned out of their courses and made them rush through the filthy building until every part of the stables of Augeas was washed perfectly clean. Then he restored the rivers to their former beds, and returned home to report this task fulfilled.

The next labour that was assigned to the hero was the capture of a mad bull given by Poseidon to King Minos. In the early days of his power, Minos had boasted that he could obtain anything that he wished from the gods; and had accordingly begged of Poseidon a bull for the sacrifices. The kindly sea-god sent a splendid offering, but when Minos saw the bull's size and beauty, he resolved to keep it. So he substituted another animal for the sacrifices. This angered Poseidon so much that he made the bull go mad; and it rushed here and there over the island, causing great terror among the people. The creature was finally caught and overcome by Heracles, who rode it through the waves to Greece. The offspring of this bull was the famous Minotaur which the hero Theseus pursued through its labyrinth, and slew.

The eighth labour of Heracles was to bring from Thrace the horses of Diomedes. These splendid creatures the king fed on human flesh; and in order to get a sufficient supply of fresh meat, he decreed that all strangers who came into his kingdom should be imprisoned, fattened up, and then served as food to the horses. To punish Diomedes for his years of cruelty, Heracles fed him to his own steeds, and then led them back to Eurystheus, who was proud to be the possessor of such a prize.

At the court of Eurystheus was the king's beautiful daughter, Admete, who loved purple and fine linen, and decked herself with all the jewels that her father's wealth could command. One day Admete heard a traveller telling wonderful tales of the girdle that was worn by Hippolyte, queen of the Amazons; and at once the spoiled princess demanded of her father that he send Heracles to procure for her the coveted girdle. So the hero set out again, accompanied by his friend Iolaus; and after a hard and perilous journey came to the country of the Amazons. These were a fierce, warlike nation of women who kept in their tribe only the girls who were born among them and disposed of the boys by killing them, or by giving them to the neighbouring peoples. The girls were trained in severe military discipline, and became a race of very redoubtable warriors whom no king cared to treat with contempt. When Heracles came before the queen Hippolyte, she received him kindly, listened to the explanation of his visit, and even promised to give him the girdle that the selfish Admete coveted. Before the hero and his friend set out on their journey homeward, the queen entertained them royally with feasting and games that lasted several days. Meantime Hera saw an opportunity for indulging her hatred of Heracles; and taking the form of an Amazon, she mingled freely with the women. By pretending to have received a heaven-sent message, she persuaded them that the stranger had used the girdle as a mere pretext for his visit, and that his real intention was to carry off the queen. The Amazons believed this artfully-contrived report, and rushed in a body to protect Hippolyte. They attacked Heracles fiercely, but he beat them off and finally escaped with his friend, but not before he had killed several of the Amazons, including the queen who had befriended him. With the dearly-bought girdle he returned homeward, and on the way he heard the proclamation of Laomedon that whoever would save his daughter Hesione from the sea-monster should receive a large reward. Heracles killed the beast and freed the maiden, but was obliged to leave Troy without the promised gold, because of Laomedon's perfidy and greed.

When the ancients looked each evening at the glowing west, they pictured it as a far-distant country, more wonderful than any ever seen by mortal eyes. Here in this land of heart's desire lay the Garden of the Hesperides, where a dragon guarded the golden apples that grew on a wonderful tree which had sprung up miraculously to grace the wedding of Zeus and Hera. In this far-off sunset land were also the Isles of the Blest, where mortals who had led virtuous lives were transported without ever tasting of death. Here the blessed of the gods enjoyed an eternity of bliss; and wandered happily over the Isles, which had a sun and moon and stars of their own, and never felt the touch of wintry winds. In this mysterious region of the west was the island of Erythea, called "the red" because it glowed in the light of the setting sun. To this spot Heracles was sent to take possession of the oxen of Geryon – a monster with three bodies. On his journey to the island, Heracles's way was blocked by a huge mountain; and with one blow of his strong oak club he cleft the opposing rock, and allowed the waters of the sea to flow through. This is now the strait of Gibraltar, and the cliffs on either side are called the Pillars of Heracles.

When the hero reached the island of Erythea, he found the oxen guarded by the giant Eurytion and his three-headed dog; but even this did not daunt the slayer of the Hydra. He boldly attacked the giant; and after a fierce battle, in which his oak club stood him in good stead, killed both Eurytion and the monstrous dog. Then he went in search of the oxen, and, after herding them closely, drove them toward his own country. On the journey homeward he passed Mount Aventine, where the giant Cacus lived in a rocky cave. One night, as Heracles was asleep near the mountain, the giant stole part of the cattle; and, to deceive the hero, he dragged them backwards by their tails into his cave. Heracles might have been tricked by this stratagem if the stolen oxen had not lowed loudly as the rest of the

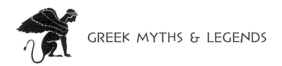

herd passed the cave, and so betrayed their hiding place. Heracles rushed into the giant's dark, ill-smelling dwelling, slew him, and recovered all the stolen cattle.

PART II

One of the most difficult of Heracles's labours was to procure the golden apples that the Hesperides, daughters of Hesperus, god of the west, guarded very jealously. At the foot of the tree coiled a fierce dragon whose nostrils poured out fire, and whose deadly breath would have slain any venturesome robber, even if he had escaped the dragon's claws. As Heracles did not know in what part of the great glowing west the Garden of the Hesperides lay, he wandered many miles before he met with any one who could direct him where to go. The first help he received was from the nymphs of the Eridanus River, who were sporting on the river bank and called to Heracles to come and join in their games. Much as he would have liked to rest, the hero dared not tarry; but he begged the friendly nymphs to tell him the way to the Garden of the Hesperides. They could not help him, but they advised him to go to old Proteus, "the Ancient of the Deep", who could tell him whatever he wished to know better than any one else. So Heracles went down to the seashore, and found the hoary god asleep in his cool green cave. Knowing the old man's wiles, the hero grasped him firmly and held him fast through all the bewildering changes by which he sought to frighten away the stranger. At last, finding himself securely caught, the Wizard assumed his own form, and asked Heracles what it was that he wished to know. The hero stated his errand, and Proteus told him, "in words that ne'er deceive", that he must find the giant Atlas who alone knew where the Garden of the Hesperides lay.

Heracles then started again on his search, and in the course of his journey came to the Caucasus Mountains, where he found

Prometheus, the stealer of the sacred fire, bound with adamantine chains to the rock, while a vulture daily feasted on his liver. Heracles killed the foul bird, broke the chains, and set Prometheus free; and in return for his deliverance the grateful Titan directed his rescuer where to find the giant Atlas. Following Prometheus's advice, Heracles travelled straightway to Africa; and on the way he passed through the land of a tiny race of warriors who waged continual warfare with neighbouring tribes, and especially with their deadly enemies, the cranes. One day, when he had fallen asleep from weariness, he was wakened by sharp prickings over his body; and looking around he saw a host of diminutive men, attacking him with their tiny weapons. The hero laughed at these brave efforts, caught up a few of the doughty little warriors, and, wrapping them in his lion skin, carried them back with him to the court of Eurystheus.

As he journeyed through Africa in search of Atlas, Heracles came to the country of Anteus – a mighty giant and wrestler, and the son of Terra, the Earth. All strangers who came into the land were obliged to wrestle with him, and if they were defeated, they were immediately killed. As no one had ever overcome Anteus, he had brought an untimely death on many a brave hero; so Heracles was eager to defeat him and avenge the unknown dead. As soon as they had grappled for the first struggle, the slayer of the Hydra knew that he had met more than his equal in strength. For a long time they wrestled, Anteus growing stronger after each fall, and Heracles growing fainter from every additional blow of the giant's hand. Again and again the undaunted hero threw his adversary to the ground, but Anteus rose with redoubled vigour and continued the unequal contest. Then, all at once, Heracles remembered the tale he had once heard told of a giant who drew strength from his mother Earth; and believing that this was the case with Anteus, he made a mighty effort and lifted the giant from the ground. Anteus struggled to get his feet again on the earth; but Heracles kept him in the air, and held him there until he felt the powerful body beginning to weaken. Little by little the miraculous strength oozed away, and soon Anteus grew so weak that Heracles easily crushed the limp form with his hands.

The hero then travelled on in search of Atlas, whom he finally found standing on the coast of Africa, with the great weight of the heavens resting on his broad shoulders. As Heracles looked up at the enormous figure, which reached so far into the clouds that nothing could be seen above his waist, he noticed that the forests had grown up so thick and tall all around that only a glimpse of the giant's huge legs could be seen through the heavy foliage. As the hero stood watching this figure that for centuries had stood here in obedience to the divine command of Zeus, he saw dark clouds beginning to gather about the giant's head, and soon a storm broke over the sea and land. Amid the beating of the rain and the crash of the thunder, Heracles thought he heard the voice of Atlas speaking to him; but it might have been only a peal of thunder. When the storm was over and the mists rolled away from the earth, Heracles saw the head of Atlas through rifts in the scurrying clouds. The snow-white hair gave the giant's face a benign look as it fell thick and white over the stooping shoulders that bore so terrible a weight. In a voice that he strove hard to make gentle, Atlas asked the hero what he was seeking, and Heracles told him that he had come to get some of the golden apples from the Garden of the Hesperides. Atlas laughed at these words, and his great shoulders shook so with merriment that a few of the stars fell out of their places. Then he told Heracles that such a feat was impossible even to so great a hero; but that if some one would take the heavens from his shoulders for a few hours, he himself would get the apples.

Heracles was delighted with this offer of assistance, and agreed to take the giant's burden while the latter went on his friendly errand. Very carefully Atlas transferred the heavens to the shoulders of Heracles, and then sped westward to the Garden of the Hesperides. The hero was a bit troubled when he saw Atlas shake his huge shoulders and stretch himself in delight at his freedom, for it would be strange, indeed, if the giant were ready to resume his burden after having tasted the joy of liberty. With some anxiety Heracles watched him step into the sea that came only to his knees though he had waded out a mile from the shore. As Atlas went deeper and deeper into the waves, at first his huge bulk loomed like a cliff against the horizon; but soon it dwindled into a mere speck, and was presently lost to view. How long he stood holding the heavens Heracles never knew; but he found himself growing very weary of his burden, and anxious over Atlas's long absence. Suddenly he saw a dark spot on the horizon, and he knew that it was the giant returning.

It had not been a difficult task for Atlas to reach the Garden, or to pluck the golden apples from the carefully-guarded tree; and Heracles, delighted with the giant's success, thanked him for his trouble and asked him politely to take the sky again on his shoulders, for the journey back to the court of Eurystheus was a long one. Now Atlas had no desire to stand for another dozen centuries with his old burden; and seeing a good opportunity of getting rid of it forever, he told Heracles that he would carry the apples to Eurystheus himself; and meanwhile the hero could keep the heavens supported until Atlas returned. Pretending that he was quite satisfied with this arrangement, Heracles bade the giant goodbye; then hastily asked him to wait a moment while he made a pad for his shoulders to ease the weight of the unaccustomed burden. The unsuspicious giant good-naturedly agreed to this, and took the heavens from Heracles; but instead of making a cushion, the hero picked up the golden apples, which Atlas had dropped on resuming his burden, and started back to his own country, leaving the giant to stand on the seashore forever, or until the pitying gods should release him.

The twelfth and last labour of Heracles was to bring from Hades the three-headed dog, Cerberus. With the help of Hermes and Athena, he descended into the dread realm of Hades, and begged that grim monarch to let him take Cerberus into the upper world. Hades was not willing at first to lose the guardian of his gates even for a short time; but at length he consented to let Heracles do as he desired on condition that Cerberus should not be bound or any weapons used upon him. So the fierce three-headed creature was carried, snarling and struggling, in the hero's strong arms; and when the pair approached the throne of Eurystheus, the horror-struck monarch implored Heracles to take the monster back as quickly as possible, for the sight of its dripping jaws, from which oozed the deadly nightshade, so terrified Eurystheus that he sought refuge in a huge jar, and would not come out until his courtiers assured him that Cerberus was safely out of the country.

When the twelve labours were ended, Heracles's term of service at the court of Eurystheus was over, and he was free to wander where he willed. He spent many years roaming through various lands and assisting other heroes who, like himself, were in search of adventures. He took part in the battle between the Centaurs and Lapithæ; joined in the Argonautic expedition; organized the first siege of Troy, and braved the terrors of Hades to bring Alcestis back to her repentant husband. The expedition against Troy was one of revenge, for the false Laomedon had never paid the gold that he had promised for the release of his daughter Hesione from the sea-monster; and Heracles now set out to punish the treacherous king. So he sailed for Troy with eighteen ships, and the city fell into his hands with but little resistance. Laomedon was killed, his son

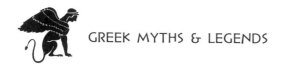

Priam placed on the throne of Troy, and Hesione given in marriage to Telamon, one of the Greeks who accompanied Heracles.

The hero's splendid career received a check, however, for in a quarrel he killed his friend Iphitus, and the gods, angry at this unnecessary bloodshed, compelled him to go once more into bondage. So for three years Heracles served Omphale, queen of Lydia; and during this time he lived very effeminately, wearing sometimes the dress of a woman and spinning wool with the handmaidens of Omphale, while the queen wore his lion's skin and wielded his renowned club. When his years of servitude were over, he set out again on his wanderings; and during one of his journeys he met the beautiful Deïaneira, daughter of Oeneus of Calydon and sister of Meleager, famous in the Calydonian hunt. Heracles immediately sought the maiden's hand in marriage; but she had another suitor, the river god Achelous, who had already obtained her father's consent. Deïaneira, however, much preferred her new lover, and begged him to free her from the betrothal with Achelous. So Heracles challenged the river-god to a wrestling match, the conditions of the contest being that he who won should have the maiden in marriage. Achelous readily agreed to this way of settling their rival pretensions, for he had no doubt as to the result of the wrestling.

The opponents were well matched as to strength, but the river-god had one great advantage, for he could assume any form he pleased, and thus bewilder any one who tried to grapple with him. Among his many changes, he took the form of a serpent; but when Heracles grasped it by the neck and was about to strangle it, Achelous became a bull and rushed at the hero with lowered horns. Skilfully eluding this unexpected attack, Heracles seized the bull by one horn and held on so firmly that when the creature tried to wrench himself free the horn broke. This decided the victory in favour of Heracles, and Achelous departed sullenly to his bed in the river. The broken horn was appropriated by Fortuna, the goddess of plenty, who filled it with her treasures, and adopted it thenceforth as her symbol, calling it Cornucopia.

There was nothing now to hinder the marriage of Heracles with Deïaneira, and the wedding took place with much mirth and feasting. After several days of festivity Heracles departed with his wife; and in the course of their journey homeward, they came to the river Evenus, which had grown so swollen and turbid from the heavy rains that it was impossible to ford it. As the travellers stood helpless on the bank, the centaur Nessus came galloping up to them, and offered to carry Deïaneira across the river in safety. Grateful for this timely assistance, Heracles placed his wife on the back of the centaur, who swam with her through the swift-flowing stream. When they reached the opposite bank, Deïaneira expected the centaur to stop, that she might dismount; but Nessus set off at a brisk trot, hoping to kidnap his fair rider before her husband could overtake them. Heracles heard the cries of his terrified bride, and as soon as he swam the river he sent a swift arrow after the treacherous Nessus. The poisoned tip sank deep into the centaur's side, and he knew at once that he had received his death-wound. With a pretence at repentance, he asked Deïaneira to forgive his rash deed; and then, as if granting her a favour, he told her to take his robe which was stained with blood, and keep it carefully, for it had wonderful properties. He assured her that if the time ever came that Heracles's love grew cold, she had only to persuade him to put on this magic robe, and his devotion to her would become more ardent than ever before. Deïaneira took the robe, but said nothing to her husband of the centaur's gift, hoping that she would never have to make use of it.

For many years Heracles and his wife lived happily together; for, although the hero went on other adventures, he was always eager to return to Deïaneira, and she had no need to be reminded of the centaur's gift. On one of his expeditions, however, he brought back with him a fair maiden named Iole, of whom his wife soon grew to be extremely jealous. Not long after the arrival of Iole, Heracles wished to offer sacrifices to the gods in honour of his safe return; so he sent to Deïaneira for a suitable robe. His wife, trembling for the success of her venture, bade the messenger Lichas carry to Heracles the magic robe of Nessus, which she had carefully guarded all these years. The hero, not knowing the history of the fatal garment, threw it over his shoulders, and as soon as it touched his flesh, the poisoned blood began its deadly work. The body of Heracles burned suddenly as if on fire, and agonizing pains convulsed his frame. He tried to unloose the fatal robe, but it clung to his skin, and he tore off part of his flesh in trying to set himself free. In his rage and pain he turned upon Lichas, the unhappy bearer of the poisoned robe, and seizing him in his still powerful arms flung him into the sea from the top of Mount Oeta, where they had assembled for the sacrifices. Then the hero tore up huge oak trees by their roots and built a lofty funeral pyre on which he stretched his pain-wracked limbs. Calmly he bade his servants apply the torch, but no one was willing to do this, even to ease his sufferings; so Heracles turned to his friend Philoctetes, and after giving him the poisoned arrows, begged him in pity to light the funeral pyre. The youth placed beside Heracles the hero's famous oak club, and covered his body with the lion's skin. Then he applied a torch to the wood, and the flames rose with a roar and cracking to the skies. But only the mortal part of the hero perished, for Zeus would not allow the divinity that he had bestowed upon Heracles to suffer extinction. Purged of his mortality, the hero took his place in high Olympus, and even revengeful Hera was so reconciled to his presence, that she gave him her daughter Hebe in marriage.

24

PERSEUS

When the wicked King Danaüs persuaded his daughters to kill their husbands on their wedding night, there was one, Hypermnestra, who refused to slay her lover, and by saving him brought upon the head of cruel Danaüs the doom that he had striven to escape. The grandson of Hypermnestra and Lynceus was Acrisius, king of Argo, a kindly ruler who dearly loved his only daughter Danaë, and kept her always near him to delight his eyes with her great beauty. Unfortunately the king chanced to learn from an oracle that he would one day be killed by his grandson; and hoping to prevent this, he shut Danaë in a high brazen tower which no one was allowed to enter on pain of death. He placed around the tower a strong guard, so that no one could get even a glimpse of the imprisoned princess; but though no mortal wooer could approach her, Danaë's loveliness was not hidden from Zeus's eyes, and as he looked down from high Olympus he pitied the maiden's loneliness and loved her for her great beauty. Fearing to frighten her if he assumed any mortal disguise, and not daring to appear before her in his divine splendour, he took the form of a golden shower, which fell softly on the sill of the tower window and charmed the lonely captive with its brightness. Each day this strange visitor came to glorify her darkened room, and Danaë looked forward eagerly to its appearance. Thus by means of the golden shower Zeus won the maiden's confidence and love, and spent many hours with her in the high tower room. Danaë was not lonely any more, but people who passed beneath her window could hear her singing to herself all day long.

One morning the astonished attendants rushed to King Acrisius and told him that in the brazen tower was a mother and child – his daughter Danaë had given birth to a son who was so beautiful that they called him Perseus. The king was enraged at this news, and threatened to put the boy to death; but as he was unwilling to stain his hands with the blood of his grandson – even though this grandson might cause his own death – he put Danaë and her infant in a cask, and set them adrift on the sea. For days the strange boat tossed about on the ever-rocking waves, and the poor frightened mother prayed to the gods to save her and her hapless child. Zeus heard her cries, and no storms came to beat the frail boat upon the rocks, nor did any rough seas imperil the voyager's safety. At last the cask was washed gently up on the shores of the island of Seriphus, where a friendly fisherman rescued Danaë and her child and took them to the king, Polydectes. This ruler received them kindly, and allowed them to live at his court; and here the young Perseus grew up into manhood, learning all the games and sports that belonged to the training of a Grecian youth.

Meanwhile Polydectes had become so enamoured of Danaë that he wished to marry her, and grew very angry at her continued refusals. His wrath was increased when Perseus forbade him to distress Danaë any longer with his unwelcome attentions. As Polydectes did not dare to kill Perseus or banish him from the kingdom – for he knew that his suit would then be hopeless – he began to taunt the youth with his inexperience, and asked him why he did not set out on some adventure to prove his mettle like other heroes. Perseus did not consider himself a hero, but he hoped some day to do great things; and the sneers of the king worked on his proud heart, as that wily old monarch had expected. The youth then demanded to have his courage and endurance put to the test, and Polydectes promptly told him to go and slay the Gorgon Medusa, and bring her head back as the proof of his valour. Perseus needed no urging to set out at once, though he well knew the danger of the undertaking. His mother implored him to remain with her, but the youth was determined not to endure Polydectes's taunts any longer, and he was eager to prove his bravery, even at the risk of his life.

There were three of the Gorgons, all of them hideous to behold; but Medusa was by far the most terrible, for besides her frightful appearance she had the power to turn those who looked at her into stone. She was once a beautiful maiden, who had had the misfortune to offend Athena, and that goddess, to punish her, changed her into a dragon-like creature with long tusks, a scaly hide, brazen claws, and instead of hair a writhing mass of snakes. To this monster Polydectes sent the young Perseus, feeling sure that he would never return home alive.

The young hero had not journeyed far before he noticed that some one was walking beside him, and, turning to look more closely at the stranger, he was at once surprised and frightened at recognizing Hermes. But the messenger of the gods bade him have no fear, for he himself had come to help in the perilous quest for the Gorgon's head. Then Hermes lent Perseus his own winged sandals, and told the youth that he would have to do some swift moving in the course of his adventures. The god also lent him a magic helmet that rendered the wearer invisible, and bade him offer thanks to Hades as the sender of this invaluable gift. Not to be outdone by the other gods in kindness, the august Athena lent Perseus her shield – the terrible Aegis of Zeus – which the warrior-goddess carried with her to battle. Thus equipped for the combat Perseus had no fear of encountering the dread Medusa of the snaky locks, and pressed forward eagerly on his journey. He had already enquired of Hermes the way to the Gorgon's cave, but the god could not direct him, and told him that he must find the Grææ and learn the way from them.

The Grææ were three hideous old women who had been grey-haired from birth – and so received their name – and they lived in a far-off land, where eternal darkness reigned. They had only one tooth and one huge eye among them, and passed these around to each other in turn. As they alone could tell him where Medusa dwelt, Perseus started northward on Hermes's winged sandals, and after flying for many days in search of the Three Sisters, he came at last to their cheerless land. He found the Grey Old Women seated under a drooping willow-tree that fell so far over them that it almost hid their shrunken forms.

> "There sat the crones that had the single eye,
> Clad in blue sweeping cloak and snow-white gown;
> While o'er their backs their straight white hair hung down
> In long thin locks, dreadful their faces were,
> Carved all about with wrinkles of despair;
> And as they sat they crooned a dreary song,
> Complaining that their lives should last so long,
> In that sad place that no one came anear,
> In that wan place desert of hope and fear;
> And singing, still they rocked their bodies bent,
> And ever each to each the eye they sent."

William Morris, *The Doom of King Acrisius.*

As Perseus approached the spot where the Grey Old Women sat
crooning to themselves, he took good care to keep on his magic
helmet, and he watched closely to see when the eye was being
transferred from one old head to the other. Just as the eldest sister
was taking out the great eye, and the one who was next in turn was
holding out her shrivelled hand to receive it, Perseus stepped quickly
between them and snatched it away. The old woman began to grope
for it in her pitiable blindness, and then arose a fierce dispute among
the sisters as to who really had the eye. To end the quarrelling Perseus
spoke gently to them, telling them that he had taken their treasured
eye, and would return it to them as soon as they had informed him
where to find Medusa of the snaky locks. For a while the Grey Old
Women pretended that they had never heard of Medusa, but finding
that the unseen speaker was determined to keep their precious eye
until he had received the desired information, they told him the way
to the Gorgon's Cave. Perseus then returned to them the huge eye,
which seemed to stare at him with a very knowing look, and sped off
on his winged sandals to the country where Medusa dwelt.

As he flew along the seacoast he saw in the distance a dark cavern
among the rocks, and in front of it, on the glaring white sand, lay a
monster which, even from his great height above the water, Perseus
could not glance at without shuddering. Remembering Athena's
caution when she gave him her shield, he used its bright surface as
a mirror in which were reflected all the objects below; and never
once was he tempted to turn his eyes toward the dreadful figure on
the beach. Its scaly hide glistened in the sunlight, its brazen claws
shone like live coals, and the snakes that lay coiled around its head
shot out their tongues and hissed whenever the Gorgon stirred in
its sleep. As Perseus drew nearer he saw, reflected in his polished
shield, the forms of men and animals that had been turned to stone
by one glance at Medusa's face. These were very numerous around

the mouth of the cave, and Perseus silently prayed to the gods that his figure might not be added to the number. Some distance away lay the other two Gorgons, Medusa's sisters, but the young hero had no thought for them. His whole attention was centred on the blow that he must deal the sleeping Medusa before the snakes hissed so loudly that she would awaken. Even in his shield the sight of that twisting, wriggling mass of reptiles was so repulsive that Perseus shuddered and was tempted to turn away; but just then he heard a whisper. "Be quick. Strike swift and sure;" and as he recognized the voice of Hermes, all his courage returned.

Grasping his sword more firmly and holding his bright shield above the sleeping monster, he swooped suddenly down upon it, and with one swift stroke cut off the great head with all its coils of serpents. It was only a moment's work to sheathe his sword and grasp the hideous trophy in his hands; but even then the danger was not over, for the snakes on Medusa's head began to hiss so loudly that their noise awoke the other two sleeping Gorgons, and they looked around to find why their sister had disturbed their rest. Seeing Medusa's headless body on the sand, they set up such terrible cries that the noise re-echoed like thunder through the cavern, and as far away as Perseus had already flown, he could hear the awful sounds that made the seashore seem like some vision in a dreadful nightmare.

As he hurried over the sea with Medusa's head held firmly in his hand, some of the blood dripped down into the white-capped waves and was cherished by Poseidon, who had once loved Medusa when she was a beautiful maiden. From these drops of blood the sea-king created the wonderful winged horse, Pegasus, who was to share in the adventures of another famous hero, Bellerophon. Some of the Gorgon's blood had also dropped on the hot African sand, as Perseus was flying upward from the Gorgon's cave, and from this sprang a brood of poisonous reptiles that ever afterward infested that region and brought death to many an unwary explorer.

The journey homeward was long and wearisome, and Perseus was often obliged to seek the seashore to rest. Once as he was flying along the coast of Africa, borne aloft on the winged sandals, he saw old Atlas standing where he had stood for many centuries with the weight of the heavens on his bent shoulders. The clouds wrapped his head so completely that Perseus could see only his immense body. Forests had grown up so high all around him that his huge legs were scarcely visible among the heavy foliage, and his broad shoulders looked like mighty boulders rising up above the tree-tops. But though his head was so far in the clouds, Atlas knew that Perseus was approaching – for giants have certain senses unpossessed by mortal men – and he shook the clouds from about his face, and blew away the mists with his breath. Then, when the air was clear, and Perseus could see the white hair that was previously hidden above the clouds, he pitied poor Atlas for his heavy punishment and stopped to speak with him. The giant looked down from his great height and begged the hero to uncover Medusa's head – which Perseus had kept wrapped in his cloak – for he was anxious to gaze upon it and become himself an image of stone. He told how weary he was of standing for all these ages without ever being able to rest, and he could not endure the thought of keeping up this torture for eternity. So Perseus lifted up the Gorgon's head, being careful to keep his own averted, and Atlas gazed long and eagerly at the dead face, with its wreath of lifeless serpents. Then slowly the giant's great bulk began to harden, and the stooping shoulders became firm, unfeeling stone. As Perseus stood there watching the strange transformation, he seemed to see no longer the floating white hair of Atlas, but a pile of snow on a mountain top; and he looked no more on the huge limbs surrounded by forests, but he saw rents and clefts on a mountain side that just

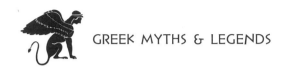

showed themselves through the thick trees. Thus was the burden of Atlas forever removed from his aching shoulders, and the heavens now rested securely on a mountain.

When Perseus resumed his journey along the coast, he soon came to a place where the cliffs rose abruptly from the sea; and as he looked down at the rocks below him, he saw, outlined against their dark surface, a figure that made him pause in his swift flight, and wonder if a sudden madness had taken hold on his fancy; for chained to the rock was a maiden so beautiful that even her constant weeping had not marred the perfect loveliness of her face. Keeping the Gorgon's head carefully concealed under his cloak, so that the captive maiden could get no glimpse of the snaky locks, Perseus flew to the girl's side, and, taking off his magic helmet, spoke to her gently. At any other time she would have been startled at this sudden appearance of a stranger; but the thought of her dreadful fate, so near at hand, drove all other fears from her mind. The spray from the sea dashed over her, and the cold winds blew on her shivering form; but of this she seemed to be hardly aware. Her eyes were fixed in wild terror upon a cavern in the rocks, where Perseus could see a huge dragon lying stretched out on the cool, slimy seaweed.

When the young hero spoke to the maiden, she did not seem to hear him, but, at his gentle persistence, she at last turned her eyes away from the dreaded cavern and told him her story. She said that her name was Andromeda, and that her mother, Cassiopeia, had angered the sea-nymphs by presuming to rival them in beauty. To punish the queen for her vanity, the nymphs sent a fierce sea-monster to devastate the homes along the coast; and when the terrified people consulted an oracle to know how they might save themselves from further disaster, they were told that the monster would not depart until the Princess Andromeda was sacrificed to its fury. So the king, her father, and her wretched, remorseful mother, and a procession of weeping attendants had led her, that very day, to the rocks, and had chained her fast to await the monster's pleasure.

Just as Andromeda was speaking, there was a rustling sound in the cave, as if the dragon were stretching its huge wings. Then came a sudden whir and rush, as the monster glided out of the dim interior of its cave, and came speeding through the water toward its victim. The scaly hide glittered in the sunlight, and the great coils of its snaky body beat up the waves as it came with incredible swiftness toward the captive maiden, whose terrified shrieks almost unnerved the young hero who had come to rescue her. Quickly he donned his magic helmet and grasped the keen-edged sword that had already stood him in good stead. As the monster's head emerged from the waves, Perseus rushed upon it unseen, and with a quick thrust pierced the creature in its one vital spot. The dragon sank back into the blood-stained water, and then made a few ineffective plunges toward its victim; but Perseus's blow had been sure, and the creature's great body finally disappeared beneath the waves. While Andromeda was thanking her deliverer with grateful tears, he struck off the chains that bound her to the rock, and led her to where her parents and an astonished group of watchers had been looking on at the strange combat. The great joy of Andromeda's father was equalled only by the mother's happiness over her rescued child; and they both welcomed the young hero who had saved her from so terrible a fate.

When Perseus had been entertained royally for several days, the king bade him demand any reward that he wished for his heroic services; and the youth boldly asked Andromeda's hand in marriage. To this the parents gladly consented, although she was already betrothed to her uncle Phineus, and the preparations were begun at once for the wedding. While the marriage celebrations were in progress, the jilted suitor, who had been too timid to attempt any rescue of Andromeda, now came forward to claim his wife. His pretensions were laughed at, however, and he left the court angry and plotting revenge. The following day he appeared with a band of followers and suddenly attacked Perseus, who had barely time to defend himself. The friends of the young hero rallied to his support, but they were outnumbered by the attacking party, and a disastrous battle might have ensued, had not Perseus bethought himself of a sure means of defence. Catching up the cloak in which he had wrapped the Gorgon's head, he cried: "Whoever is my friend, let him turn away his eyes." The courtiers of King Cepheus, and the men fighting around Perseus obeyed him; but Phineus and his followers believed this to be a mere trick to gain time, and looked on while Perseus unveiled Medusa's snaky head. Some of the gazers had their spears in uplifted hands; some were fitting arrows to their bows as they turned their eyes a moment toward Perseus; but in whatever position they stood, just so they were suddenly turned into stone. By some chance Phineus had been watching his men instead of looking at the Gorgon's head; and when he saw their dreadful transformation, he fell on his knees before Perseus, and with outstretched hands implored the hero to spare his life. But Perseus forced him to look upon the hideous face of Medusa, and he became a stone image with averted head and supplicating arms.

Having thus disposed effectively of his enemies, Perseus covered up his death-dealing trophy, and the wedding ceremonies were resumed. Later he departed with his bride to the country of Polydectes, where that king had been keeping his mother a prisoner until she would consent to marry him. He had long ago believed Perseus dead, and was therefore much astonished to see him appear unharmed and victorious. Hearing of the cruel treatment his mother had received from Polydectes, the young hero determined on a swift revenge. In the presence of the king and his court, he suddenly displayed the head of Medusa; and the whole company, just as they stood, were turned into stone. Then Perseus set sail with his wife and mother for his own country; but before he left he returned to Hades the magic helmet, to Hermes the winged sandals, and to Athena the wonderful Aegis. The august goddess of wisdom seemed to have taken a strange fancy to the Gorgon's head, so Perseus gave her this trophy of his victory, and she fixed it in the middle of her shield.

When Perseus, with Andromeda and Danaë, arrived in Argo, they found that old Acrisius had been driven from his throne, and that a usurper was enjoying the kingdom. It did not take long for the hero who had slain Medusa to kill the unlawful claimant, and reinstate his grandfather. The old man had been languishing for years in prison, and was hardly able to endure the great joy of his release at the hands of one whom he had long since believed to be dead. Things seemed to be settled very happily in spite of the oracle; but the decrees of the gods are sure to be fulfilled, and one day when Perseus was playing quoits, he accidentally threw one wide of the mark. It struck Acrisius, who was looking on at the game, and killed him instantly. This unfortunate mishap so preyed upon Perseus's mind that he could not remain in Argo, but exchanged his kingdom for that of Mycenæ, over which he ruled for many years very wisely and well. When at last Perseus died, the gods placed him among the stars with his wife Andromeda, and with Cassiopeia, who had long since been cured of her vanity.

25

BELLEROPHON

At the court of Proetus, king of Argos, there dwelt as guest of honour a young prince named Bellerophon. He was a kinsman of Proetus and a grandson of Sisyphus, king of Corinth, so much honour was shown him. As he was strong, brave, and fearless, he was a leader in all the games; and his beauty won such favour at the court that Proetus's wife, Queen Anteia, sought his love. Since the youth could not in loyalty return her affection, he found it difficult to remain in Argos; for the queen was not content to receive only the courtesy due her, but importuned Bellerophon for his love. He tried many times to find some pretext for leaving his kinsman; so when Proetus proposed that he should make a journey to Lycia to deliver some important messages to its ruler, the youth was eager to go. Meanwhile the queen, angered at his indifference, had told her husband that Bellerophon delighted in treating her with contempt in return for all her kindness, and that she could not endure his presence in Argos any longer. She demanded further that Proetus should put the young man at once to death, but that he should not let Bellerophon suspect that she had been the instigator of the deed. The king readily believed his wife's artfully contrived story, and declared that the insolent youth should be made to pay dearly for his ingratitude. As Bellerophon was already a hero at the court, Proetus dared not condemn him openly to death; so when the prince departed on his journey to Lycia, he carried with him some letters whose purport he was far from suspecting; for the sealed message that he bore so light-heartedly was a request to King Iobates to put the bearer at once to death.

King Iobates was the father-in-law of Proetus; and the ruler of Lycia had often relied on his powerful relative as an ally in time of war; so the king of Argos was confident that his instructions would be carried out. The expedition to Lycia might, therefore, have had a different ending had not Bellerophon forgotten to deliver his letters for several days. Meanwhile King Iobates, supposing him to be on a friendly visit, received him very hospitably and made him a member of the royal household. After much feasting and entertainment, the young prince suddenly remembered the sealed message entrusted to his care, and hastened to deliver it to Iobates with many apologies for his forgetfulness. When the king read the letter, he was surprised and horrified at its contents, for he could not, in cold blood, kill the guest who had sat at his table; and yet he did not wish to refuse any demand made by Proetus. When the courtiers saw his white face and troubled looks, they wondered what the message contained; but no one suspected its real import.

At last a solution of the difficulty came to the king's mind, and he began to praise Bellerophon for the bravery and courage that had made the young prince famous throughout Greece. He lamented that no such fearlessness dwelt among the men of Lycia, for otherwise the Chimæra would not be living in security and laying waste the king's lands. When Bellerophon heard what terror was inspired by the mere mention of the Chimæra's name, he wondered whether he would be afraid to face this fearful creature with its lion's head, goat's body, and dragon's tail. When he expressed surprise that no hero had slain it, the wily Iobates at once implored him to help the stricken country and to go himself to fight the Chimæra. Bellerophon might have been eager for this adventure, had he not learned to love the king's daughter Philonoë, who had found the handsome stranger more to her liking than all the youths of Lycia. He was, therefore, loath to leave the princess and depart on so perilous a venture; but at the repeated urging of Iobates, he began to make preparations for the journey.

Before setting out he first consulted the soothsayer Polyidus, who advised him to procure the winged horse Pegasus if he hoped to succeed in slaying the Chimæra. This advice was probably well-meant, but it was very discouraging; for how could Bellerophon expect to bridle the famous immortal steed that had never known the touch of any man's hand? He knew too well that Pegasus was rarely seen by mortal eyes, for he dwelt on the calm heights of Mount Helicon, a spot sacred to the Muses, and seldom came to earth except to visit the fountain of Pirene, near Corinth, whose clear waters sometimes tempted him to leave his lofty home. Very few people had ever seen the snow-white horse, with his wonderful silvery wings that carried him through the air as buoyantly as an eagle in its flight. Whenever Pegasus deigned to come to earth to taste the sweet waters of Pirene he sped over the grassy meadows so swiftly that even the fleetest runner could not hope to catch him. He had never been bridled in all his wild, free life, and for beauty and strength and sheer joy of living there was nothing like him in the whole wide world. "Sleeping at night as he did, on a lofty mountain top, and passing the greater part of the day in the air, Pegasus seemed hardly to be a creature of the earth. Whenever he was seen, up very high above people's heads, with the sunshine on his silvery wings, one would have thought that he belonged to the sky, and that, skimming a little too low, he had got astray among our mists and vapours, and was seeking his way back again.... In the summer time, and in the beautifullest of weather, Pegasus often alighted on the solid earth, and, closing his silvery wings, would gallop over hill and dale for pastime as fleetly as the wind."

When Bellerophon was advised to catch this glorious winged steed, it was no wonder that he felt discouraged, for nowhere could he find an old man, a maiden, or a child who had ever had so much as a glimpse of the snow-white Pegasus. Some one told him, however, that the immortal steed had once been tamed by Athena, and owed obedience to her; so he went immediately to the temple of the warrior-goddess, and begged her to help him. For many hours he prayed before Athena's shrine, but there came no answer to his petition; and, at last, worn out with fatigue and discouragement, he fell asleep on the steps of the temple. When the first rays from Apollo's golden sun-car fell on the white marble pillars of the temple, Bellerophon awoke, and to his great astonishment he found in his hand a golden bridle. Believing this to be the answer to his prayers, he set out hopefully on his search for the winged horse; and before journeying very far, he came to the fountain of Pirene, where the beautiful, clear stream bubbled up beside a grassy meadow so redolent of ripening clover that it might tempt a far more fastidious horse than the immortal Pegasus. Bellerophon spent many days beside the fountain, but he never caught a glimpse of the white-winged steed, nor saw any mark of his hoofs upon the sod. Once an old man stopped to ask him why he was lingering so long beside the fountain, and then shook his white head incredulously when Bellerophon spoke of Pegasus and his silvery wings.

At last the young hero grew so discouraged that he decided to return to the court of Iobates; but on the very morning that he was intending to leave Pirene, he chanced to wake just at dawn, and, leaning over the fountain to bathe his flushed face he saw reflected in the water an image that made his heart beat fast with hope and joy. It seemed like a great white bird, flying high up among the clouds, where the sunlight shone on its silvery wings. Nearer and nearer it came, sweeping the air in great wide circles, and at last it alighted beside the fountain. Bellerophon meantime had hidden himself in the bushes, and now he watched the beautiful creature as it folded its gorgeous wings and bent its arching neck to drink the clear water. Then Pegasus daintily cropped a few clover blossoms, shook his long white mane, and began to run up and down over the meadows, capering madly like a colt just set free in the pasture. After rolling luxuriously in the thick grass, and racing like the wind across the meadow, Pegasus grew tired of his play, and folding his snow-white wings, trotted quietly up to the fountain to take one more drink before flying back to his home on Mount Helicon.

Then Bellerophon crept noiselessly out of his hiding place, and while the unsuspicious Pegasus was drinking the cool water and his eyes were no longer watchful, the youth boldly sprang upon his back and took firm hold of the thick mane, being careful meantime not to let Athena's golden bridle slip from his fingers. Bellerophon had ridden many a horse, but never one as wild and spirited as this; for the glorious Pegasus had not known, until now, the ignominy of bearing a mortal rider on his back, and he did not intend to submit to the disgrace. When he felt the touch of Bellerophon's knees on his broad flanks, he made a tremendous bound into the air, and before the youthful rider could realize what had happened, he found himself hundreds of feet above the earth. The winged horse snorted, and shook with anger, and tried to unseat his rider by every trick known to equine ingenuity. He bounded forward with a sudden jerk, reared, turned over and over in the air, until half the time Bellerophon was riding with his head downward; but in spite of all his efforts, he could not throw off the strange thing that clung to his back. All at once Bellerophon saw his chance to slip the golden bridle between the maddened horse's teeth, and suddenly Pegasus became as gentle and tractable as if he had always obeyed the will of a master.

Happy to find the conflict over, the young hero turned the head of his white-winged steed toward the mountain-region where the dread Chimæra dwelt. It was a wild and rocky part of the country that Bellerophon looked down upon, and he saw all around him the evidence of ruin wrought by the fire-breathing monster. The dwellings of the peasants were in smoking ashes; carcasses of half-eaten cattle were strewn about the barren pastures; and human bodies were also to be seen, torn and mangled by the Chimæra's ruthless claws. On the mountain side was a deep hole in the rocks, and from it issued clouds of black smoke that had a horrid stifling smell as it rose up from the cavern's mouth. As Bellerophon descended nearer to the earth, the delicate nostrils of his horse dilated at the first contact with the foul smoke, and he found it hard to persuade Pegasus to fly closer to the Chimæra's den. When they did approach through the thick clouds of smoke, Bellerophon saw the monster's great body stretched out at full length in the cave, while all the three heads lay on half-eaten carcasses that were strewn about the floor. The lion and the goat part of the Chimæra were asleep, but the snake was wide awake; and when it saw Bellerophon approaching on his winged horse, it raised its head and began to hiss so loudly that it roused up the other creatures until they too were intent and watchful.

Then the smoke poured out of the cave more thickly than before; and if Pegasus had not carried him quickly away from the poisonous fumes, Bellerophon would have been suffocated long before he was able to get near enough to deal the Chimæra a mortal blow. But the brave horse bore him out of danger, and kept him far above the thick smoke until the monster crawled out of its lair. Then like the swift rush of air, Bellerophon swooped down upon the Chimæra and cut off its three horrid heads with his sword; but even then the danger was not over, for the headless creature sprang into the air, and clutched wildly for its enemy with its long claws. So sure an instinct for destruction did the Chimæra have that, mangled and dying as it was, it struck directly at Bellerophon and would have torn him into pieces had not the faithful Pegasus borne him swiftly out of reach of the deadly claws. After a few vain attempts to grasp its destroyer, the Chimæra's great body gave a convulsive shudder, and fell back stone-dead upon the blood-soaked ground.

Then Bellerophon sped back to the court of Iobates and announced that the Chimæra was dead. The king was glad to hear that the monster could no longer devastate his land, but he was sorry to see Bellerophon returning unhurt and victorious, and with such a wonderful prize as the winged horse, Pegasus. Most people had never believed that this immortal steed really existed, and had thought that the stories about it were merely old wives' tales. Iobates did not dare to kill so popular a hero as the young prince became after this adventure, but he sent him off on other perilous journeys, hoping that on one of them he might meet his death. Bellerophon, however, never came to any harm, for he had always the sure help of Pegasus, and he returned safe from each expedition with trophies to lay at the feet of his beloved princess, Philonoë. At length the king was convinced that Bellerophon was under the special protection of the gods, and, hoping to win their favour, he gave the young hero his daughter in marriage, and appointed him his successor to the throne.

For several years Bellerophon lived happily in Lycia; but his many victories with Pegasus had made him presumptuous, and he felt that his true place was with the immortals. So one day he mounted his winged steed and flew far above the earth into the white clouds that wrap the top of Mount Olympus. Angered at this insolence and daring, Zeus sent an enormous gadfly which stung Pegasus so cruelly that he gave a sudden leap forward, and this unexpected movement threw his too-confident rider from his back. The luckless Bellerophon felt the reins slip through his fingers, and he plunged downward through mist and clouds many, many miles to the earth. This terrible fall would have killed any one but a mythological hero, but Bellerophon, though bruised and shaken, only lost his eyesight. Ever afterwards he wandered through the fair places of the earth, lame and blind and lonely, lamenting the foolish pride that had led him to risk the anger of the gods. What his end was no one ever knew, but he probably died in some distant land, alone and forgotten, while Pegasus went back to the sunny slopes of Mount Helicon and never visited the earth again, even to drink the sweet waters of Pirene.

26

THE STORY OF JASON

PART 1

In Thessaly there once ruled a wise and good king named Aeson, who dwelt happily with his wife Alcimede, and his little son Jason. The king's reign did not last long, however, for his wicked brother Pelias collected a band of armed warriors and made war upon Aeson, who, after a feeble resistance, surrendered his throne to the invader and escaped secretly from the kingdom with his wife and child. The dethroned monarch took refuge in a distant country, and lived in concealment until Jason was old enough to be sent to some place of greater safety, for they knew that the cruel Pelias would try to seek him out and kill him. So they entrusted the boy to the care of the centaur Chiron, after telling that wise teacher who the lad really was, and begging him to bring Jason up with the desire some day to avenge their wrongs.

Chiron instructed the youth in all the arts of which he himself was master, and when the young prince reached manhood, he was one of the bravest and most skilful of the centaur's pupils. Jason had been told many times of his uncle's tyranny, and he burned to avenge the wrongs of his parents; but his wise teacher cautioned him to wait until he had strength and power enough to face the wicked usurper. When he deemed the youth sufficiently trained to leave his care, Chiron sent Jason forth, bidding him satisfy now his desire for revenge. He advised his pupil, however, to be careful and to do no harm to any one except the man who had wronged him. Jason promised to obey his tutor's instructions, and, girding on his sword, set out on the journey to his native city.

It was springtime when Jason turned his steps toward his father's kingdom, and the rains had swollen all the streams, making them difficult to ford. One day as he stood on the bank of a river, wondering where he had best attempt to swim across, he saw an old woman looking despairingly at the rushing, foaming water. Jason spoke gently to her, and offered to carry her across the river. This unexpected assistance was gratefully accepted, and Jason bravely waded into the shallowest part of the stream. The swift current and his unwieldy burden made the crossing very difficult, so that when Jason at last reached the opposite bank, he was glad to rest. He did not mind the wetting, but he was sorry to find that he had lost one of his sandals in the river. As it was useless to try to find it, he set off with only the remaining one, but first he stopped to say goodbye to the old woman. To his surprise he no longer saw a bent and trembling figure beside him, but he stood in the presence of a beautiful, imperious woman, whose royal bearing would have proclaimed her a goddess even if the startled youth had not seen beside her the peacock that ever attends the stately Hera. Jason trembled at this transformation of his aged passenger, but Hera smiled graciously upon him and bade him have no fear, for she had come to promise him her aid and protection.

Before he could render suitable thanks, the goddess had disappeared, and Jason continued his journey, full of courage and confident of success. Soon he came to his native city, where he found a great crowd of people assembled at the temple, for Pelias, the king, was offering on that day special sacrifices, and a public festival had been proclaimed throughout the city. Jason joined in the crowds that were hurrying to the temple, and stood quite near his uncle, while the king, unconscious of his presence, was performing the sacrifices. When the ceremony was over, Pelias glanced around at the assembled company, and started back pale with terror when he saw Jason; for although he did not recognize his nephew, he had been warned by an oracle to beware of a youth who would appear before him wearing only one sandal. Trembling, but striving to hide his fear, Pelias spoke to the stranger and asked him his name. Then Jason confronted his uncle boldly, declared his own parentage, and demanded that the usurper should at once resign his throne and restore old Aeson to his rightful place in the kingdom.

Pelias did not dare openly to defy this fearless youth, but neither did he intend to give up his power and wealth; so being a crafty man he sought to beguile Jason with soft words, and promised to send at once for the absent king and queen. He urged his nephew to remain meanwhile at the court, and invited him to join the royal household that evening in a splendid banquet. Jason needed no persuasion to eat, drink, and be merry; and as the wily Pelias plied him with rich viands and the choicest wine, his heart warmed toward his uncle, and he felt less eager to carry out his long-cherished vengeance. During the feast the bards sang of brave deeds done by heroes, and one old musician told of the famous golden fleece that many had sought to take by stealth; but of those who went on the quest, no one ever came back to tell why he had failed.

Jason listened eagerly while the old singer told how the famous fleece once belonged to a ram that the friendly Poseidon sent to Phryxus and Helle to enable them to escape from the persecutions of their stepmother Ino. This was the same Ino who cared so tenderly for the infant Dionysus; but to her stepchildren she was very cruel. Their own mother Nephele had been sent away by King Athamas because he had wearied of her, and wished to marry Ino; and when the banished mother learned how neglected and ill-treated her children were, she begged Poseidon to help them. So the sea-god sent a golden-fleeced ram, which Phryxus and Helle mounted and thus escaped from their cruel stepmother. Only Phryxus reached the land of Colchis, however; for when the ram flew over the sea, Helle grew frightened at the sight of the waves tossing so far beneath her, and suddenly lost her hold on the golden fleece. Her brother reached out to clutch her as she slid from the ram's back, but it was too late, and the unfortunate maiden fell into that part of the sea that is since known as the Hellespont. Phryxus reached Colchis safely, and here he sacrificed the ram to Poseidon, and hung its golden fleece on a tree under which he placed a dragon to guard it night and day.

As Jason listened to this story he felt as though here was a task worth his mettle; and it needed no urging from Pelias to make him declare himself ready to set forth on the adventure without further delay. The wily king praised Jason's courage, and prophesied that he would be called the greatest among heroes, while in his heart he felt assured that the troublesome nephew would never return alive. He promised to render Jason every assistance in his power, and offered to fit him out with a well-manned ship; but the young adventurer had been thinking over the matter more calmly, and had begun to distrust his uncle's apparent kindness. So he went for counsel to the shrine of Zeus at Dodona, where there was an oracle called the Speaking Oak; and, on consulting this, he learned, to his great satisfaction, that Hera was still watching over his welfare, and would aid him in the quest of the golden fleece. The Speaking Oak then bade him cut off one of its great limbs, and carve from it a figurehead for his ship. It told him also that the ship in which he was to sail should not be made of timber cut from any ordinary trees, but should be built of the wood taken from pine-trees that grew on Mount Pelion.

When Jason had carved his figurehead, he found that it had the gift of speech and could counsel him wisely in all his affairs, so as soon as the ship was ready, the figurehead was fastened to its prow, and Jason set out on his memorable voyage. He called his ship the *Argo*, and himself and his fellow adventurers the Argonauts. Among his companions were many men famous for their brave deeds: Heracles, Admetus, Castor and Pollux, Meleager, Orpheus, and Theseus. All these were eager for new adventures, and no one doubted that with so many heroes to aid him, Jason would succeed in winning the golden fleece. Even Pelias, as he watched the voyagers sail away, wished that he had sent the daring youth on a still more perilous journey.

The voyage to Colchis was full of strange happenings, both on land and sea. The first disaster that overtook the Argonauts occurred when Heracles went ashore to get some fresh water, with a youth of the party named Hylas. There had been several occasions on which it was necessary for some of the heroes to land in order to get food or water, but the delay had been brief and the voyage quickly resumed. This time they were in need of new oars, so Heracles offered to procure them, and took with him his favourite companion Hylas. While he himself was felling trees, he sent Hylas in search of fresh water; and the youth, after wandering about for some time, came at last to a fountain whose waters were so pure and cool that he lingered long beside it. The nymphs who lived in the fountain were charmed with the beauty of Hylas, and determined to keep him with them; so when he bent over the water, they drew him gently down into its clear depths. Heracles, after waiting long for the lad's return, went in search of him; but no trace of Hylas could be found anywhere in the lonely forest. Though he called again and again, no voice answered him; for Hylas lay in the green bed of the fountain, and his ears were deaf to the cries of his friend. Heracles's grief was so great over the loss of Hylas that he refused to accompany the expedition any further, and made his way home alone and on foot.

On another occasion Jason landed in Thrace; and here he learned that the blind King Phineus was tormented by some Harpies – creatures half woman and half bird – that ate or befouled all the food placed before the wretched king. The only meals Phineus could take were by stealth, and the poor king's life was rendered miserable by the constant presence of these foul monsters. When the two sons of Boreas, who were happily gifted with wings, heard Jason relate the story of the Harpies to his companions, they promptly offered to help the blind Phineus; and, flying at the loathsome birds with drawn swords, the brothers drove them out of Thrace into an island so far away that they never came back to trouble the king.

PART II

O nce, in the course of the voyage, Jason was attacked by a flock of brazen-feathered birds that showered their sharp metal plumage down on the Argonauts, and wounded some of them sorely. Jason soon found that weapons were of no avail against these formidable enemies, so he consulted the figurehead that had always counselled him wisely. In obedience to its advice the heroes clashed their swords and spears furiously against their shields until the birds, terrified by the noise, flew away and never returned.

When the *Argo* approached the Symplegades – or Clashing Islands – Jason remembered the words of Phineus, who had advised him to let free a dove, whose speed was less than that of his swift vessel, before he attempted a passage. If it flew easily between the rocks, then the ship could safely follow it with no chance of being ground to pieces as the islands clashed together. When the Argonauts reached this dangerous spot, Jason sent a dove out before him. He watched its flight anxiously, and when it glided between the rocks with only a tail feather caught, he guided the ship so close behind it that, as he slid through the opening made by the rebound of the islands, the deadly rocks merely grazed his rudder. Since their destructive power depended on allowing no vessel to pass them unharmed, the evil force that the islands possessed was now broken, and they were henceforth chained fast to the bottom of the sea.

At last the *Argo* reached the shores of Colchis, and Jason made known to King Aeetes his desire to possess the golden fleece. The owner of that wonderful pelt was very naturally not ready to give it to even the boldest stranger; but he treated the Argonauts kindly, and even promised to bestow upon Jason the coveted fleece if he could catch and harness to a plough two brazen-hoofed, fire-breathing bulls. Then, having done this, he must plough up a certain piece of ground sacred to Ares, and sow the field with dragon's teeth just as Cadmus had done. Last of all he must conquer the armed giants that would spring up in the field after the sowing, and then slay the dragon that guarded the golden fleece. This was certainly enough to daunt any hero, but Jason, relying on the help of Hera, agreed to the king's terms and went down to the seashore, where his ship lay, to consult the figurehead who had never yet failed him. On the way he met Medea, the king's daughter, who was much taken with the young stranger's beauty, and hoped to induce him to marry her. Medea herself was very beautiful, and being also a sorDemeters she was an invaluable ally in the adventure that had brought Jason and his friends from a far-distant land. So before many days had passed Medea plighted her troth to the young hero who needed help sorely and the king's daughter promised to give him the aid of her magic arts.

On the day appointed for the great task, Jason boldly approached the fire-breathing bulls, for Medea had given him a charm by which the fierce brutes were rendered harmless, and were easily yoked and harnessed to the plough. Then, in the presence of the astonished spectators, who expected to see him crushed beneath the brazen hoofs, Jason ploughed the field; and having sown it with dragon's teeth, stood ready, sword in hand, to meet the attack of the giants who sprang up out of the ground clad in full armour. When he saw the glittering spears turned toward him, Jason's heart began to quail lest, after all, Medea's help should prove ineffective; and even the sorDemeters herself felt a momentary doubt of her own power to save her lover from his foes. As the armed men were about to rush upon him, Jason threw a stone in their midst, according to Medea's instructions, and the giants turned against each other and began a furious battle that ended in the destruction of the whole armed host.

Then the hero, accompanied by Medea, hastened to the tree where the golden fleece hung, and here a charm was needed to lull to sleep the dragon that guarded the treasure. As soon as the great eyes that had never been known to close began to shut one by one, Jason stepped softly up behind the monster and cut off its head. It was but a moment's work to tear the fleece from the tree where it had hung for so many years, and to bear it in triumph to the *Argo*, where Jason's friends stood anxiously awaiting his coming. The men were already at the oars, for he had told them to be ready to sail at a moment's notice when he should appear bearing the golden fleece. In spite of Aeetes's promise the hero did not trust him, and so made his preparations for departure very secretly. When he and Medea boarded the *Argo* with their prize, the rowers bent with all their strength to the oars, and the ship slid silently and swiftly out of the harbour.

Aeetes soon learned that the Grecian vessel had left his shores, carrying on board the golden fleece, his daughter, and – worst of all – his only son and heir Absyrtus; so he hurriedly manned his royal barge with rowers, and set out after the Argonauts. Although the fugitive vessel made good speed, the king's ship began to gain on it; and as Jason watched the distance between the vessels growing less and less, he was filled with despair and begged the sorDemeters to aid them with her magic. Medea did not care what fate befell the Argonauts, but she had no desire to leave Jason and return to her father's court; so she did not hesitate to resort to any means of preventing the king from overtaking her. She therefore killed her brother Absyrtus, and, cutting his body into pieces, dropped them one by one over the side of the vessel. Aeetes, seeing the remains of his only son floating on the water, stopped to collect them so that the body might have suitable burial; and by this delay the Argonauts were allowed to escape. The wretched king then returned to Colchis, where he buried Absyrtus with prayers to the gods to bring vengeance upon his inhuman daughter.

When the *Argo* with its triumphant crew reached Thessaly, they found that their arrival caused great surprise as well as joy, for King Pelias had never supposed they would return, and felt himself secure against any further trouble from the youth with only one sandal. He was therefore much dismayed at seeing Jason return, especially as he came unharmed and bearing so rich a trophy as the golden fleece. The usurper knew that his days of power were over, and when Jason again demanded the kingdom in his father's name, Pelias was forced to resign his throne to the lawful king. Old Aeson was then summoned from his place of banishment, and restored to his rightful place; but he was so weak and decrepit that power had no charm for him, and he accepted his throne very reluctantly.

So Jason begged his wife to use her magic in behalf of the old king; and Medea, anxious to please her lover, willingly promised to restore Aeson to all the vigour of manhood. To prepare the magic potion that was to bring youth and health, the sorDemeters went out into the meadows on nine successive nights beginning with the new moon, and gathered herbs whose magic properties she alone could tell. Then she set a cauldron in the deepest part of the woods, and built under it a slow fire that burned always night and day. In the cauldron she threw the magic herbs, flowers with acrid juice, stones from the far east and sand from the all-surrounding ocean, hoar frost gathered by moonlight, a screech-owl's head and wings, and the entrails of a wolf. Then she added some bits of tortoise shell and the liver of a stag – for these animals are tenacious of life – and the head and beak of a crow that outlives nine generations of men.

All these she boiled together, stirring them with an olive branch; and when she lifted out the branch, it was full of new leaves and heavy with young olives. These preparations being finished, and the time being full moon, Medea went forth alone into the forest with old Aeson, just at midnight when all creatures slept, and no breath of wind stirred the trees. She laid the old man on a bed of herbs, and after putting him into a deep sleep, cut his throat and let out the sluggish blood of age. Then she poured into the wound the juices from her cauldron; and when these began to flow through the king's weak frame, he underwent a wonderful change, for his hair and beard lost their whiteness and took on the glossy hue of youth. His paleness changed to the ruddiness of manhood; and his feeble limbs felt all the vigour of a hero in his prime.

When the daughters of Pelias saw this miracle of old Aeson transformed into a stalwart man, they begged Medea to use her magic in restoring their father to his former youthfulness; and the sorDemeters promised to help Pelias just as she had the father of Jason. So she prepared a cauldron full of boiling water, and pretended to put into it the necessary ingredients for the magic potion; but when the devoted, though too-credulous daughters of Pelias killed their father, and put his body into the cauldron, as Medea had directed, they did not restore him to youth, but merely ended very effectively the life that they so ardently wished to prolong.

Though Medea's great beauty and her power as a sorceress kept Jason faithful to her for many years, he at last grew weary of her and prepared to wed a maiden named Creusa. Pretending to approve of his choice, and concealing her rage at Jason's heartlessness, Medea sent the bride a beautiful, though poisoned, robe. The unsuspicious Creusa was delighted with this rich gift; but as soon as it rested on her shoulders the hapless maiden was seized with terrible convulsions, from which she shortly died. Then Medea killed with her own hands the children that she had borne to Jason – so that she might have no reminder of his falseness – and fled in her dragon-car to Athens, where she sought the protection of King Aegeus, the father of Theseus. Here she lived many years, for the king, not knowing her history, and being enamoured of her beauty, married her and made her his queen.

Jason, filled with remorse and despair, now led a most unhappy life, and spent most of his time on the seashore beside the great hulk of the Argo, which was slowly rotting away on the beach. One day a sudden gale detached a loose beam from the vessel, and it fell on Jason's head, killing him instantly. Thus ended forever the voyages of the Argonauts.

27

THE CALYDONIAN HUNT

One of the heroes of the Argonautic expedition was Meleager, son of Oenus and Althæa, king and queen of Calydon. When Meleager was born, his mother saw in a vision the three Fates spinning the thread of her child's life; and she heard them foretell that he would live until the brand then burning on the hearth should be consumed. Althæa, terrified by the vision, awoke; and snatching the brand from the fire, she plunged it into an earthen jar full of water. When she saw that the last spark was extinguished, she carefully hid the brand on whose existence depended the life of her son. Meleager, thus saved from death, grew up into splendid and vigorous manhood, and was welcomed by Jason as a fitting companion for the famous voyage to Colchis.

While his son was absent on this expedition, Oenus offended Artemis by omitting to offer to her the customary yearly sacrifice; so the angry goddess sent a fierce boar to devastate the country. This creature was of such enormous size and strength that no hunters dared attack it, and it laid waste the fields of Calydon by trampling on the young corn, rooting up vines and olive trees, and devouring flocks and herds, thus creating wild confusion among the panic-stricken people. When Meleager returned from his voyage, and learned of the disaster that had overtaken the land, he summoned a band of heroes and set out to slaughter the wild boar. Jason, Nestor, Telamon the father of Ajax, Theseus and his friend Pirithous, Peleus (afterwards the father of Achilles), the twin brothers Castor and Pollux on their snow-white horses – all these and many others came at Meleager's call to join in the hunt.

With the youths came also Atalanta, daughter of Jasius, king of Arcadia. This princess had been left when an infant on Mount Parthenium, and exposed to the hunger of wild beasts, for her father was angry at finding that the gods had sent him a daughter instead of the longed-for son. Atalanta was not devoured, however, nor did she perish from cold, for a kindly she-bear nursed the deserted infant, and she grew up strong and fearless. Later on some shepherds found the sturdy little maiden in the woods; and taking her to their rude home, they cared for her, and taught her to follow the chase. Thus she had grown up like a boy, fearless, bold, and skilled beyond most youths in the use of the bow and spear.

When the company of heroes saw Atalanta ready to join them in the chase for the wild boar, they were disposed to scoff at the idea of a maiden taking part in an adventure whose dangers might make a brave man fearful; but Meleager, won by Atalanta's beauty, welcomed her eagerly, and begged her to share in the hunt. Then the company set forth into the forest, and they did not have to wait long for their quarry, for, as soon as the wild boar heard the barking of the dogs and the sound of snorting steeds, he rushed out of his lair and savagely attacked the hunters. One after another of the heroes was gored by the boar's long tusks, or thrown down and trampled on by the cruel hoofs, or put to flight. Jason threw his spear, but it only grazed the boar's side. Telamon rushed forward, but stumbled over a projecting root and fell to the ground. Nestor, thrown headlong by a furious attack from the boar, sought safety in the branches of a tree. Theseus hurled his lance, but it was caught by a bough and turned aside. Then an arrow from Atalanta's bow pierced the brute's side, and blood flowed from the wound. The infuriated boar turned savagely upon her, but Meleager, who was ever near the maiden, hurled his spear with so true an aim that the boar fell dead upon the bloody and trampled ground.

Then the heroes crowded around Meleager, congratulating him on his victory; but he refused to accept the honour of having slain the boar, and gave to Atalanta its head and rough hide as trophies belonging to the victor. His companions were angered that such honour should be given a mere girl, and they feared the scorn and ridicule that would be heaped upon them when they returned to report the success of the hunt. Meleager, however, did not heed their murmured threats, nor did he listen to the reproaches of his two uncles, Plexippus and Toxeus, who had accompanied him. To see themselves thus rivalled by a boyish girl was too humiliating for the pride of these two princes; and they began to insult Atalanta by chiding her for joining in the sports of men, and showing such unmaidenly boldness. Then they attempted to snatch from her the trophies of the hunt; and at this Meleager, who had been incensed at their taunts to Atalanta, turned upon them in a blaze of fury, and killed them both with his sword.

Meanwhile Althæa had heard that the boar was slain, and was on her way to the temple with a thank-offering when news was brought her that her two brothers had been killed – and by the hand of her son. Then the sister's desire for vengeance crowded out of her heart the mother's love for her son; and she brought out of its place of concealment the brand on whose existence depended Meleager's life. She lit a fire, and then hesitated for a moment whether to commit this dreadful deed or not; but the thought of her murdered brothers hardened her heart, and she threw the brand into the fire. As the flames wrapped around it, Althæa fancied that she heard it give a groan and, seized with remorse, she was about to snatch it from the fire, but the memory of her dead brothers stayed her hand, and she sat by the fire watching the flames consume the brand. While this was going on, Meleager suddenly felt his body seized with deadly pangs; and, though not knowing the cause, he was certain that his death was at hand. Then, like a brave man and a warrior, he lamented that he must die in this mysterious way and not meet his death fighting like the heroes of old. He called upon his mother and father, upon his sisters, and upon his loved Atalanta, but no one could save him from his fate. When the last bit of the brand fell into the ashes, Meleager died; and his mother, now filled with horror and remorse at her deed, committed suicide.

Atalanta, having won fame and the spoils of a celebrated hunt, was now welcomed at her father's court and returned there to live. But though she spent much time at the palace, she could not be induced to give up the chase, and roamed the forests as before, glorying in her freedom. Her father could not persuade her to marry, although many noble suitors sought her hand; for an oracle had once warned her that marriage would be her ruin. To her father's continued insistence she at last returned this answer – that she would wed the suitor who could beat her in a foot-race; but the conditions of the race were to be that the runner, if defeated, should lose his life. Rather than accept these terms, many of the suitors withdrew; but some remained to run the race, for the maiden's beauty was worth a great venture. None of them, however, succeeded in beating the fleet-footed Atalanta; and each man paid the price of defeat with his life. In vain the old king implored his daughter to alter the hard conditions, but Atalanta was determined never to wed.

At one of the races a youth named Hippomenes was made the judge; and when he learned the terms of the contest, he turned to the competitors and asked them why they were so foolish as to risk their lives for the sake of a maiden's beauty. As he was speaking, Atalanta appeared dressed for the race, and when he looked at her, Hippomenes said: "Pardon me, youths, I knew not the prize you were contending for." When the race was over, and the defeated runners put to death, Hippomenes, undaunted by this result, boldly asked that he might try his fate. Atalanta looked at him pityingly, for he was a youth of noble bearing, and she felt a strange reluctance to see him go so blithely to his death. She would not admit to herself that she could fall in love so quickly with a stranger; and yet she half hoped that in this race she would not come first to the goal. As Hippomenes prepared himself for the running, she thought: "What unkind god wishes to bring disaster upon this youth, and commands him, at the risk of a life so dear, to seek this marriage? In my own opinion I am not of such great value. It is not his beauty that moves me, though he is good to look upon, but I pity him because he is still a boy. He himself cannot affect my sympathies, but his youth moves me." Then she tried to persuade Hippomenes to give up the race; but the more he looked at Atalanta, the more determined he was to win her, and he demanded the right to compete alone with the fleet-footed maiden.

Reluctantly Atalanta prepared for the race, and as Hippomenes waited eagerly for the sound of the trumpet he breathed an ardent prayer to Aphrodite to help him win the peerless maiden. Aphrodite, the patroness of lovers, heard his prayer, and, unseen by any watchers, slipped into his hand three golden apples gathered from a wonderful tree on her own island of Cyprus. When the signal was given for the start, each runner shot forward like an arrow from the bow; but Atalanta soon outdistanced her lover, and his fate seemed assured; but just as she passed him he threw in front of her a golden apple, and the maiden, surprised at this unexpected interruption, stopped to pick it up. Hippomenes pressed eagerly forward, but Atalanta soon overtook him and as she sped by him he tossed another golden apple in her path. Caught by its glitter the maiden stooped again, and while she paused to recover the apple, Hippomenes shot ahead. This advantage was soon lost, however, for again Atalanta outran him and was speeding past him toward the goal. Then the lover, with another prayer to Aphrodite, threw the third golden apple; but by this time the maiden had begun to fear that she might be beaten by the handsome stranger, and so hesitated to stop for the tempting golden fruit. Aphrodite impelled her, however, to pause long enough to snatch the apple quickly from the ground, and in that moment's delay Hippomenes passed her and reached the goal.

Thus for the first time the race was won by another than Atalanta, and Hippomenes claimed the maiden as his rightful reward. Triumphantly he carried off his prize, and for a long time he and Atalanta were so happy that the words of the oracle seemed unlikely to be fulfilled; but unfortunately the lovers forgot to do honour to Aphrodite, and the goddess was so angered at their ingratitude that she caused them to give offence to Cybele (Rhea) by desecrating her sacred grove. To punish them for this impiety, Cybele changed them into a lion and lioness, and yoked them to her car, which they were ever afterward compelled to draw.

28

THESEUS

PART 1

Theseus was among the heroes who joined Jason in the famous Argonautic expedition; and he also accompanied Meleager on the Calydonian hunt. Thus it seems that he was well-known throughout Greece for a brave and daring youth who was ready to follow his friends into any adventure, no matter how dangerous. When Theseus was a mere child, his father Aegeus, king of Athens, went on a journey to some distant country, taking with him his wife Aethra and his little son. He returned alone to Athens, leaving Theseus and his mother in the stranger's land; but before he departed he hid his sword and sandals under a large rock, and bade Aethra leave them there until she deemed her son strong enough to raise the stone. If Theseus proved equal to the test, he was to take the sword and sandals and go straightway to his father's court at Athens, where he would be acknowledged as the king's son and heir.

Aethra carefully obeyed these instructions, and when the time came that she considered Theseus strong enough to meet his father's test, she led him to the rock and bade him raise it. With a mighty effort the youth lifted the huge stone, and to his surprise he found beneath it a pair of sandals and a fine sword – both so perfectly preserved that they might have been placed there only the day before. Then Aethra explained the presence of these gifts, and told her son how the king, his father, had placed them there beneath the rock, so that he might know whether Theseus was to be a future hero or a weakling. While his mother was speaking, the youth eagerly girded on the bright sword and put the sandals on his feet, and he needed no urging when Aethra bade him set out at once for his father's kingdom. She warned him of the perils that beset the road to Athens, for giants and robbers would bar his way, and many other dangers lay in wait for the traveller; but Theseus was young and fearless, and he would have faced greater dangers than these to reach King Aegeus and the wonderful city of Athens.

He had gone but a few miles on his journey, when he was accosted by the giant Periphetes, son of Hephaestus, who stood in the road, with his huge club in his hand and refused to let Theseus pass. When the young hero pushed boldly forward, Periphetes raised his club to strike the youth to the ground, as he had done many another wayfarer; but as he lifted his arm for the blow, Theseus plunged his sword quickly into the giant's side, and Periphetes fell dead upon the very roadway where he had been for so long a terror to all travellers.

Elated with his victory, Theseus took the stout club of his fallen enemy and continued his journey to the Isthmus of Corinth, where he found that the road soon grew very narrow and led along the edge of a rocky precipice. Here he encountered a famous robber named Sciron, who compelled all those who passed his way to wash his feet. When the terrified traveller, unable to refuse, was thus occupied, the robber would suddenly raise his foot and kick the man over the side of the cliff into the sea below, where a hungry tortoise lay waiting with ever-open jaws. When Theseus was told the condition on which he would be allowed to pass, he drew his sword and set upon his enemy so fiercely that Sciron quickly withdrew his demand, and offered to let the hero go on his way undisturbed. Then Theseus, as he held his sword point at the robber's throat, commanded Sciron to perform the same menial task that he had set so many others; and when the robber, not daring to refuse, was kneeling before him, Theseus hurled him over the precipice and gave one more meal to the hungry tortoise, who never again was able to feast on the bodies of luckless travellers.

The next adventure that befell the hero was with a cruel giant called Sinis, or the Pine-Bender, because he delighted in bending over some tall pine-tree until its top reached the ground; and having done this, he would call to some unsuspicious passer-by to help him hold it down. The stranger usually complied with this request, and then the giant would take his great hand from the tree, which would at once spring back to its upright position, hurling the unfortunate helper into the air, and often dashing him to pieces against the rocks. When Theseus encountered the giant and was asked for his help, he remembered that his mother had told him long ago of this brutal giant's jest, and he determined that travellers should no more be killed or even terrorized by this curse of the highway. So when Sinis bent down a particularly large and strong pine-tree and begged Theseus to help him hold it, the hero deftly fastened the giant himself to the tree which sprang upward as soon as it was released and dashed the huge body against the mountain side, crushing it to pieces.

After disposing of the giant, Theseus continued his journey and next encountered Procrustes (called the Stretcher), a fearful giant who, under the pretence of hospitality, lured travellers into his house. Though an offer of food and entertainment was so unusual that it might have aroused suspicion, most of those who passed Procrustes's house accepted his invitation and entered. In the house was an iron bedstead on which the giant forced all his guests to lie. If they were too short, he stretched their limbs to suit the size of the bed; and if they were too long, he cut off their legs to make them fit its dimensions. Theseus entered Procrustes's home, and partook freely of the food set before him. Then he suddenly fell upon the giant, who was unprepared for such an attack, bound him to his own bedstead, and by making his huge body fit into it, inflicted on Procrustes the same cruel death that he had delighted to visit on others.

When Theseus finally reached Athens, he went straightway to the palace, and on his way he learned that his father had married the sorDemeters Medea. When he arrived at the royal apartments and came before Aegeus, his cloak so completely hid his sword that the king could not possibly recognize it as the one he had left for his son. Nevertheless he welcomed the stranger, who seemed a brave and handsome youth, and bade him take a place at the banquet-table. But though the king did not know whom he was entertaining, Medea, the sorDemeters, was perfectly well aware of the stranger's identity, and mixed a deadly poison in the wine-cup that was intended for the guest. Handing this to Aegeus, she bade him honour the youth with a cup of their choicest wine; and the king, suspecting nothing, was about to offer the poisoned drink to Theseus when he suddenly saw the sword beneath the stranger's cloak. Looking down at the youth's sandals, he recognized them as the ones that he had buried under a rock long ago, and he knew then that the sword was also his own. With a cry of joy he started forward to embrace his son, and as he did so the cup of wine that he held in his hand was overturned and its contents poured on the table. Some of the drops of poisoned wine fell on a dog that was lying at the king's feet, and immediately it gave one convulsive shudder and died. Realizing that the deadly draught had been meant for him, and knowing that only the jealous Medea could have dared to commit such a crime, Theseus sprang toward her with drawn sword, intending to put an end to her wickedness; but the sorDemeters fled from the banquet-hall, mounted her dragon-car, and escaped to a distant country, which was afterwards called by her name Media.

King Aegeus was delighted to find that his son had grown to be such a brave and handsome youth, and he listened with pride while Theseus related all the adventures that had befallen him on the way to Athens. Then the king made a great feast in honour of his son, and publicly proclaimed him his heir. The time passed very happily to Theseus until the day when he saw a sad procession of weeping people wending its way through the streets, and observed in the midst of them seven youths and seven maidens dressed in funeral garments. He enquired where this solemn cortège was going, and was told that the casting of lots had just been concluded and the victims had been chosen for the Minotaur. Then the young prince learned for the first time that since Minos, king of Crete, had conquered the Athenians in a recent war, he had exacted of them a terrible tribute. Each year seven youths and seven maidens were offered to the Minotaur, an insatiable monster that dwelt in an intricate labyrinth built for its special use by King Minos, and designed by the celebrated architect Dædalus.

The labyrinth was so intricate that no one who entered it could ever hope to find his way out; and the victims which Athens supplied each year were probably killed by terror and suspense as they threaded their way through the labyrinth's tortuous windings, long before the fearful Minotaur came upon them. The architect who designed this wonderful cave should have earned the lasting gratitude of Minos; but Dædalus unfortunately lost the king's favour, and for some slight offence was shut up in a tower with his son Icarus. The boy gave himself up for lost, but the father began at once to contrive some means of escape, and ingeniously fashioned two pairs of wings, which were to gain freedom for himself and his son. When the last feather was adjusted, Dædalus fastened one pair of wings securely on Icarus, and cautioned him not to fly too high lest the heat of the sun should melt the wax with which the feathers were held together. The youth, impatient to be free, paid slight attention to these warnings; and as soon as his wings were fastened, he sprang boldly from the tower window and flew straight toward the clouds. Higher and higher he rose, exulting in this glorious motion, and soon the heat of the sun's rays began to soften the wax on his wings. When it was too late, Icarus realized his danger and came nearer to the earth; but the wax was melting fast, and in a moment the feathers separated and the adventurous boy was plunged headlong into the sea. His body was never recovered, but that part of the sea was afterwards called the Icarian Sea. Dædalus enjoyed a happier fate than that of his son, for he reached Sicily in safety and built a temple there to Apollo. In the temple he hung up his wings as an offering to the god.

PART II

When Theseus heard the story of the Minotaur and its wonderful labyrinth, he determined that it should no longer exact its yearly tribute of human lives, for he would offer himself as one of the victims and end the terrible sacrifice by slaying the monster. When he announced this intention to his father, the king sought to persuade him to remain at home; but Theseus joined the youths and maidens who had been chosen by lot to go to Crete, and they set sail for the country of the Minotaur. According to the custom, the ship hoisted only black sails, which Theseus promised to change for white ones when he returned unharmed, having slain the monster.

Nothing befell the voyagers until they reached the coast of Crete, but here the ship was stopped by the giant Talus, whose body was made of brass and was always so red hot that if he held any one in his embrace, the victim was burnt to cinders. This giant was a very effective guardian of the island, and kept off all strangers who had no business along that coast. As he knew that the black-sailed ship brought to his master, King Minos, the yearly tribute from the Athenians, he let the vessel pass; and the voyagers, having landed, were led before the king. The cruel mouth of Minos relaxed into a smile when he saw the youths and maidens, for they were all young and beautiful – the very flower of the Athenians – and it gave him special satisfaction to consign such a chosen company to death. Beside Minos stood his daughter Ariadne, who looked compassionately at those who were destined for the sacrifice, and when she saw Theseus, she pitied him above all the rest, and wished she might save him from his loathsome fate.

When the young hero asked that he might go first into the labyrinth, and alone, King Minos smiled at what he considered a child's boast – for he had heard that Theseus hoped to slay the Minotaur; but when he learned that the bold youth was his enemy's only son, he gladly allowed him to do as he wished, although it was contrary to all custom. Theseus was therefore placed alone in a cell of the prison, and here he did not feel quite so bold or so eager to face the Minotaur as he had when he talked over the adventure at his father's court. His sword had been taken away, and he had no other weapon with which to fight the monster, so his confidence was somewhat shaken; and as he watched the night deepening the gloom of his prison, he felt disheartened and almost unnerved for his coming battle. Just then the door of the prison opened softly, and Ariadne, the king's daughter, entered. To Theseus's great surprise she gave him a sharp sword and a ball of thread – two things that she assured him were necessary for him to have if he hoped to come alive out of the labyrinth. She bade him fasten one end of the thread to the entrance of the cave, and keep the ball tight in his hand, so that it might lead him back through the intricate windings after he had slain the Minotaur.

Theseus was very grateful to Ariadne for her assistance, without which he would never have been able to encounter the monster or to escape from its wonderful labyrinth. He assured the maiden that his father would send her a generous reward of gold and jewels; but she refused to accept any return for her kindness until Theseus ventured to suggest that if she would become his wife, he would be proud to take her back with him to Athens. To this Ariadne gladly agreed, and they plighted their troth in the murky darkness of the prison. When at dawn of the following day the hero, now full of courage and sure of success, was led to the labyrinth, he fastened one end of the thread to the entrance. Then, with his hand on his sword, which was hidden under his long cloak, he stepped boldly into the cave from which no human being had ever come out alive. The passage was narrow and dark, and strewn everywhere with whitening bones, so Theseus stepped very cautiously, with his ball of thread held fast and his hand ever ready on his sword. Suddenly the Minotaur rushed upon him at an unlooked-for turn in the road, and though the hero had no warning of its presence he met it boldly. A terrible battle ensued, in which Theseus struck fiercely at the Minotaur, wounding it mortally, while the pain-maddened brute tore gashes in his flesh and almost suffocated him with its deadly breath. At last the hero gave a swift thrust with his sword that cut through the monster's great head, and in a moment the Minotaur lay dead among the bones of its former victims.

With the help of the thread, which he had never lost, even in the thick of the fight, Theseus was able to retrace his steps and to reach the entrance to the labyrinth, where he found Ariadne anxiously awaiting him. At the sight of the blood-stained sword she knew that her lover had slain the Minotaur, and together they hurried to the black-sailed ship, to which Ariadne had already conveyed the youths and maidens who had been Theseus's companions on the voyage. As quickly as possible the ship sped out of the harbour; but before they could quite clear the Cretan shores, the giant Talus came upon them, and, seeing that some of his master's prisoners were escaping, he tried to catch hold of the vessel by its rigging. As he leaned forward to do this, Theseus dealt him such a mighty blow that he toppled over into the sea and was drowned. At this spot there were later discovered some thermal springs, which gave evidence of the terrible heat in the giant's brazen body.

Only once did the vessel stop on its swift voyage homeward, and this was at the island of Naxeos. Here the whole company landed to explore the beauties of the island, and to find some spring from which to get a supply of fresh water. Ariadne wandered apart from the gay company, and being weary, threw herself down on the bank of a stream to rest. Here she fell fast asleep, and when Theseus later found her there, he at once conceived the treacherous idea of deserting her. So he summoned all his companions, and went stealthily down to the ship, where he embarked, leaving Ariadne alone on the island. For some days the deserted maiden sat on the seashore watching in vain for the Athenian ship to return; but she did not mourn her faithless lover long, for the gods sent her a greater happiness than she could ever have had with the fickle Theseus. The island of Naxeos was the favourite spot of Dionysus, god of wine, who landed one day with a merry company of followers, and found the weeping Ariadne. In a short time he won her love and confidence, and persuaded her to be his wife. The wedding celebrations so occupied Ariadne's mind that the treacherous Theseus was soon forgotten.

The Athenians had been so eager to return to their native city that they had no thought but to reach home as quickly as the vessel could bear them; and Theseus forgot his promise to his father that, in case of success, white sails should replace the black ones that were hoisted on the outgoing voyage. Old Aegeus went each day to the seashore, and stood on a high rock, watching the sea for some sign of the returning ship. When, at last, he saw it loom up on the horizon, with its black sails showing ominously against the sky, he at once concluded that his son was dead; and in his grief over this great loss he threw himself into the water, which has since been known as the Aegean Sea.

When Theseus entered Athens in triumph, the first news he heard was the tidings of his father's death; and realizing that it had occurred through his forgetfulness, he was filled with remorse. Though this misfortune made him king of Athens, he allowed the city no rejoicings on his accession to the throne; and the power and wealth at his command gave him no happiness, for his conscience still accused him of causing his father's death. He tried to divert his mind by absorbing himself in state duties, but soon found that nothing would bring forgetfulness as long as he stayed in Athens; so he set out again in search of adventures, and led an expedition against the Amazons, who had been harassing his land. After a long and fierce battle he defeated them and took their queen, Antiope, prisoner. The Amazons then attacked Athens, and penetrated into the heart of the city, but were finally driven out. Shortly after this Theseus married the queen, Antiope, and a son was born to them whom the delighted father named Hippolytus. When, later on, the Amazons again made an invasion into the country under the pretext of rescuing their queen, Antiope was killed by an arrow sent at random into the court of the palace.

The next adventure in which Theseus engaged was to lead the Athenian army against Pirithous, king of the Lapithæ, who had been secretly carrying off some of his herds. Full of anger at these continued plunderings, Theseus came suddenly upon the marauders as they were boldly making off with their booty; but as soon as he and Pirithous were brought face to face, they were seized with such an admiration for each other that they had no longer any feelings of enmity. They threw down their weapons, clasped each other's hands, and swore eternal friendship. To prove his devotion to his new friend, Theseus agreed to accompany him to the court of Adrastus, king of Argos, and to be present at the marriage of Pirithous to Hippodamia, the daughter of the king. Many guests came to the wedding, and among them were Heracles and a number of the centaurs. The beauty of the bride so won the admiration of the centaurs that they determined to kidnap her, and a terrible battle ensued between them and the Lapithæ, who were aided by Theseus and Heracles. Finally the centaurs were driven away, but not before many of them had been killed or wounded. The bride who had been the cause of this strenuous fighting did not live long, however, and Pirithous soon found himself like Theseus, a disconsolate widower.

Having been so unfortunate in their wives, the two heroes determined not to seek again any king's daughters in marriage, but to choose some one of divine parentage. So Theseus decided upon Helen, the child of Zeus and Leda whom the ruler of the gods wooed in the form of a snow-white swan. Pirithous's choice fell upon Persephone, the wife of Hades. Theseus succeeded in carrying off Helen; but as she was at that time a mere child, he left her in the care of his mother Aethra until she should be old enough for marriage. Meanwhile Helen's twin brothers, Castor and Pollux, having discovered who her abductor was, waited until he was absent on the venture with his friend Pirithous, and then went to the rescue of their sister, whom they took forcibly from Aethra, and carried triumphantly home to Sparta.

Of these twin brothers, Castor was mortal, and some time later was slain in battle. Pollux, who was immortal, then begged Zeus to let him die also, that he might not be separated from his brother. The ruler of Olympus, touched by this evidence of devotion, allowed Castor to return to life on condition that Pollux would spend half of his time in Hades. Later on both brothers were translated to the heavens, where they form a bright constellation, one of the signs of the Zodiac.

Although Theseus's attempt to win an immortal bride was unsuccessful, the two friends were not discouraged; and the hero accompanied Pirithous to Hades when he made the bold attempt to carry off Persephone. Hades, having discovered their intention, was so enraged at the insult that he fastened Theseus to an enchanted rock, and bound Pirithous to the ever-revolving wheel of his father Ixion. When Heracles went down to Hades to ask Hades's permission to carry the three-headed dog Cerberus to the court of Eurystheus, he freed Theseus from the enchanted rock and thus enabled him to return to Athens.

Though somewhat advanced in years Theseus decided to marry again, and chose as his bride the beautiful Phædra, a younger sister of Ariadne. An embassy was accordingly sent to ask for the maiden's hand in marriage, and later she was brought to Athens; but she was not at all pleased with her elderly husband, and much preferred his handsome young son Hippolytus, whose years were better suited to her own. She tried to persuade Hippolytus to elope with her, and when he indignantly refused to be so disloyal to his father, Phædra's affection for him turned to hate, and she determined to make him pay dearly for thus scorning her love. So she went to the king and told him that Hippolytus was trying to persuade her to desert the husband she adored; and the infatuated Theseus, believing her story, vowed to punish the youth for his treachery. Learning that his son was then driving his chariot along the seashore, the king implored Poseidon to avenge his wrongs; and the obliging sea-god sent a huge wave over the chariot, which dashed it against the rocks and threw the lifeless body of Hippolytus on the beach. When Phædra saw what had happened as the result of her false accusations, she was filled with remorse and despair; and after confessing her wickedness to the king, she hanged herself. One story relates that Artemis, pitying the innocent Hippolytus, restored him to life with the aid of Aesculapius; and, to remove him from the power of his irresponsible father, placed him in the care of the nymph Egeria.

Theseus, having grown bitter from his many misfortunes, now became so stern and tyrannical that his people began to hate him and to wish for another ruler. At last, driven to desperation by his harsh measures, they banished him to the island of Scyros, where the king Lycomedes treated him at first with great kindness; but he soon grew tired of the old man's presence and decided to get rid of him. So one day when Theseus was walking along the cliff's edge, a servant stole up behind him and threw him into the sea. When the Athenians heard of the fate that had befallen their king, they repented of having sent him into banishment; and now, in a sudden revulsion of feeling, they made him a national hero. Later on he was deified as a sort of demigod; his bones were brought piously back to Athens; and a magnificent temple was erected in his honour on the Acropolis.

29

OEDIPUS

Laius and Jocasta, king and queen of Thebes, were very happy when the gods gave them a little son, and they sent to the oracle at Delphi to learn what auspicious omens attended the child's birth. To their horror they were informed that the boy would kill his father, marry his mother, and bring great misfortune upon his native city.

Hoping to avert this dreadful calamity, Laius commanded a servant to take the child away and kill him; but the man, not wishing to commit so heartless a crime, hung the infant by his ankles to a tree, and left him there to perish of hunger or from the teeth of wild beasts. The king, believing that his command had been carried out and that the boy no longer lived, was happy in the conviction that the oracle would never be fulfilled. Meanwhile the helpless child was left hanging to the tree until a shepherd, chancing to pass by, heard his pitiful cries and went to his rescue. The kindly peasant then carried the infant to his master Polybus, king of Corinth, who befriended the little stranger and later adopted him as his son and heir, for he had no children of his own. He called the boy Oedipus, which means swollen-foot.

The young prince grew up in entire ignorance of his real parentage, and never suspected that he was not king Polybus's son until one day, at the royal banquet, a guest, drunk with wine, was heartless enough to tell him that he was only an adopted child. At first Oedipus believed this statement to be just a malicious invention; but as he saw the glances that the other guests exchanged, he was filled with dread lest the words might be really true. So he went in haste to the woman he had always called his mother, and demanded the truth about his birth. The queen, fearing that Oedipus might kill himself if he knew that he had been deceived about his parentage, assured him that he was indeed her son. The youth believed her repeated assertions, and yet he was not wholly satisfied; so he went to consult the oracle at Delphi. From this he could learn nothing but the terrible prophecy that he would kill his father, marry his mother, and bring misfortune upon his native city.

Determined not to be forced into committing any of these crimes, Oedipus fled from Corinth and became a wanderer. Once, while he was walking on the high-road, bewailing the cruel fate that drove him away from the people he loved, he was met by a chariot in which sat an old man and his servant. This was Laius, king of Thebes, who was journeying thus far from his native city to consult the oracle of Delphi. The servant who drove the king's chariot commanded Oedipus to move out of the road, and flourished his whip to enforce his demand. The young prince was not accustomed to be thus ordered about, and refused to move so that the king's chariot might pass. The driver then struck Oedipus with his whip, at which the youth grew so enraged that he avenged the insult by killing the servant with his sword. The king hurled his spear at Oedipus and called loudly to his other servants, who were some distance behind; but before they could come to their master's rescue, Laius was stretched dead in the road. Thus the first part of the prophecy was fulfilled.

When the attendants came hurrying to the king's assistance, they were horrified at finding both him and his charioteer dead; but although they searched everywhere, no trace of the murderer could be found. Oedipus meanwhile had escaped and was on his way to Thebes, whither the servants were now preparing to carry their dead master. Though strangers were usually noticed as they came through the city gates, Oedipus was scarcely observed during the many days that Thebes was in mourning for the dead king. When the funeral ceremonies were over, the young stranger heard one day a herald proclaiming in the streets that the throne of Thebes should belong to him who could kill the Sphinx and thus free the country from its baneful presence. The hand of the queen Jocasta was also promised as a further reward.

When Oedipus asked one of the natives what this creature called the Sphinx might be, the old man to whom he spoke turned on him a look of surprise, and remarked that he must indeed be a stranger to Thebes if he did not know that the city was suffering from the presence of the Sphinx. This monster, he said, was half woman and half lion, with the claws and wings of a huge bird; and it had stationed itself just outside the city gates, where it crouched upon a rock so close to the high-road that no traveller could pass it unseen, especially as it kept watch both night and day. To each passer-by the Sphinx propounded a riddle, and those who solved it could pass undisturbed, but those who failed were at once torn to pieces by the monster's claws. Thus far no one had been able to solve the riddle, and many travellers had already been destroyed.

When Oedipus heard this story, he determined to seek the Sphinx and try his fate. Even if he himself were slain, he would not regret having given his life to the nation that had befriended him, especially since the oracle had prophesied for him such a series of crimes that he had no love for life. So, sword in hand, he went out of the city gates, and walked boldly along the road to the rock where the crouching Sphinx lay in wait for its prey. As soon as it saw Oedipus,

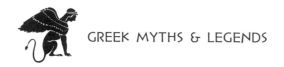

it stopped him, and demanded that he should answer the riddle or else lose his life.

"Tell me your riddle then," cried the hero, boldly; and the Sphinx replied:

"What is it that in the morning goes on four feet, at noon on two feet, and in the evening upon three?"

For some minutes Oedipus did not answer, but he crept nearer to the Sphinx, with his sword gripped firmly in his hand. The monster began to lick its cruel lips, and stretch out one long claw toward its victim, when Oedipus answered:

"It is man, who in childhood creeps on hands and knees, in manhood walks erect, and in old age moves with the help of a staff." The Sphinx, with a cry of rage and disappointment, spread its wings, preparing to fly away to some other place where it could find new victims; but Oedipus suddenly rushed upon it with his drawn sword, and drove it over the edge of a precipice which was so steep that the monster was instantly killed by its fall.

When Oedipus returned to the city and announced that he had slain the Sphinx, the people greeted him as their deliverer. They placed him in the royal chariot, proclaimed him their king, and carried him in triumph to the palace, where the queen Jocasta welcomed him. Shortly after this she married Oedipus, thus fulfilling the second part of the prophecy.

In spite of the crimes that he had unknowingly committed, Oedipus reigned many years in Thebes, and proved himself so wise and just a ruler that the people never regretted having chosen him for their king. Two sons were born to him and Jocasta, and two beautiful daughters. The former were named Eteocles and Polynices, and the latter Ismene and Antigone. Oedipus himself was so content that he almost disbelieved the fatal prophecy at Delphi; but his happiness was destined to be short lived, for the city was suddenly afflicted with a pestilence and famine which caused such distress throughout the land that the stricken people came flocking to Oedipus, praying him to deliver them from the scourge. The king sent at once to consult the oracle at Delphi, and his messengers returned with this answer from Apollo:

"The plague, he said, should cease,
When those who murdered Laius were discovered,
And paid the forfeit of their crime by death
Or banishment."

Every effort was then made to discover who had slain the former king Laius, and it was not long before the crime of Oedipus was revealed. At the same time the old servant who had been commanded to kill the infant son of Laius and Jocasta was found, and made to confess his part in the tragedy. Oedipus was now convinced of his real parentage, and discovered to his horror that he had already been guilty of the three crimes that the oracle had foretold. In vain he had fled from Corinth to escape being near his supposed parents; and in vain, too, had he sought refuge in another city, believing that the one he had left was his birthplace. When the queen Jocasta realized the full horror of her relationship to Oedipus, she committed suicide; and the king, rushing into her apartment at the sound of her cries, saw her lifeless body on the ground. In despair at this sight Oedipus, the unwilling cause of the tragedy, was seized with a sudden madness and put out both his own eyes, declaring that the sunlight would be forever hateful to him.

Blind, penniless, and on foot, he left the palace and the city on which he had brought such disaster, and wandered over the land accompanied by his devoted daughter Antigone, who clung to the fallen king the more lovingly because of his misery and disgrace.

After many days of wandering in the rain and cold, begging their scanty food and resting in any wayside spot that offered them shelter, Oedipus and his daughter came to Colonus, a village near Athens. Here was a deep and almost impenetrable forest, which the Greeks believed to be sacred to the Furies. In this gruesome spot Oedipus declared that he would stay the rest of his days; and bidding his daughter farewell, he entered the dark forest alone. Antigone, weeping and clinging to her father's arm, besought him to let her stay beside him, for what could he – old and blind and helpless – do in that fearful spot but perish? Oedipus gently released her clinging hands, and refused to allow her to go any farther with him, assuring her that to him who lived ever in the eternal night of blindness, there were no terrors in the darkness of the forest.

So Antigone sadly returned to Athens, and the blind king groped his way among the thick underbrush and fallen trees. At nightfall a terrible storm came up, and its forerunner, the wind, shook the forest as if it were some child's toy; but still the old king felt his way among the trees, and the lightning, as it flashed into the dark places of the forest, illumined a figure bent and shaking, but grim, determined, and unafraid. The next day when the storm was over, a party of men sent by Theseus, king of Athens, went in search of Oedipus, but no trace of him was ever found; and the ancients believed that the Furies dragged him down into Hades, where he received a fitting punishment for his crimes.

The plague having been removed from Thebes by the death of Oedipus – according to the words of Apollo – the city returned to its former prosperity; and then began a fierce dispute between the king's two sons as to which of them should succeed to the throne. A compromise was finally agreed upon whereby the eldest son, Eteocles, was to reign for one year, and at the end of the year the second son, Polynices, was to accede to the throne and rule for the same length of time. The dispute being settled amicably, Polynices set out for adventures in foreign lands during his brother's reign; and at the end of the year he returned to claim his right to wield the sceptre of power. Eteocles refused, however, to relinquish the throne; and with the help of the soldiers, drove Polynices out of the city.

Furious at this treachery, but unable to retaliate single-handed, Polynices fled to the court of Adrastus, king of Argos, where he was hospitably received. On relating the story of his wrongs, he so won the sympathy of the king that the kindly monarch promised to help him regain his kingdom. Later on the banished prince married Adrastus's daughter, and the king equipped a large army to go with Polynices to Thebes. At the head of the troops he placed seven valiant chiefs who were determined to win the city from the usurper, or perish in the attempt. These leaders gave this celebrated expedition the name of "The Seven against Thebes".

If courage and boldness were enough to overthrow a city, the besiegers would have won an easy victory; but their bravery was of no avail against a place so well fortified and defended as Thebes. After a seven years' siege the leaders of the attacking forces grew weary of espousing a hopeless cause, and decided that the quarrel between the two brothers must be settled by a duel. Accordingly Polynices and Eteocles met face to face, and fought so fiercely that both of them were killed. The only one left in the city who could rightfully assume the reins of authority was Creon, the father of Jocasta, who was now proclaimed king of Thebes. By Creon's order the body of Eteocles was given all the honours of a royal burial; but the corpse of Polynices was left on the battle-field a prey to dogs and vultures. Then the king issued a proclamation that if any one dared to touch the body of the dead prince, he would be buried alive. The friends of Polynices did not venture to defy this edict; but his sister Antigone, horrified at the thought of leaving her brother's body to suffer such disgrace, determined to ignore the king's barbarous decree. As she was unable to procure any assistance, she dug a grave with her own hands and buried Polynices, performing such funeral rites for the repose of the dead as she could accomplish alone.

While she was engaged in this act of devotion she was seen by the soldiers of Creon, who dragged her at once into the presence of the king. Although Antigone was one of his own family, and was also the promised wife of his son Haemon, the relentless monarch condemned her to death. Haemon pleaded with his father to spare the life of his betrothed, since her deed, though in defiance of the king's order, had been one of praiseworthy devotion; but Creon would not revoke his decision, and condemned Antigone to the most horrible of deaths – that of being buried alive. While this inhuman sentence was being carried out, Haemon leaped into the grave where Antigone was kneeling, and declared that he would die by her side. As the terrible process of walling-in the lovers was slowly completed, Antigone died in Haemon's arms; and when he felt her lifeless body lying limp in his embrace, he ended his own life with his dagger.

30

THE APPLE OF DISCORD

Zeus, father of the gods, once fell in love with the beautiful sea-nymph "Thetis of the silver feet", the daughter of Nereus and Doris. Before he arranged for the marriage, the ruler of Olympus first consulted the Fates to see whether any misfortune was likely to attend his nuptials; and the three sisters who spin the thread of life night and day declared that Thetis was destined to be the mother of a son who would be far greater than his father.

Although Zeus could not imagine how any god could supplant him in Olympus, he was nevertheless unwilling to act in defiance of what the Fates decreed; so he gave Thetis in marriage to Peleus, king of Phthia, who had long loved her and had sought her hand in vain. The sea-nymph was not very well pleased at having to accept a mere mortal as a husband, even though he was a king, after having been wooed by the greatest of the gods. To induce her to consent to the marriage, Zeus promised that he and the other gods would come down from high Olympus to attend the wedding; and the prospect of this great honour soothed the pride of Thetis so that she consented to marry Peleus.

The preparations for the wedding were begun in the coral caves of her father Nereus, and all the ocean-deities and sea-nymphs helped to beautify the palace under the sea. When the wedding day arrived, Zeus, with all the attending gods, came to grace the marriage feast. The guests took their seats at the well-filled table, and pledged the bride in brimming cups of wine. There was nothing to mar the joy of the occasion until suddenly an uninvited guest appeared in the banquet-hall, and the laughter died away into an ominous silence. This unexpected visitor was Eris (or Discordia), the goddess of discord, who had not been asked to the wedding because her hideous face, snaky hair, and vicious temper made Thetis fear that her presence would anger the other guests. The strife-breeding goddess regarded this omission as an insult, so she went unbidden to the marriage feast, determined to vent her wrath and spite on those who had received the coveted honour. For a moment she stood looking at the assembled company with glances full of hatred, and she laughed mockingly when she saw them shrink away as she breathed over them her poisonous breath. Then she threw on the table a golden apple, and immediately vanished.

The guests were eager to see the beautiful fruit, and as they passed it about among themselves they were surprised to find engraved on its smooth surface the words "For the Fairest." Immediately there arose a lively discussion as to whom the apple should rightfully belong; and each of the goddesses present was inclined to believe that the fruit was intended for her. At last all the contestants for the golden apple withdrew their claims except Hera, Athena, and Aphrodite – each of whom disputed hotly for its possession. Hera contended that her power and majesty gave her the best right to the prize; Athena claimed that the beauty of wisdom surpassed all other charms; while laughter-loving Aphrodite asked who could rightfully be called "the fairest" if not the goddess of beauty.

As the dispute grew more and more bitter, the goddesses called upon the other guests to decide their respective claims; but no one was willing to assume this responsibility. Since the apple could be given to but one of the three, the other two would be sure to vent their anger and disappointment on those who made the decision, each believing that the judges willfully refused to admit her superior charms. So, at the suggestion of one of the company, the entire wedding party adjourned to Mount Ida, where the beautiful shepherd Paris was tending his flocks. Zeus appointed him to be the judge of the contest. The bewildered shepherd took some moments to recover from the surprise of having this brilliant company break in upon his solitude; and he stood watching them in awe and reverence, not daring to speak in the presence of the immortals.

Paris was not, however, an uncouth peasant lad, for although occupying the lowly position of shepherd, he was really the son of Priam and Hecuba, king and queen of Troy. When he was a mere infant, he was left on the mountain to perish, because an oracle had foretold that he would cause the death of his family and the destruction of his native city. But though so inhumanly exposed to cold and the hunger of wild beasts, the child did not die, for he was found by a shepherd, who adopted him and brought him up to follow his own calling.

When Paris grew to manhood he was so handsome that the wood-nymphs, who were his companions, all sighed for love of him. Among them was the fair and gentle Oenone, whom Paris secretly married, and with whom he lived happily on Mount Ida. Though his foster-father had told him the story of his birth, Paris had no longing for the glitter and grandeur of palaces, for he felt sure that king Priam would wish to kill him if he learned that the son he feared and hated was alive.

Paris had grown so accustomed to the solitude of the mountain that when the wedding party suddenly came upon him, he stood fearful and silent while Zeus, showing him the golden apple with its inscription, bade him judge which of the three goddesses should receive it. Before he could make any answer, Hera told him if he gave the apple to her he would thereby win great wealth and honour. Athena promised him the gift of wisdom far exceeding that of mortal men; but laughter-loving Aphrodite whispered in his ear that if he awarded her the apple, he should have the most beautiful woman in the world for his wife. Whether it was the alluring beauty of Aphrodite that blinded his judgment, or the reward which she offered that tempted him, it is impossible to tell. Perhaps it was for both of these reasons that Paris turned quickly and placed the coveted apple in Aphrodite's hand. This decision brought upon him the wrath of both the discredited goddesses, who began from that moment to cherish a hatred for the house of Troy, and to plot its destruction.

Aphrodite told Paris that in order for her to fulfil her promise, he must now go down to the city of Troy and make himself known to his parents. She assured him that he need have no fear of his father, for she herself would so order his affairs that the king would welcome him and acknowledge him as his son. Later on she would arrange that he should be furnished with ships in which to sail to Greece, for to this country he must inevitably go, since Helen, wife of Menelaus, king of Sparta, was the most beautiful woman in the world. Obeying carefully all the instructions of the goddess, who had now become his protectress, Paris left his shepherding and went down to the court of his father, King Priam. He was so blinded by the vision of his glorious future that he did not think how heartless he was to desert the loving and faithful Oenone, who mourned for him until the hills echoed with the sound of her cries.

To tell the story of Paris's return to his native city, of his voyage to Sparta, and of his abduction of Helen, would be to tell the story of the Trojan war and of how dearly Paris and his household paid for the most beautiful woman in the world. When the sons of Priam were falling, one by one, beneath the fierce blows of the Greeks, Paris was wounded by a poisoned arrow shot by Philoctetes, who had received these famous weapons from Hercules when he lit that hero's funeral pyre. As the poison entered Paris's veins, and he knew that he had received a mortal wound, he sent at once for Oenone, who had always loved him so dearly that he believed she must have forgiven his treachery and desertion. He knew how skilled the nymph was in the use of healing herbs, and she had once told him, in the happy days of their love on Mount Ida, that if he ever were wounded, he should send for her and she would heal him. Paris therefore dispatched a messenger in all haste to bring his wife from her home among the hills; but Oenone refused to accompany the messenger, for she knew that it was not for love of her that her husband desired her presence. So Paris died of his poisoned wound, and when Oenone heard of his death, she went down to the city and saw the funeral pyre with its flames leaping toward the sky. Filled with remorse at her refusal to come to his aid, Oenone could not look on at the sight of Paris's burning body and live; so she sprang upon the blazing pyre and perished beside her lover.